JULIE OLIVIA

IN TOO DEEP

JULIE OLIVIA

Copyright © 2019 by Julie Olivia

julieoliviaauthor@gmail.com

www.julieoliviaauthor.com

All rights reserved.

No part of this book may be reproduced in any form or by any electronic or mechanical means, including information storage and retrieval systems, without written permission from the author, except for the use of brief quotations in a book review.

This is a work of fiction. Names, characters, places, and incidents either are the product of the author's imagination or are used fictitiously. Any resemblance to actual persons, living or dead, events, or locales is entirely coincidental.

Edited by Merethe Walther

Cover Photo from DepositPhotos

Cover Design by Julie Olivia

For J.R.

*With fronds like these
well, who needs anemones?*

CONTENTS

About "In Too Deep"	ix
Playlist	xi
1. Grace	1
2. Grace	9
3. Grace	16
4. Cameron	24
5. Grace	30
6. Cameron	36
7. Grace	40
8. Cameron	54
9. Grace	57
10. Cameron	61
11. Grace	69
12. Grace	78
13. Grace	86
14. Cameron	91
15. Grace	96
16. Cameron	120
17. Grace	132
18. Grace	138
19. Grace	150
20. Cameron	160
21. Grace	164
22. Cameron	168
23. Cameron	172
24. Grace	176
25. Cameron	179
26. Grace	181
27. Cameron	190
28. Grace	194
29. Cameron	202
30. Grace	209

31. Cameron	216
32. Grace	228
33. Grace	238
34. Grace	244
35. Cameron	248
36. Grace	254
37. Cameron	259
38. Grace	262
39. Grace	267
40. Cameron	271
41. Cameron	275
42. Grace	282
43. Grace	290
44. Grace	295
45. Cameron	302
46. Grace	308
Epilogue	311
Nice to See You!	315
Acknowledgments	317
About the Author	319

ABOUT "IN TOO DEEP"

In Too Deep is a full-length, standalone romantic comedy! It is the first book in the *Into You* Series.

———

They say not to stick your pen in company ink. Does that apply to graphic designers as well?

This year, I decided to check off a couple life-altering items: Ditch the cheating ex, move into my own apartment, and finally pursue my dream career. When I land a graphic design job at Treasuries Inc., the start-up darling of the marketing world, I think I have it all figured out.

Oh, naïve little me.

I, Grace Holmes, am not related to the great detective, Sherlock. If I were, maybe I could solve the mysterious case of why the universe gave me my dream job, but then paired it with my new boss, Cameron Kaufman.

Cameron Kaufman is a man with a plan--if that plan is attempting to stilt my career. He's arrogant, cynical, and ready to spit sarcasm any chance he can. But, most of all, he is swoon-worthy to a degree of unfairness. Seriously--dimples and a winning ass? Give me a break here!

So, of course, we're hit with a big project on my first week. Of course, now my boss and I have to spend late nights together. And, of course, I'm getting more attracted to his snarky comments as each day passes.

We both have mouths that could kill. My only problem is that I can't stop picturing what else he can do with his, or whether my job is worth risking to find out.

PLAYLIST

"Holdin' On" - Rooney
"Unsquare Dance" - Dave Brubeck
"Get Over It" - OK Go
"Monster" - dodie
"Our Deal" - Best Coast
"Hot Volcano" - Pearl and the Beard
"It's Only Temporary" - Harley Poe
"All These Things That I've Done" - The Killers
"Universe & U" - KT Tunstall

1
GRACE

Does love even exist beyond dogs?

In my case, definitely not.

I hear that golden retrievers are one of the smartest breeds. If that fact is true, then maybe my dog Hank would have had the common sense to leave Joe earlier than I did.

Even now, mere feet away from me with his graying fur and wise old age, I bet he's wondering if I'll ever learn.

Master Yoda's got nothing on this pup.

He walks over and plops himself beside me, laying his head inches from mine so I can scratch behind his ear.

I roll over on my stomach and reach out to swipe at the laptop laying inches from my fingertips. With a groan and all the strength I can muster, I curl my toes and push myself just the one extra inch I need to snatch the computer, slide it in front of me, and pop it open.

Hank army crawls closer to me as I go straight for my email, whining softly as if he doesn't think I should look at them, either. Told you: Smart as a whip.

"I know I shouldn't," I say, reaching down to poke his nose. "But I'm a glutton for punishment."

I open the inbox and find exactly what I thought I would find: Another email from Joe. Ten, to be exact. He's deteriorated the formal structure of emails into that of a three-year-old. I can commend his effort, at least.

"Grace, answer my calls," "I'm a huge douche," and the coveted: "I miss you."

"Yep, definitely punished myself with that one," I mutter with a half-hearted smile, reaching over and ruffling Hank's ears until he wags his tail. The old boy leans over and lays his paw over my hand, adding in a lick on my cheek for good measure. He doesn't gloat about the fact that he was right because he's a gentleman, damn it.

The worst thing about being a relationship in your late-twenties is the inevitable process of moving out once you and your once fabulous beau break-up. It gets even trickier if you've bought a house together. It's kind of dumb to buy a house with your unwed significant other, but I am just that brand of stupid.

The custody battle between the ex and I for my loyal golden retriever wasn't even a discussion. Hank was my high school graduation gift and I'd throw Joe off a cliff before I'd give up Hank. But who wouldn't want an excuse to throw their ex-boyfriend off a cliff anyway?

But here I am now: A lonely, twenty-seven-year-old woman lying on the floor of a mostly empty apartment. I'm waiting on my friend Ramona to arrive in a moving truck with some hand-me-down furniture to fill this place, but as of right now I only have a suitcase full of clothes, my old laptop, various art supplies shoved into a box, and my trusty dog, Hank.

I look to my watch and see that I have a bit of time to sketch, and there's no time like the present to focus on something much more enjoyable. I whip out my trusty tablet and pen and begin sketching anything and everything. Lines, dots, swirls... What do they make? What's my heart telling me?

That's a bunch of hippie nonsense, I think with a roll of my eyes. This line tells me, "Grace, be better," and this one says, "You're talking to yourself again; stop it."

That's an "aggressive line," as my former art professors would say.

I'm still getting back into the groove of it all, to be honest. I've been in a relationship for the past two years. It was happy until it wasn't. For the record, a woman not being happy due to a man is just her telling the world that it has successfully beaten her down, and I will not have that.

I bite the end of my drawing pen, trying to brainstorm something new; something original. I sketch out a couple things—mostly drawings of my lazy dog—when I hear the squeak of wheels coming from a heavy vehicle that most likely hasn't been oiled in a year. I get up, pace to the front door, and open it to find Ramona and her husband Wes hopping out from each side of the moving truck.

Ramona looks up, shielding her eyes from the sun. Her shorts are mega-short, accentuating thighs muscled from years of running. She's almost never caught dead without a crop top with self-printed text saying something pseudo-clever. Today's winning outfit has a cow with text below saying: *Moo-ve it or lose it.* I have no doubt in my mind she made this shirt specifically for moving day.

"There's my sunshine!" she yells up at me, waving her hand around wildly.

"My day did not breathe life until I saw you!" I call down, and she laughs.

Wes throws me a quick wave, then comes up behind her and picks her up, walking both of them to the back of the truck, pulling the handle down, and releasing it back up to reveal the packed trunk. He is inarguably a very good-looking man: high cheekbones, brilliant green eyes, and toned arms covered in tattoo sleeves that could never be misconstrued as anything other than pieces of art.

Ramona and Wes met during their freshman year of college, and they've been inseparable ever since. They shared everything together: They started as undeclared majors, ended up going through the same psychology degree, and now they own a practice together with Ramona conducting behavioral therapy in children and Wes handling couples' counseling. They're a powerhouse couple if I've ever seen one, and I'd be lying if I said I wasn't jealous of their perfect little life.

I close Hank up in the kitchen so he can't run off and then trot down to the parking lot.

"You didn't take anything?" Ramona asks, pulling me into a hug before I even finish stepping off the last stair.

"Nah," I say, falling into her embrace. There's nothing more reassuring than the hug of a close friend—especially one taller than you with larger tits. I don't care who you are; they're like pillows just waiting to provide comfort. "The furniture didn't really mean much to me. But can I have the house itself back?"

"That isn't how it works, *chica*."

"Yeah, I know. But I put my heart and soul into that house."

"Well, even that beautiful house couldn't save your relationship, I'm afraid." Ramona exhales, pulling away and scanning me up and down.

Wes shifts some items in the back of the truck and calls down to me, "Sorry he's a cheating asshole, Grace."

I shrug. "Any surprises there?"

"No, not really," Wes responds without skipping a beat, and a weak smile pulls on my lips. "He wore a flipped-up collar"—Wes hops down from the back—"who *does* that?"

"Joe," Ramona and I chorus in response.

Thankfully, it has no edge to it that could instill some form of confidence in the human being attached to the name.

Ramona runs her hands through my thick red locks and cringes. "Geez, you look like you haven't washed your hair in a week."

"Rude." I laugh, then run my own hands through the knotted mess, which halts my sense of humor. *Yeah, okay, it's been a couple days...* "I was gonna do it today."

"That's what we all say," Ramona says, touching her flawless curly black hair.

I narrow my eyes. My gingery red hair betrays me every time I so much as sweat for a minute like it's shouting, "*Hear ye! Hear ye! Girl with unwashed hair!*"

"Hank was supposed to remind me," I mumble. *Dog traitor once again!* "And hey, this doesn't have to do with Joe!" I say, defensive the second I get a side-eye of pity from Wes. "I'm over him."

"It was a long time coming," Ramona says with a reassuring head nod, looking away from me.

Although her face was turned away from me just so I honestly can't tell if she's being sarcastic or not. She knows her expression will give her away every time.

"It was!" I call up to her as she hops on the back of the truck to grab a box and hand it down to me. "I think."

I *am* over Joe. I'm pretty sure. Listen, after months of not sleeping together, it's like the post-mortem had come and gone, and the only thing I had left to focus on was getting the heck out of there as soon as I could before my soul ripped apart even more.

Lesson to all ladies: Love is a lie. Men will find some way to seek out other women. Let's all just get dildos and call it a day.

"Fuck him," Ramona shrugs then laughs. "Well, don't, but... screw him."

"I get your point."

We spend the next few hours going up and down the staircases to my new second-floor apartment with everything from living room side tables to a decorative giraffe that has wide eyes and kind of makes me uncomfortable.

"No," I say, shoving it into her arms the second I pull it out the box. "Absolutely not. Either you take it back or it will be going in the kitchen cabinet before I find it in the doorway of my bedroom at two in the morning."

"Oh, we got that in Africa!" she says clapping her hands together. "It's some tribal..."

"Yep, gonna cut you off there." I shake my head.

"Guess we won't be using the camera we installed in there." Wes winks at me.

Ramona sighs. "So much work down the drain."

I place the box I'm carrying down next to the crisp black new TV. "I'm beginning to think this isn't just hand-me-downs."

Ramona and Wes cringe at each other. They try to hide it, and I know they're being nice.

"I'll take you to some fancy restaurant," I say. Well, given that my bank account statement nearly made me sob, I'm not sure that's a great idea—even *if* my pride is bleeding at the thought of being a charity case.

I'm sure they can see the hesitation, though, and I want to kick myself for my emotions showing on my face so easily. The last thing I want is for them to feel bad.

"Just pizza works for us," Wes says. "No need to bother."

"I'll at least order a really fancy takeout pizza," I offer. "None of that commercial chain-restaurant stuff. I'll get real classy."

"Perfect!" Ramona says with a hand clap. "Pineapples too, please!"

"Girl, you know it." We high five as Wes groans.

That no-good pineapple pizza-hating man.

"So, how are the interviews coming along?" he asks.

I groan. "On a scale of one to natural disaster, it's about a hurricane of a billion killer whales. There's only been one so far, actually."

The interview was for a company looking for printing press operators, which I am definitely *not*. Screen printing classes were never my forte, as I'm also the kid that screamed when I touched glue during arts and crafts in preschool. How I pursued and loved paints instead, I'll never know.

Given a fight or flight situation, such as, oh I don't know, my horrible unemployment dilemma, I like to think my redheaded tenacity has always guided me in the right direction. I am a fists-up, *bring it on, baby!* fighting kinda gal. When I settled for a simple customer service job—which eventually developed into a collections role—my days were filled with "Please pay your balance or else your account will be on hold," statements and I decided after five years of that junk, all I really wanted was to pursue my true passion. I quit my collections job, instantly upgraded my resume, took some new designs I've been perfecting and some old paintings from college (conspicuously erasing the year I actually created them), and then sent out my portfolio to the world.

"Ian said they're hiring over at his job," Ramona says, placing a papasan down. "A design position, actually. I think they just promoted someone and need a replacement."

Ramona's older brother Ian is just like her: Successful, incredibly in tune with health and working out (which, admittedly, I need to get better at), and bit of an asshole. But like, a lovable asshole. Needless to say, we actually get along quite well.

"I'm willing to take any interview at this point," I say, lugging in a box filled with who-knows-what.

"Oh yeah," Wes chimes in, "he's at Treasuries Inc."

"Treasuries Inc.?" I gawk, almost tripping over the threshold and knocking into Ramona. "Treasuries Inc. as in the upcoming marketing firm? The marketing firm we went to that mixer at? The one where they were all like, 'Yeah, every Friday is Beer Friday because we're super cool and hip?' The start-up culture-beast darling of the city, and I'll be damned if I don't try my shot at it? That Treasuries Inc.?"

"Holy overload of information, Batman." Wes laughs. "How much stalking have you done on that company?"

"Don't even get her started." Ramona rolls her eyes.

"How are you just now telling me about this?" I'm almost offended this is the first I'm hearing about the opportunity. How could she! Withholding information from your best friend is a federal crime!

"Get your panties out of a wad," Ramona says. "I already told him you're interested." This elicits a slow grin to spread across my face as she starts mocking my missing reaction. *"Thank you, Ramona. You're such a wonderful friend. Oh, no, you are, Grace. I'm happy to be of service."*

I bolt toward her and jump into her arms, legs wrapped tight around her waist. "Thank you, thank you, thank you!"

"We got you covered," she laughs.

My head is swimming with possibilities: A place with a future. A place where they give promotions. An actual design gig in some cool, trendy job with progressive people who probably eat kale salads and do hot yoga. I'd kill to be one of those people. Literally, murder someone.

I decide right then and there the position that "may or may not exist" is totally mine.

2

GRACE

A TYPICAL THURSDAY NIGHT. Yet instead of lying on my empty apartment floor, I'm relaxing belly down on my mom's couch, laptop propped against the armrest, Hank chilling on the other side. His paw hangs off the end and twitches as a result of his deep sleep. I feverishly sift through my emails—ignoring those from Joe—and refresh the page over and over before realizing just how desperate I seem.

Ramona's brother, Ian, must have been feeling gracious a couple weeks ago when she sent him my resume. Two days later, Ian sent me an application, which I'd like to say I completed in record time. Instead, I spent two more days mulling over how to word my cover letter, fretting about which art to put in my portfolio, and taking maybe a bit too much time on my signature for the paperwork itself. First impressions are everything; I don't need my calling card looking like a crayon doodle.

Though maybe that's "in" now? Design trends are so weird.

"Will you get off that laptop for one second and help me?" Mom asks, holding a slightly threatening knife and waving it over as an invitation to join her in the kitchen.

My mom has the same flaming red hair, thin figure, and short fuse that I have, so it's no surprise where I got it all from. But at her core, she is the loveliest woman alive, trust me.

"Are you finally gonna use that kitchen of yours?" I ask, raising an eyebrow and sticking out my tongue.

Her own eyebrows raise up as she points the knife at me once more. "That mouth is going to get you into trouble one day, missy," she says. "And yes, I refuse to let this house go to waste."

I definitely inherited my love for redecorating homes from Mom. She's spent years since my dad passed away redoing the entire house. She pulled up the carpet, stripped the paint, and spent way too much money on an entirely new kitchen, despite her rare desire to actually cook.

"I'm sure the kitchen appreciates the love," I snark, and she shoots me another menacing look.

On the flip side of the equation, my mom and I have always butted heads. We've always blamed it on our red hair. We said we're feisty and fire doesn't mix well with fire. Whatever that means. It's cooled down since I've gotten older, but I was mostly just a little shit of a teenager. Teachers always commended my parents for raising such a lovely girl, but that's just because I saved all my angst for my parents.

What was it that Usher said? Lady in the streets, complete heathen she-devil behind closed doors? No, that's not it…

I was a force to be reckoned with. At least I thought I was. Mostly I just stayed out at friends' houses until four in the morning—especially once I'd gotten my beat-up old Volkswagen; a car I still drive to this day. My parents were obviously worried, but I was just so damn cool with my car.

Yeah, I still cringe thinking about it, too.

Bless my mom for still being with me today.

I close my laptop and walk across the open floor plan to the kitchen island where I pull up a bar stool and lean my elbows on the counter. It's the one part of the kitchen that doesn't *quite* match her more modern décor. I run my hands along its scarred wood surface and memories of Dad wash over me. I used to sit on it and watch him cook here. He never really said much, but occasionally, he'd throw me a homemade French fry or two while I doodled. I miss being near him; I'm glad she kept the island.

"So, what's on the menu?" I ask, reaching to grab a piece of a sliced cucumber. She bats my hand away.

"Tacos."

"Ooh yum." I say, wiggling my shoulders. "And why tacos this time around?"

"They seem easy," she says with a sigh. "If I'm going to learn, I've got to start simple, right?"

"Well, it's good to know that after renovating everything that can possibly be renovated, you've decided to conquer the art of cooking," I say, trying my hand at stealing another slice; she catches me again. I laugh and she winks.

The kitchen shelves are lined with cookbooks containing lofty recipes, but unfortunately for me, when she's normally done cooking, the outcome isn't nearly as appetizing as the pictures.

In our small lull of silence, I start to get itchy with anticipation of hearing about the job again. I unlock my phone and look at my emails, pulling the screen down to refresh.

"Leave it alone," Mom says with a chuckle. "If you get an email from them, you'll get an email. It won't go anywhere."

"Yeah, I know," I say through a heavy exhale. "But I'm not exactly the most graceful person."

With her mouth half open, I know my mom is about to make some clever come back about how "Grace is always graceful," but I point at her to stop before she can start.

"The HR person asked how I handled stress and I totally lied," I say.

"Did you say you handle it well?" my mom asks, still chopping. Why is she asking if she knows the damn answer?

"Yeah."

"Definitely a lie," she says without missing a beat. She tries to wink at me again, but I twist my mouth into the corner, undeterred by her teasing.

"Well, the creative director and I talked about my history in design and eventually discussed my ambitions," I say. "I think that's where I nailed the interview." While I say this, my anxiety gives me a thousand reasons as to why maybe I actually *didn't* nail it.

My mom lets out a small breath of air. "Wait, do you remember that time you wanted to go to that concert... oh, what was it..."

"The Backstreet Boys?"

"Yes!" she says, throwing her hand in the air. "Backstreet Boys. And you insisted your father buy you tickets."

"He didn't."

"Well of course not. You were six. But you being the spunky girl you are, off you went! Backpack full of stuffed toys and one peanut butter sandwich. You were determined to make it to that concert."

"Blindly walking in no direction at all," I comment with a smile. "Not much has changed."

"Yes, but I firmly believe that if you put your mind to something, you *will* do it. It may not be this company, but you will be a designer."

My mom has always been a glass half-empty woman, and my dad was the family optimist. When he passed, I think his positivity somehow osmosed into her and now her sunshine and rainbows outlook on life is like a full glass of water I could drink in every day.

We exchange smiles and she returns to chopping. Me, on the other hand, I can't help but whip out my phone again.

"In my day, we had to wait on calls and if we missed it, poof, you missed it." She nods matter-of-factly before slicing into a cucumber—nearly chopping her fingers off. She's still learning.

"Mom, you know I lived during those times too, right?" I say, putting my phone down after another glance yields zero responses.

"Millennials don't know how good they have it," she continues, pretending I didn't say anything rational at all. "And will you please grab that pepper and help me out?"

I lean forward on the counter to withdraw a knife from the block and scoot the green pepper toward me. But before I can even start, my phone buzzes. I look down to see an email from a sender using an address ending in treasuriesinc.com.

"Holy shit," I breathe, ignoring Mom's immediate reply of "Language, young lady!"

I gulp—almost a cartoony sound that makes my mom's disappointment in my choice of words switch to excitement.

"Well, are you going to open it?" she asks.

"Just... give me a second, Mom," I say.

I stare at the unopened email, trying to come to terms with how let down I will be if it holds bad news. Taking a deep breath, I click the message.

Grace Holmes,

We are pleased to offer you the position of Junior Designer with Treasuries, Inc. Attached, you will find your offer letter and background authorization form. Please complete and return both documents to our HR Manager, Nia Smith. She is copied on this email.

We look forward to working with you.
Regards,
Cameron Kaufman, Creative Director

The biggest childlike grin spreads across my face and my fingers go from shaking to practically dancing off my hands.

"Mom!" I scream, causing my poor old, sleeping dog to bolt upright on the couch, wide awake. "I'm in!" I jump up, run to my mom, and grab her hands. "I'm a designer!"

"That's fantastic!" she yells, joining me as I jump up and down in excitement. "See? I knew things would turn around for you."

I smile and rush over to my phone to look down at the email once again and read out loud, "Regards, Cameron Kaufman."

"Who is Cameron Kaufman?" Mom asks, returning to her haphazard vegetable cutting.

"I think he's the guy they just promoted?" It's a question more than a definitive answer. "I don't know. It says 'creative director' in his signature, but I definitely didn't meet with a dude named Cameron."

It's impossible to forget the old man who actually interviewed me. I think he could cough dust into his handkerchief.

"Sounds proper," she says.

"And professional," I muse, looking down at myself and realizing I haven't changed clothes in a couple days... nor have I showered.

"I need a new outfit," I say, and Mom squeals.

Clothing is the only thing she hasn't had to revamp in her life because her style has always shifted with the times. In seconds, she's redirecting me on my phone to some fancy online shop.

The clothes are strictly within a price range that starts with a fifty dollar minimum (because hey, I can totally support that now), so we buy the exact well-tailored outfit the model is wearing on the front page from their "#GirlBoss" collection. I look down at my own shirt and realize that "#GirlBoss" sure beats the hot pink "#BlessThisMess" shirt Ramona gave me.

The website's cart reads well over a price range I can afford, and the price is bumped even higher when I select two-day shipping. But the spiffy suit just screams, "I have my life together!" so I click "purchase," ignore the sinking feeling in my gut that knows I spent too much, and scoot myself back into the bar stool.

Mom begs me to "please finish cutting the darn pepper, Grace!" but I just keep smiling while I look at the email. While I may not know much about clothing, budgeting, or helping in the kitchen, I do know one thing: This is my new start.

3

GRACE

My hands haven't stopped shaking since I received that email. They shook when I turned off my alarm clock this morning, they shook when I packed my laptop bag, and they continue to shake while I turn the wheel into an empty parking lot in an effort to get back on the road in the actual direction I'm supposed to go.

"Rerouting... turn left onto State Boulevard—"

"Shut up," I groan to my phone's GPS. It's been trying to direct me to Treasuries, Inc. for nearly thirty minutes in what should have been a ten-minute drive. I thank my lucky stars I had the good sense to leave as early as I did or else this could have been an entirely different day.

"Rerouting... turn right onto State—"

"Stop!" I furiously tap my phone to exit the app and reopen it.

Everyone knows that always solves the problem.

After turning left then right then left again, swerving into grocery store shopping center, and making a quick stop at a gas station to break up the nervous energy (yes, I may have looked in the mirror and said, "You can do this, Grace! You are a super hero!" but we don't need to talk about that), I'm finally facing the front of a warehouse building with the words "Treasuries, Inc." displayed in bold, beautiful letters across the garage door entrance. All with ten minutes to spare.

My old-fashioned yellow VW bug normally sticks out in a business car park, but in this lot full of eclectics, it fits in nicely. I spy on some other individuals walking into the building. They're all wearing blue jeans, casual shoes, band t-shirts, and some women are even wearing those flowy skirts that seem to say, "Sure, I could live in a van and go on meditation retreats." I look down at my own attire and groan.

I definitely overdressed. What woman in this day and age goes into a new graphic design position with the notion of, "I must dress my best?" Nobody. That's who. You know what women do now? They go to Anthropologie or, hell, *Goodwill* and make themselves look "chic."

Is that the word? Oh, hell.

Tons of unnecessary money I do not have just went right down the drain.

Wait—no! I am a confident woman. I overdressed because I mean business. This shows I'm serious, dang it! I'm taking my life by the balls and squeezing it into submission.

I snatch my phone from its holster on my dashboard, slam the car door shut, and lug my bag right up to the front door. But with confidence. Obviously. Always with confidence. Because I am a suit-wearing female with a plan.

The double doors slide open the second I walk in, and before I can mentally make some snarky comment about whether this is some renovated grocery store, a woman at a beautifully curved front desk raises her eyebrow at me, scans me up and down, and smirks.

She's just as trendy as everyone else I've seen so far. Her platinum blonde hair is perfectly curled and a piercing hugs the curve of her nose as if it's always belonged there. Dang, she even looks super cool with her choker necklace and collared tee that seems both professional and like it'd be right off the back of a mannequin in Forever 21. But more impressive than the receptionist's beauty is the building itself.

The interior is already massive, but it appears even larger with its exposed ceiling fifty or so feet off the ground. The desks are gathered in clusters, but it doesn't feel crowded. There are no cubicles. There is no musty carpet. Just clean, open space. Where there aren't conference rooms closed off by clear windows, there are walls coated in vibrant colors with designs blended in both graffiti and pop art styles. Painted on the central back wall is a giant treasure chest surrounded by a circle of the repeating statement: *Work Hard, Play Hard.*

A bit cliché, but I can get behind it.

I had no idea that an office space could look this cool.

The girl behind the counter clears her throat.

"May I help you?" she asks.

She has this weird mix of both irritation and an obligation to sound as nice as she can for her job. No clue how she pulls that off. I think it's her stunning beauty that gives her an edge.

"Y-yes!" I stammer. Goddamn it, who really stammers? Not confident women. That's not who stammers. And I am a confident woman with my too-high heels and my too-sharp suit. "My name is Grace Holmes. I'm here to see Cameron Kaufman."

The girl peers behind her cat-eye turquoise-tinted glasses (God, can she get any cooler?) and swishes her eyes over to her laptop screen, rapidly clicking on the keyboard.

"He's not in yet," she says, her tapping fingers settling. "But take a seat over there. He should be in shortly."

She points to a set of very stiff beanbag chairs in varying colors of orange, and I choose the one that will expose the least amount of thigh when I plop down into it. But I was mistaken. They may look stiff, but the bag swallows me whole the second my butt hits the seat. So much for not having my skirt ride up too much.

After I've sufficiently taken in the remaining scenery and the couches where employees casually complete work while wearing massive headphones over their heads, I start to feel like a significant amount of time has passed.

Am I in the right place? Of course I am. This is Treasuries Inc., and by golly, I've made it here. I work here!

But I look at my watch and, yes, time surely has passed.

9:20.

Yikes. Is this guy kidding? I'd pictured this Cameron Kaufman guy as a prompt man: He arrived at 7:00 in the morning, on the dot—maybe earlier. He wears suits sharper than mine and way less comfortable, if that's even an option. But so far, I see no promptness and no sharp suit. Zero for two, Mr. Kaufman.

I glance over at the sliding glass door and watch as more employees trickle in. There's a blonde man with a bag slung over his shoulder bobbing his head back and forth under his headphones, a young Asian woman wearing a t-shirt dress and popping gum to the beat of every third step, and finally an older man that comes in, waves to the trendy receptionist, and keeps walking.

Was that Mr. Kaufman? He walked right past me. Would the girl have told him I was sitting here? I'm honestly not sure, given her attitude.

I look down at my watch again.

9:30.

More happy employees walk in, with me wishing I was one of them instead of my current role as the lone dope chilling on the beanbag I'm slowly sinking into.

This beanbag is my destiny, and my soul is the uncomfortable sewn edge now making a mark into the side of my thigh where the skirt has rolled up.

While I'm focused on making sure my skirt returns to an appropriate length, footsteps squeak across the laminated concrete, and if this weren't my first day on the job and I wasn't trying to maintain my professionalism, my jaw might have hit the floor when I see the man approaching.

I'm pretty sure it's absolutely unfair to be that good looking.

His jawline can probably cut glass, but it's lightly covered by a layer of stubble that softens his features just enough that I can imagine running my hands over his chin. His hair is shaved closer on the sides, but it's thick and mussed up at the top with just the slightest bit of gel—or maybe it's still wet from the shower.

His denim shirt is tucked into cream-colored chinos, and he wears dark leather oxfords, which add just a bit of business sense to the otherwise casual look. But unlike other employees, his clothes are slightly more well-fitted, as if he's gotten them tailored. Or maybe he's just built exactly how the designers imagined a perfect man to look.

He stops at the front desk and the girl directs him over to the prison of beanbags where I'm sitting. She looks equally as distracted as I am by his presence. As he approaches the corner I have thus begun to claim as my own desk area, I find myself starting to sweat and I pray to the good lord above that my black suit won't reveal armpit stains.

He sits in the beanbag next to me, crossing his ankle over his other leg. His pants come up just enough to reveal corgi-patterned socks peeking out.

Be still my heart.

This body connected to a jawline turns to me, as if he's going to speak, but I nervously blurt out, "Is this your first day, too?" before he even has the chance to get any sound out.

Wow, dummy. What are the odds? But I'd rather have the first word in this conversation where I know I have only an eighty-percent chance of looking like a fool rather than my usual one hundred percent chance of looking like a complete moron.

He stares at me for a second, squints a bit as if considering, then smiles. Boy oh boy, if I wasn't dead yet, those dimples would have just done me in.

"Uh, no, I'm here for"—he pauses, glancing at his watch—"an interview, actually. How long have you been waiting?" His voice is deep, but it's equally smooth and calming.

A voice that feels familiar; like he's the boy next door you've been swooning after your whole life. Unattainable, but welcoming.

I break my gaze away to glance down at my own watch.

"Thirty minutes," I say, and then I shrug. "Which if you ask me is a bit too long."

Great job, Grace. You really can't filter your thoughts right now? Seriously? I'm kicking myself knowing that I'm completely incapable of hiding the frustration at how long I've had to wait.

But come on! Half an hour? On my first day? What is this, the DMV?

His eyes widen in surprise and he laughs. "Won't be a secret if you say it much louder."

I smirk in a knowing glance, even arching my eyebrow as if testing him.

"So, thirty minutes, huh?" he asks. "Who are you waiting on? Some hot shot exec, I bet."

As he talks, his eyes slip down to the part of the beanbag that's tugging on a corner of my pencil skirt and exposing an immodest amount of thigh. I awkwardly adjust and he averts his gaze.

"Cameron Kaufman," I say.

He cringes. "Does this guy know he's incredibly late? Did he remember it's your first day?"

"Well, that'd be irresponsible if he didn't, wouldn't it?"

"Very. You know," he says, leaning in a bit closer and lowering his voice, "if that's how they act around here, then I sure as hell don't think I want to interview."

I can't help but let his scent of body wash waft over me. Is that some type of artificial campfire? Maybe mahogany? Whatever it is, I'm pretty sure I have a candle with that scent.

I can tell he's joking by the way he smiles wider, and I find myself attracted, rather than off-put that he was willing to walk out here and talk to me on a whim. Maybe it's the risk of it all; a man taking risks isn't the worst thing that's happened in the world.

He looks down at his watch again and shakes his head. "9:45. They're really pushing their luck with you."

"Thankfully I'm fairly patient," I say.

He looks down at my bouncing leg that I was unaware of until just now and laughs, "Clearly."

I cave. "Okay, so sure, I've got a bit of a patience issue, but forty-five minutes? Get real." I'm not trying to trash this Cameron guy, but I'm totally trashing this Cameron guy, despite the fact that part of me knows I should be thanking my lucky stars I'm even here to begin with. That calms me down a bit.

"Well, you've convinced me." He stands up, clapping his hands as if announcing his imminent departure, and I instantly long for him to stay. He's so wildly impulsive.

No, don't abandon me with these lonely beanbag chairs, Mr. Gorgeous Man.

He holds out his hand to me. "It was nice to meet you, Miss...?"

"Grace. Grace Holmes." I shake his hand.

"Are you related to Sherlock Holmes?" he asks with a grin.

Not the first time I've heard that, but he's just so damn good looking that I'll give it to him.

"Distant cousin." I smile. "Always second best. But hey, I try."

He nods. "Well it's nice to meet you, Grace."

I refuse to let this man leave without getting a name, a number, an address, a hand on those forearms...

"I'm sorry—what did you say your name was?" I ask.

"I didn't. I'm Cameron Kaufman." The most shit-eating grin flashes across his face and my heart sinks. "But most people just call me Cam."

Shit.

4

CAMERON

My name is Cameron Kaufman, but most people just call me Cam. If you needed to use it in a sentence, it could be said as: "Hey Cam, I have these new layouts for you," or "Cam, don't forget we have the new girl starting on Monday!" and, "This is the third time you've been late this month, Cam." Human Resources loves that one.

What most people don't realize is that brand new Mr. "Boss Man" Cam has a lot going on right now. First, there's the promotion. Then, the crazy responsibilities. Oh, and I'm not getting laid even though I'm in a relationship. That's a big one.

Let's just say that, even though I let off some steam joking around with the new girl, her first day is the least of my worries, and Human Resources needs to understand that. Though, in reality, our HR lady Nia is quite nice. She bakes cookies.

But as I'm looking at my shiny new official write-up, complete with both mine and Nia the HR Manager's swoopy glamour signature, I hear a kick on my door followed by long legs striding into my office.

Some people start their weekdays with coffee. I start mine

with Ian Chambers. Ian is gregarious, as tall as that dumb bellhop from the Addams Family, and he's got the humor of a frat boy, but the man frequents the gym religiously and could sweet-talk a toad into boiling water.

"Good morning, Cam!" he sing-songs into my office, running a hand through his jet black, curly hair. "Finally got that third warning you've been aching for?"

"Months and months of being late time and time again, and all I get is a silly piece of paper!" I jest, waving it in front of his face. "Where's my medal? Where's my face on the wall of *Slacking Employee of the Quarter?*"

"Nobody wants your face on a wall," Ian says, snatching the paper out of my hand from a few feet away. He skims it over, his glasses sliding down the end of his nose; he looks like a sixty-year-old man in a thirty-five-year old's body, but he's still one of the sharpest sons-of-bitches I know.

I'm on the creative side of Treasuries, Inc., but he's our in-house lawyer. Ian conducted part of my orientation week about five years ago, and as a young, budding designer I thought it would be funny to ask legal advice on what to do if a client asks for graphic nudity in their design. He replied that the client is always right, we should do what they like, and then asked if I was taking commissions.

We've been best buds ever since.

"They put you on probation?" he asks, letting the paper fall to his side. "For being late a couple times?"

"I have to volunteer at Beer Friday for the next two weeks," I groan. "You know, I thought being promoted to creative director would grant me some immunities, like not being bitch boy to the whole company."

"But you love Beer Friday," Ian says, peering up from his glasses.

"Exactly! I would prefer to be *drinking* the beer rather than *pouring* the beer."

Ian quirks an eyebrow at me. "You should not be a manager."

"I'm a damn good manager," I say, pointing a finger at him. "I just also like booze."

Ian rolls his eyes and places the document back on my desk, patting it as it rests.

"Damn, this is beautiful documentation," he says, looking at the paper as if it were wearing a two-piece string bikini. "You told Nia I love her, right?"

I smirk. "Of course not."

"Darn," he says. "She'll never know."

"Bullshit she won't," I say. "You've been bugging her for as long as I've known you. HR or not, you're playing with fire."

He motions his hand open and closed like a yapping mouth, mocking. "Don't need your judgments, Cam. I'm a lawyer. I know what I'm doing."

"Sure ya do."

"So," he says, narrowing his eyes and changing the subject. "How's your sleep?"

This is what I get for not indulging him. Let's delve into my love life instead. Perfect.

"Getting better," I lie. I shouldn't have told the bastard about my relationship issues.

"You were late to work again," he says, folding his arms across his chest.

I scoff and shake my head, averting my eyes and shuffling papers on my desk. What even are these? Please give me something to avoid this conversation.

"Nah," I laugh. "I was only late by like, five minutes."

"Forty minutes," he corrects.

"I got caught in traffic."

If looking guilty was a sport, I'd be the national champion. I can feel my eyebrows pinching together in the middle, holding the weight of my bold-faced, nasty, no-good lie.

Ian knows Abby and I are struggling, and he's trying to be a good friend. But there are multiple issues popping up left and right that even *I* have a hard time comprehending—let alone trying to explain.

"Fine," I sigh. "It sometimes feels like Abby is arguing for the sake of arguing."

"You think she's just going through something?" he asks.

"I think she's just made up her mind to hate me."

"Women, am I right?" he says with a grin.

Don't get me wrong—Abby's not a bad girlfriend. We've been through a lot together. She's practically my dog Buddy's stepmother. I think she may walk him more than I do. Much to her disdain.

"It's not like it's unwarranted," I say.

But the real point of contention—the elephant in the room...

"So you still haven't proposed, huh," Ian says.

Bingo.

It's not like she's not "the one," but even after five years together, the idea of a ring, vows, a wedding... Potentially committing to a lifetime of something inescapable makes me sweat; makes me feel like I'm wearing the thickest, highest turtleneck on a beach in August.

Some might say it's a fear of commitment. But I say I have a healthy caution about accepting things that will last a lifetime.

But think about this: I wanted a tattoo that was an exact replica of The Rock's bull head tattoo when I was seventeen. Did I get it? Absolutely not. That shit would still be on my arm today—some dumb token representing a teenage dream about becoming a professional wrestler.

The Rock may not have fully inspired me to pursue my wrestling dreams, but he sure taught me that slapping a really shitty tattoo, or in this case a ring, on my finger for the rest of eternity is a dumb idea.

I open my mouth to argue my answer but, as if on cue, Nia pokes her head into my doorframe, forcing the door open and leaning her hips to the side.

"The new girl's ready for you," she says.

If I didn't know any better, I'd say she was showing off her thin figure with the way she moves, but this chick is as hard and ruthless as they come. She follows her self-written company policies to a "T." Strong women are definitely my type, but I tend to veer away from the law-abiding, goody-too-shoes kind.

How dare she walk into my office after giving me probation? I demand some sort of privacy after that lashing.

"Oh, right, Grace," Ian says, snapping his fingers and breaking his fixed gaze on Nia.

The name gives me pause. Grace Holmes. The new girl with an attitude. Maybe I shouldn't have tricked her, but she's too feisty and confident for her own good.

"How do you know her?" I ask Ian.

"I got her to apply," he says.

"Oh really?"

"Yeah, she's my sister's best friend."

"Boys," Nia snaps, "reel it in."

"Is she still in your office?" I ask.

I turn on professional Cameron: The personality I should have given to the new girl this morning rather than tricking her. I can be myself around Ian, but I know it's better to approach Human Resources with "Is she still in your office?" rather than, "I'm really fucking sleepy, Nia."

Yeah, that wouldn't go over too well.

Nia shakes her head, sending her blonde hair swishing from side to side. "She's had most of her orientation, but she's still filling out some paperwork. She's at her desk in the back corner near the printers."

Lucky girl. That was my old desk. Before I had this office, it was impossible to concentrate with our office's open structure. I negotiated for that desk, purchasing the UX Designer, Gary, gummy bears for an entire month so he'd switch with me.

"I'll be there in a second to show her around," I say.

"Perfect," Nia replies with a snap. Every word with her is a direct statement. Just one more checkmark on her list before moving on to the next task.

The conversation clearly over, she leaves the room and Ian sighs. "That woman."

He plops down on the small sofa in the corner of my office. His long legs dangle over the edge of the arm rest and touch the floor.

"All right, out of my office, bud." I open the top drawer of my desk to pull out the new girl's design brief for the company and walk toward the door. "I'm heading out."

He barks out a laugh. "You're such a stiff now. I hate manager Cameron."

"I'm just here to do my job," I call back.

"You've changed!" he says, getting the last word in.

Damn him.

He's not wrong. I used to be just another designer until a month ago. Just another dreamer. But then I got the offer of creative director, and all these high expectations got placed in my lap. I've quickly learned that the jump from being a cog in the machine to being the handle that powers it results in having to put on a face that may not be your own.

It's just a job, I guess.

5
―
GRACE

My first week on the job flies by in a whirlwind of meetings, lunches, and learning the names of people I know I won't remember for at least a few months. But I love every second of it—the PowerPoint presentations showing every recent project they've produced, sketches and design processes, and even the catered lunches are to die for. I ask too many questions, I'm sure, but my desk neighbor, Gary, is happy to answer any inquiries I have. Plus, sometimes he rewards me with the jar of gummy bears at his desk.

I ain't complaining.

It wasn't until Friday that I finally touched my computer and tablet, but even that didn't last very long.

It was the sacred Beer Friday.

I got introduced to the warehouse at exactly five o'clock when my team members close their laptops and exit the designer's bullpen, leaving their stuff behind. The beautiful, chill receptionist, who I now know as Saria, walks in and rolls a finger at me for me to follow her.

If Beer Friday could have a chapel, it would be the warehouse. The back of the building holds no production or storage but is simply dedicated to the glorious celebration of alcohol. Ten beer pong tables are spread around the back. Bars to both the left and right of the entrance feature handles for craft beer on tap, shelves of wine, and rows of displayed sample shots with unique names like, "Speed of Light," and, "Down the Hatch."

Who even comes up with this stuff?

Saria leads me around and introduces me to some more people I won't remember: Sales guys who eyeball me a bit too close for comfort, the accounting team that's shy yet seemingly genuine, and customer service, which mostly consists of outgoing individuals who chatter too loudly for my tastes. Eventually, Saria eyes the bar, takes my order, and goes to file in line. Thanks to that, I'm left to fend for myself. Great.

Over the course of this week, I've gotten very good at pep talking myself into anything I need to do. *Que sera, sera!* I'm not just some awkward new girl sitting in the back-corner desk. I'm a bold, fiery red head with things to say. Important things. Things that will get me remembered.

My phone buzzes and I look down at it. My chest sinks. It's a text from Joe. I'd gotten accustomed to his constant barrage of emails, and I was getting comfortable with the routine of no longer receiving texts. But like most things in life, that must not have been good enough for him.

Joe: Let's meet up.

I almost respond, but then my frustration takes over and I decide to pocket my phone so roughly it almost brings my pants down past my hips. No, he will not ruin tonight. This is *my* night.

Confidence is key, remember?

I look around and spot the tallest man in the room. I'm kind of tall myself, and even taller with my combat boots on. After settling back into my default attire once I realized that Treasuries Inc.'s "business casual" policy is heavy on the "casual," I whipped those puppies out real quick. But regardless of my height, this man is still intimidating. But damn it, that's exactly what I need. If I approach the most intimidating person here, then I have conquered Beer Friday.

Beer Friday will be my bitch.

I make it over to him and almost start talking, but behind this guy's tall, muscular frame, I see the one man I have attempted to avoid all week: My boss, Cameron Kaufman.

It was bad enough I insulted him before I even knew who he was, but every time I see his beautiful, sharp jawline move as he produces wonderful words during meetings, I slink my way back to my corner desk and pretend to be reading whatever documents I've been given that day.

But I've noticed a couple things about Mr. Cameron Kaufman during my week-long observations. I've noticed that his hair is always perfectly tousled. I also noticed that he keeps his face shaved with the perfect amount of brown stubble leftover. And although every other employee dresses in casual wear—including myself with my no-nonsense combat boots—he veers more on the business side of things with his charming denim tops and clean-cut chinos.

Even now, as he stands here with one hand in his pocket and the other holding a beer, a small smile plays on his face and just beneath the stubble, I spot a hint of dimples. Good lord almighty above, I swear by the Beer Friday gods, this man is beyond the appropriate levels of attractiveness, having dived deep into unfair territory once again.

So instead of following my original plan where I step in and say super fun, interesting things to make me immediately likable, an odd silence falls over the two of them because I am just too stunned by Cameron's Cameron-ness. But the tall man turns and, thank God, I recognize him.

"Ian!" I say, relief washing over me. Ramona's brother is a breath of fresh air.

"Grace!" he says, his long arm swallowing me in a side hug while he balances a small plate of food in the other hand. "Glad you could make it."

"Yeah, me too," I say, glancing around. My eyes stop on Cameron. He's smiling at me. I didn't even know it was possible to be charming without saying a single word.

"No drink?" Ian asks, nodding to my empty hands.

"Saria is in line." I jab my thumb toward the bar.

We all turn to look, but it's one of those unnecessary head turns that mostly just gives us something to do. I can feel that in two seconds we might already be running out of things to say. Or maybe my rude interruption just made things awkward.

"I should get a refill too," Cameron says, speaking for the first time. "I have to start my shift soon anyway."

"Shift?" I ask. If it's going to be uncomfortable, I'll just go the whole nine yards. That's me: Pushy human extraordinaire.

"He's been late to work too many times," Ian says. "He got in trouble with HR and now he's a volunteer."

"It's not really volunteering if you're being forced to do it, right?" I ask, and Cameron smirks.

"We'll call it volunteering for fun," he says.

"So, are you normally late to work?" I ask. There I go again. Putting my foot in my mouth. But, hey, he smiled and I panicked. What do you expect me to do?

Ian laughs, but Cameron doesn't show the same appreciation of my humor.

"I mean..." I laugh. Yeah, I screwed up this time. "I just—"

"No, I'm only late on the days new hires get here at nine a.m." he says, sarcasm dripping down his lips. "It's like I wake up and think, 'Nah, I don't need that responsibility in my life right now,' and then I toss right on over."

"And do you normally trick new hires into thinking you're

someone else as well?" I retort, cheeks flushing at his biting remark.

"Excuse me?" Ian asks, raising his eyebrows to his hairline and chuckling. "Is there a story here?"

"Call it a test of character," Cameron says, ignoring Ian and holding his drink up to me in a toast. "And I have a question: Do you normally insult your bosses on your first day?"

"I've generally had bosses that arrive on time," I shoot back, crossing my arms with a smirk. "In fact, isn't it called 'leading by example?'"

"Maybe I prefer a different approach to management," he says, crossing his arms in a mocking motion to mirror me, his beer bottle hanging from between his fingers.

"And what would that be?"

"Shaming employees into submission," he says, and I wonder if there's a hint of a smirk tugging at the edge of his lips.

I also feel a pull between my legs at the idea of submission. I like that word coming out of his mouth. "And how is that working out for you?" I ask.

Cameron's eyes narrow. *Shit, I might have taken it too far.*

Ian's eyes dart between the two of us, amused.

"Well, I'll be," Ian says, holding out his free hand to let me high five it. "I almost forgot why Ramona likes you."

I'm not sure if joking with my direct supervisor in such a way was exactly a good thing to do, but the in-house lawyer is congratulating me, so I guess I'm not fired.

Yet.

I land the high five and keep looking at Cameron, who's shaking his head back and forth. "That mouth is going to get you in trouble one day," he says.

I smile. "So I've been told."

Maybe I'm just imagining it, but I swear for a second, I see his eyes dart down to my lips and then back up. It's subtle, but I can feel the heat rising up my body beneath his gaze. It's intoxicating; I wonder if he knows just how much tension he can put on a person. Or if he even cares.

"I'll see you later," he says to Ian, patting him on the shoulder before turning back to me. "And you, Holmes"—he points at me with his index finger as if demanding me to follow his next order—"might want to spend the weekend getting that attitude under control."

I hesitate for a moment, wondering if this is a request from a boss or a warning, but all I can think to say is, "Maybe."

He rolls his eyes and stalks off.

Oh yeah. Beer Friday is my bitch.

6

CAMERON

BEER FRIDAYS normally go like this: Chat with Ian, drink a bit, play beer pong, drink a bit, play darts, drink a bit, rinse and repeat. But it seems like the next two Fridays will consist of drinking only a little and then working behind the bar pouring said drinks. And unfortunately, I didn't get any time to play beer pong or darts before coming back to volunteer, since I was interrupted by Grace Holmes.

The new girl is a little firecracker and probably the last person I need under me as a new manager. I can tell we're going to have issues, and even if I'm ready for the challenge, I'm a bit irritated that it exists this soon into the game. Even those combat boots of hers really add to the whole "watch out I'll take you down" vibe.

I'll be damned if some new girl is going to undermine me in my first month as a manager. I get enough shit at home with Abby constantly on my case about who knows what anymore. Judging by Grace's response, I doubt she took my warning to heart, but that's on her. She'll be in for a rude awakening soon enough.

I spend the rest of Beer Friday slinging drinks and trying

not to think of Grace's attitude. But once that leaves my mind, all I have left are thoughts that encompass a weekend full of Abby's disagreeable self. After five years, I'm tired of late-night fights over who did the dishes and why they weren't done sooner, or why I don't pursue my dream of architecture design, or who took Buddy on a walk most recently. The poor dog doesn't need to see fighting parents that often—if you would even call Abby a motherly figure to him.

I bet she went out tonight. I bet she's wearing that top that makes me fucking crazy. Or maybe the other one that shows most of her toned back. God, I miss looking at that back from behind. She may be a menace as of late, but that doesn't mean she's lost any of her looks.

I try and remember the last time Abby came to Beer Friday with me and frown. It's been about a year—since she started her cycling class and made some friends there. I miss seeing her hanging around the warehouse—especially in some of her sexier outfits—but I'm glad she's getting some time in with her girlfriends. She doesn't have many, as it is. Still, it wouldn't hurt seeing her walking around in that top, beer in hand, smiling at me from across the room...

Tonight has gotten me far more worked up than I need to be. Unfortunately for me, volunteers work until the company stops partying at around midnight, and then they have to help clean up. By the time I get back home near one, she'll be in pajamas and passed out.

I wave over Ian at around eight o'clock and convince him to take over for me for the rest of the night. This may have taken some bribing and promises that I'll pay for lunch next week, but by the time I head out, it's nine o'clock. I should be able to make it home just in time to set up a candle or two before Abby gets back from hanging out with her friends. Then, who knows? I may not get laid—because that seems like an impossibility nowadays—but at least she'll think it's sweet and I'll see her smile.

Not sure the last time I saw something shot in my direction that wasn't a scowl from that woman, but it's worth a shot.

I drop by the convenience store, pick up some candles, and hurry home.

When I pull up to the driveway, Abby's little black Audi is already there. Shit, she must be intending to drink a lot tonight if she's getting a DD to take her out.

But when I open the front door and hear the unmistakable sound of *Kitchen Nightmares*, confusion sets in. *So she's home?* Honestly, I'm a little irritated she's watching it without me because it's *our* show, but oh well. I'm here with candles, and hopefully it will be a good time regardless.

I hop up the stairs, realizing that even the thought of my girlfriend in her little sheep pajamas is getting me excited. But there's no sexy girlfriend sitting in her animal print pjs on the sofa; only a man.

A *naked* man.

A naked man who's sprawled out all over my leather couch.

His gross, bush-covered balls are on my leather couch, and in his hand is my glass Abby got me for our anniversary last year—the one that says "#1 Boyfriend."

Is that my fucking *brandy*?

My stomach drops down into my balls and then plummets even farther into my legs. There's buzzing in my ears, my temperature rises; I'm having trouble thinking words—let alone saying them.

"Who the hell are you?" the stranger demands, a thick French accent obscuring his words so that I almost can't understand him.

Of course he's fucking French.

I don't know what's worse: The fact that he doesn't know

this is my house, or that he's so confident in himself he doesn't even consider covering his privates.

"Frank, it's your turn to walk the dog," Abby calls. "He keeps barking. I'm fucking tired of his shit."

She walks in, just as naked as I was imagining her. Toned, beautiful... and definitely not in her birthday suit for *my* pleasure. She stops and her jaw drops.

"Fuck."

I'll take the honest reaction. At least she didn't come up with an excuse; the evidence is damning enough.

I grimace. "Yeah. Fuck."

The French guy starts yelling, "Abby, who is this dick?"

I say nothing as Abby bites her lip in response. She looks up at the ceiling and her eyelashes flutter. *Is she seriously fighting back tears?*

Around the corner comes Buddy, my golden retriever and best friend. He rushes toward me, tongue lolling out of his mouth happy as can be, unaware of the situation. I want to take him and run, but with a small yelp, Frank the French man yanks Buddy by the collar.

"No, bad dog."

Bad dog? *Bad dog?!*

They say your life flashes before your eyes when you die, and I sure hope Frank can look back on his life with regret. Blood pumps through my veins like fire and every step I take toward him only fuels my rage. I can't see anything around me through my tunnel vision except his hook-nosed, tiny mustached, weasel face.

So, I do what any good American would: I punch the guy.

7

GRACE

IF YOU TELL me I'm going to spend a Saturday night out in bars with booze and dancing, I'll say, "Sure, I guess I can make it." But tell me I can instead come home and have hot tea with my old dog, and I'll be zooming out of the parking lot before you finish your sentence.

I spent my Saturday doing exactly that: Cuddling with Hank, ordering too much food, and flipping between old episodes of *Sex and the City* and *21 Jump Street* (A young Johnny Depp? Swoon). Hank prefers *Sex and the City*—that's not my choice, I swear! It might make lazy Saturdays a bit lazier than they need to be when I switch from show to show, but I'm willing to make sacrifices as needed for his sake.

By Sunday night, I've finished one season of each show, devoured two large pizzas, and burned off all the calories by going on occasional walks with Hank. At least, I like to think I burned off all the calories. It helps me sleep at night.

I've switched to grapes because I need some type of healthy balance after the junk food. I'm still popping them in my mouth and imagining I'm instead being fed by some Greek man next to a pool when my phone rings.

"Hey Ramona."

"Did you catch up on *The Bachelor* yet?" she asks.

"What are you talking about?"

There's a beat of silence between us. "Wait, is this Grace?"

"Yeah," I laugh.

"Shit, I meant to call Corinne. It's *The Bachelor* night." This isn't surprising. Ramona—ever the fast-paced sort of girl—commonly calls the wrong person when she's in a rush to gossip. I wish I could say this is the first time it's happened with *The Bachelor,* but I'd be lying. I should probably watch it with her and Corinne from the amount of times I've been mistaken for my cousin. "Anyway, how are you settling in, girl?"

"Well, I haven't been through *The Bachelor,* but I've demolished some *Sex & the City* this weekend."

"Big and Carrie's love is to die for," she swoons.

"Too complicated." I scrunch my nose. "Give me Charlotte and Harry's any day. They're friends first, he's goofy, and you can tell it's true love through and through."

Another moment of silence and Ramona clears her throat. "How are you, really? Without Joe, I mean. You haven't lived alone in two years."

"Just fine," I say. I wrap a string from my hole-riddled lounging tee around my finger. "I do miss that house, though."

"I believe it." She laughs.

Our house was a pet project for both of us, and Ramona spent too many weekends helping me paint and repaint every wall in that place. Joe was always a little less interested and rarely helped with the renovations. I made the big decisions.

It started as a beautiful two-story bullet home. Skinny on the sides and lengthy where it counts, but I added so much character to it. In the end, it could have rivaled the pad of a celebrity YouTube star with too much money to spend. Ramona and I covered the kitchen in chalkboard paint, tore out the walls on the top-most floor so that the master bedroom became a loft overlooking the den, and even transformed the cupboard under the stairs into a bedroom for Hank.

Joe and I lived in it for a stellar two years and then a not-so-great four months that involved no sex at all. Nothing. Nada. Not even a I'm-frustrated-we-haven't-had-sex-so-let's-get-it-on, rough sex kind of deal. Just barren ground. There could have been tumbleweed going through that bedroom. But sometimes, and only sometimes, he would roll over in our pallet-style bed and plant a small kiss on my forehead. The bastard gave me hope.

"Do you think you miss the house or the man?" Ramona asks.

"Don't use your psychologist voodoo on me, ma'am." Whenever Ramona's day job bleeds over to our conversations, it's never good. Maybe it's because she's right most of the time.

"I'm just curious!" she says.

"Whatever, I know I'm too good for him," I say. "He isn't worth my time. I am a new person. I'm a designer. I go to work events and stuff. I went to my first Beer Friday yesterday. It was a great time."

Joe and I used to go to his work events, too. But that's beside the point. *This is growth, dammit!*

"That sounds fun!" Her voice raises a pitch as if she's trying to lighten the mood again. "Did you see Ian?"

Sure, Ray's brother was there. But so was Cameron. Gorgeous, sarcastic, demanding Cameron. I've really got to stop thinking of him that way.

"Yeah, he seems like he's doing good," I say, deciding not to mention Cameron. He's just my weird boss. Uninteresting.

"Let's all get together again soon," she whines.

"Would it be weird without Joe?" I ask.

"Ian never really liked the guy anyway," she scoffs. "Remember that time he refused to play *Monopoly*? Who refuses *Monopoly*?"

"Most of the world. It's like, a two-hour game, Ray."

"And why are you defending him?"

"I'm not!"

Hank peers up at me from his bed. If he was capable of raising an eyebrow in disbelief, he would be.

"I mean, he's reached out to me less and less, which is nice." Thankfully, his ignored text on Friday prevented any more from coming through. Now I only get an email once or twice a day. He's gone from one full sentence down to two-word sayings: "Love you," and "Miss you."

"If you're over him, why are we still talking about him?" she asks.

"Because I'm totally fine. Hank and I are absolutely loving our weekend alone. It's fine. Everything is fine."

"Okay, well, let's plan a date together. I gotta go. *The Bachelor* is almost back from commercial. And I have your cousin to vent to."

"Go for it."

Once she hangs up, I toss my phone on the floor and lay back on the couch. Ramona left me to simmer. I don't like simmering.

Joe. Joe, Joe, and more Joe.

I don't need memories of our stupid relationship and our stupid house. I wonder what he'll do with it. A lot of my money went into the reconstruction, and I should probably ask him how we're going to split the sale. Or is he still living there? We didn't discuss what would happen to it, but I guess a conversation is hard to have when I'm so adamantly ignoring him.

Am I not ready to talk to him? No, I could if I wanted to. This isn't about willpower. This is about being stubborn.

My phone rings again. Good Lord, did she misdial Corinne's number again? The woman is in her late twenties and can't work a phone to save her life. I pat the floor beside me until I find it and answer without looking.

"Ramona, it's still Grace," I say.

A much deeper voice responds, and my body breaks into chills.

"Hey, it's Joe."

"Oh, damn it," I blurt out.

He chuckles. "I guess that explains why you answered."

"What do you want?" I spit out. My neck hair stands on end and I feel cold. I reach for the bundle of blankets I've accumulated at the other side of the couch and tug them over me.

"Just calling to talk," he says. His fun-loving tone makes me pull the sheets up to my chin. His charm stretches even over the phone. Not surprising given that he charmed other women over the phone while we were dating. "We should get dinner."

"I don't want to." I close my eyes tight and cringe. I sound like a child.

"We have to eventually."

"Do we? Talk to me again when you're not a cheater."

"Come on, Gracie." The nickname makes me fist the sheets tighter, and I hang up without saying any pleasantries. He doesn't deserve them. Joe knows that nickname belonged to my Dad, and he used it as a weapon against me. Strike number fifty thousand, Joe.

I roll over to face the back of the couch, shoving my face between the cushions. Hank's collar jingles as he jumps up. The cushions depress under his paws from one side of the couch to the other until he reaches me and places his head on my hip.

"I *am* over him," I mumble, but words feel bitter and untrue.

MONDAY ROLLS around and my computer at work is just as I left it—on my desk surrounded by papers. The only exception being a new calendar event from Mr. Cameron Kaufman slated for today at 9:00 a.m.

I make my way to Cameron's office about five minutes before our meeting, hoping to re-establish my first impression, but instead I see him, head down on his desk. I knock on the door to announce my presence.

"Cameron?" I ask. I still only see the top of his head as his face is pressed into the desk. I wonder if I misread the calendar event. *Geez, is he sleeping?* "Are we still set for our meeting at nine?"

Cameron's head shoots up and a groan like a bear coming out of hibernation escapes his throat. His hair is wild as he blinks himself awake. He quickly runs his fingers through the locks, but it doesn't fix much. It instead gives him the look of a punk rocker just coming off stage from a concert. Weirdly enough, this is still just as attractive as his normal hairdo. Then I notice the left side of his face is surrounded by purple, blue, and hints of green. His eye is bruised. Bad.

Oh, so I guess he *can* look unattractive.

"Jesus!" I let out, covering my mouth and dropping my papers. "What happened to you?"

He moans, lowering his head to the desk again and using his free hand to wave me in. "Come in and shut the door," he grumbles.

I close it behind me and walk over to his couch, taking my seat slow, so not to disturb the beast.

"Bad weekend?" I ask.

His lifts his head to meet my eyes and his face is filled with annoyance.

"What did I say about that mouth on Friday?" he says through an exhale.

"I'm not the one with the bruise, *sir*," I respond, crossing my arms. "I mean, geez, you look terrible. Are you okay?"

"Let's not talk about it," he says, as if I didn't just tell him he's a sitting piece of trash. *Whoops.*

He opens his top drawer, sifts through some papers, and pulls out a packet that he slides to the edge of his desk. I stand up, take it, and sit back down.

"Not talk about what?" I say, trying to redeem any sense of professionalism I lost in that snotty comment.

He smirks at me and his dimples do the job they were born to do by slaying my soul.

"Very cute," he monotones.

Is it bad his half-beaten face—combined with a lack of interest in what I'm saying—is totally turning me on? Yes, I realize. This is exactly how I ended up with Joe, and I already know how that turned out.

"Anyway, listen up, we have a huge project coming up. I'll be honest with you, as the new designer you'll be doing a lot of the grunt work, but it'll help you in the long run. I was in your position, and these kinds of projects are the best things to happen to a new hire. You're lucky you're jumping in when you are."

He briefs me on the project at hand and I'm trying to avert my attention from his bruise so I can focus on all these expectations and the inevitable long nights that are ahead of us. But this isn't news to me. The old creative director told me similar things in the interview with the whole "work hard, play hard" mentality being their driving force for the company's success.

"I want to know now whether this will be an issue," he says, his eyes boring into my brain as if testing me to go against anything he just said.

"Maybe if I had a family this would be an issue," I say. "But that's not really the case right now, so I'm more than prepared to dive in."

"Perfect, any questions?"

I want to ask about his bruise. He doesn't seem like a

fighter, but what do I really know about this guy? Nothing at all.

He raises his eyebrows, waiting, and I shake my head. "No —no questions."

"Good."

The meeting ends unceremoniously as he gets up and opens the door for me. We pretend there is absolutely no giant, elephant-sized bruise in the room lurking between the two of us.

The door shuts behind me and all I can do is send thoughts his way.

Whatever good that does.

WHEN I GET BACK to my desk, I have a missed call and a voicemail from my mom who insists on getting dinner later. Not that I was going to turn down the offer, but she says she already made reservations for a place nearby, so I guess the plans are set in stone for me whether I like it or not. That's both the wonderful thing and the biggest issue with us Holmes women: We want something, so we go for it.

Getting food? *Boom*. Reservation. Want to see a movie? *Pow*. Tickets bought in advance. Tired of your job? *Shazam*. Guess we'll start at a new company and make bad impressions with the new boss.

I'm definitely not kicking myself right now.

I head out right when five o'clock hits. When I arrive at the restaurant, it doesn't take long for me to see my mother frantically waving her hand, but this is mostly due to the fact that I could hear her wrist bangles knocking against each other before I even see them.

In the seat across from her sits a tiny white gift bag with the handles wound and tied together with giant pink ribbon, complete with tulle and lace. I wonder if she spent more on the gift or the packaging.

"Now how am I supposed to open that?" I ask, picking it up and giving it a small but harmless shake.

"Oh, hush and come here, girlie!" she swats at me, readying her arms for a big hug, which I crumble into.

We unhook ourselves from each other and I sit across from her, taking the gift bag and placing it in my lap. I look down at the bow and frown.

No, but seriously, how do I open this?

Mom sees my pained expression and reaches across the table to take the bag from me. Around the side of the bag is a tiny clip which she unhooks, making the bow release its wrapping from the bag's handles. It unravels as if being *Wingardium Leviosa'd* out of there.

What is this sorcery?

"Thank you," I exhale with relief.

I part the handles, sift through more pink tissue paper, and pull out a small brooch in the outline of a golden retriever. The silhouette is filled in with the same creamy color as Hank's fur, and the edges and lined details in the dog's coat are trimmed with gold. The dog's face has a smile painted on it that is very reminiscent of Hank's, "I just ate your shoe and I can't wait until you find the damage" smile, and arched across its body are the words:

"Life is Golden?" I read, laughing.

"Do you like it?" she asks, grinning from ear to ear knowing full well that she really hit it out of the park this time. It is definitely gaudy, but it's just my type of gaudy.

"I love it!" I say, unhooking the back of it and pinning it to my corded black cardigan. With the shimmer of its gold edges, the color pops against my monotone attire and coordinates perfectly with the canary yellow shade of my blouse underneath.

"I saw it and thought it looked exactly like Hank," she continues, explaining her gift. She never understands that there's no need to have a reason for every gift. I can like it just the same without an explanation. "And I figured you needed a little piece of him during the day."

But bless her for having one.

"Thanks, Mom. I love it." I repeat, taking the other side of my cardigan across my chest to wipe the pin clean and let it shine.

"How's your job going?" she asks.

"Good! First week in the bag," I say. "I actually got a new project today. New opportunities."

"And how's Hank doing?" she asks, picking up the menu in front of her and letting it cover her face. This is the move of a shameful woman. This can only mean one thing: She's somehow about to make things awkward.

"Hank is doing well," I answer, slow and skeptical.

She's seconds away from asking about Joe. She knows I know she is going to ask about Joe. I know she knows I know.

"And is he missing Joe?"

So predictable.

"No," I spit. "He hates Joe. Joe was a horrible human-dad." I shove my menu up to my face as well.

"Oh, baby don't cry!" she wails out, lowering her menu and reaching across the table to take one of my hands holding the menu.

She fires the first shot. She wins as always.

"Mom, I'm not crying!" I insist, lowering the menu and pointing at both of my eyes as if to prove zero tears have fallen from them. "See? Nope. No sadness here!"

It's like she wants me to feel more emotion from my breakup with Joe. I did feel a lot. In fact, I felt so much emotion I sent her an onslaught of texts for the first month after. But it's been a while, and those texts have stopped. I think she's still in the mourning state even after I'm trying not to be.

"He didn't deserve you and Hank," she huffs—ever the strong-willed woman I know. She says she's feistier than me simply because her hair is a deeper red than my ginger locks. I don't see how that makes much of a difference but arguing against the fact is pretty much useless. "Tell him he was supposed to give me a grandbaby. Almost three years of work down the drain."

And there it is. I know at the core of it all, Joe was the shining beacon of hope she had for a son-in-law. He was someone who could eventually provide her a grandchild that isn't a golden retriever. I don't blame her, really. I'm twenty-seven and according to my conservative family's standards, I'm far behind on the whole "giving babies" game. It doesn't help that I'm an only child.

"Mom, way to lessen my pain!" I say, putting down my menu with as much self-restraint as I can muster to not slam it down in anger. I've done so well not thinking about him. Work has been a brilliant distraction and the last thing I need is guilt. "Plus, I hate to break it to you, but kids weren't even on the agenda. Joe didn't want any to begin with."

She stares at me. I could have just slapped her in the face, and I don't think she would be as surprised as she is now.

"How dare he!" she says, slamming her menu on the table. She doesn't show nearly as much restraint as I do.

I shrug as if it means nothing to me; it meant everything.

I never told my mom about his aversion to children or marriage—mostly because I didn't want to believe it myself. Joe and I had multiple conversations about children, and we both agreed that it didn't really matter at the end of the day. We had Hank, and that was good enough. Good enough for *him* anyway.

"He called me," I admit.

"And what does the man want?" she hisses. Her eyes dart as she reads the menu. There's no way she's taking in any of her meal options. It's unsurprising that the mention of having no grandchildren would cause her mood toward him to shift entirely.

"He says he misses me," I say, "and that he loves me."

"Well he should have said that months ago, shouldn't he?"

"He keeps wanting to meet up."

It's silent for a moment then she says, "Do it."

Huh?

"Wait, what did you just say?"

"I said you should do it. You meet up with the jerk and give him a piece of your mind. You tell him he's made a mistake and that he's not welcome in the Holmes household again. Not under my roof."

"I don't even live with you, Mom."

"You're my baby." The way she says it is sweet but also borderline threatening.

Here's the thing: Mom is a steadfast advocate and constant quoter of the "Live, Laugh, Love" mantra. It is displayed in, at minimum, thirty different places in her house. Almost more than Bible quotes. But if we're all being honest with ourselves, we both know she could bite the head off a snake if it even side-eyed her. I'm not sure how I feel about that bit of trivia. My mom is a dangerous woman.

It's the dark red hair, I tell you.

"I don't think meeting up with him would solve a thing," I say.

"Or maybe it would give closure," she insists.

"What even is closure?" I exhale. "Not answering texts and not feeling guilty about it? 'Cause I already feel very guilt-free about the whole thing."

I am a liar. Of course I feel guilty.

"Guilt isn't the point, Grace. You have no reason to feel

guilty. It's getting him to pay for a dinner while you tell him how... how ridiculous he is."

If my mom allowed herself to curse, I'm sure she would have used better expletives to describe exactly what he is.

"That's harsh," I laugh.

"Is it?" she asks, her eyebrows cinching in the middle. "He cheated on you."

"He didn't cheat on me," I correct, holding my finger up in a corrective stance. "He downloaded a dating app and sexted other women. Very different."

"So why are you defending him?"

"Why do I keep getting asked that?"

Admittedly, it's a good question. But I don't need to think about it. In fact, the way my mom is looking at me irritates me rather than comforts me. I've thought about the whys and what-ifs for a couple months now. I'm tired of thinking what I may have done wrong or, hell, why I'm still defending someone who was compelled to send dick pics to other women. Which, by the way, I saw. Were they flattering? No. He took it at an angle that made it look like some bald guy sitting a few seats in front of you on a train with a wrinkly skin-toned shirt and Wookie pants. *Very* unappealing.

Whatever happened, happened, and there's nothing I can do about it. The last thing I want to do is make him spend a bunch of money on me if I'm not even going to give him the time of day. If I'm going to feel guilty about anything, it would be that.

"I'm not defending him," I say. "I just don't think I have the heart to be that vindictive."

"If you say so. Oh, this has gotten me so worked up, I swear I'm having hot flashes. Where's the ladies room?"

I point to the left side of the restaurant, but she still does the dance of walking from one corner of the restaurant to the other trying to find the restrooms before disappearing into the hallway.

My phone buzzes and, damn it, speak of the devil...

Joe: We at least need to discuss splitting the house. I'm selling.

I hesitate. He sure knows a way to get me hook, line, and sinker.

If all we're discussing is the house, that can't be bad, right? Plus, I can handle anything he might throw at me. I'm a badass chick now. Maybe it's the strength of my killer combat boots, or maybe it's the power of the golden retriever pin having Hank's old, wise dog energy flow through me, but I respond with an answer even I don't expect.

Grace: Fine. Let's do dinner.
Joe: Perfect. Details later. :)

Pin be damned. My heart sinks and I know I shouldn't have agreed. But it's just about the house. That's all. It won't be some fancy dinner. We'll just go to some quickie place like McDonald's, meet for twenty minutes, and call it a day. Then I'll go home and bury myself in a design once again. No muss, no fuss.

But that smiley he just sent definitely says a different story. And maybe he believes he made a mistake. He's only human.

And maybe I'm just a sucker.

8
CAMERON

"This is it?" asked Ian.

"This is it."

"A beanbag chair is your couch?"

"A beanbag chair is my couch."

Ian eyes my new, nearly bare, apartment with his arms crossed and look of disgust—or maybe pity—across his face.

"Well, you are definitely living the bachelor life," he says, shrugging.

I want to think he's just being an asshole, but when I look around the apartment, it *is* sort of sad.

In the middle of the floor are three boxes—one filled with various technology like remotes, a Kindle, and my trusty old Gameboy. Another box holds important work gear: Art supplies and the like. The last one is random stuff I felt the need to pile in last minute when I got the hell out of my townhome with Abby. I think there might be a *Terminator* DVD in there, but who knows. At the time I remember thinking, "Wow, even the Terminator gave a thumbs up while drowning in lava."

If that's not inspiring, I don't know what is.

My mattress is leaning against in the wall in the master

bedroom and there's another box in the middle of the floor overflowing with mismatching sets of sheets and blankets. In the corner is Buddy's dog bed—that quite frankly looks even fancier than all of my junk combined.

The only stuff I've fully unpacked is in the area surrounding my drafting desk. It's a couple rulers and pencils, as well as the blueprints I've been working on of a hotel I've had in my mind for a while—all in front of the sliding glass door leading to the balcony. Other than the fact that the apartment was the only place immediately available so close to work and at such short notice, the patio was the selling point. It gives me a clear view of the cityscape, which is a perfect place for brainstorming new buildings. I need all the motivation I can get nowadays.

Buddy comes up and drops a stick at Ian's feet, looking up at him expecting any form of play. He's about five years old, but still acts like a puppy. If someone isn't playing with him, then why are they even here?

"Okay, it's official," Ian says. "You live in the slums. I mean, where the heck did this dog get a stick inside your apartment? Seriously."

"Nah, finding sticks is just a weird talent Buddy has. Isn't that right boy?" I bend down with open arms and my beautiful, wonderful golden boy gallops into my arms and licks my face. His entire body sways from the force of his wagging tail and sheer happiness. Moving might have been uncomfortable for me, but he's been fine for the entire process.

"Who needs a girlfriend when you have a dog?" I grab him in my arms and give him a noogie repeating, "Who's a good boy? Who's a good boy? You are!"

Buddy twirls in a circle. He is in disbelief such wonderful compliments could be given to him. That, or he has no idea what I'm saying. I'm sure I could call him an asshole in the same tone, and he would be equally as overjoyed.

We really don't deserve dogs.

Ian's black eyebrows furrow in the middle as he shakes his head. "Yep. Bachelor life it is. I'll see you on the other side in two weeks when you decide you need a wingman."

He reaches his hand up for a high five and I ignore it. "You're just jealous of Buddy," I say.

"A dog doesn't match up to a one-night stand, my friend."

Sex. What even is that anymore? Some mythical, unattainable source of pure bliss; something I haven't experienced in about six months. Six months and two days. Six months, two days, and eight hours. But who's counting?

Ian drops onto the beanbag chair. It's one of the classic ones —not one of those fancy ones the size of a king-sized bed. It's almost nostalgic hearing the unsettling crunching sound the chair makes when you fall in. The only part of Ian that fits is his butt and half his torso. The rest of him is sprawled out. With his long limbs, he looks like a spider settling into its web for the day.

"Hey at least you're only fifteen minutes from work now," he says, looking around as if trying to justify anything he's seeing that doesn't quite meet his standards. The dude owns a sports car. What did I expect? "Could do worse."

"Oh, stop. You're making me blush."

"So, are you buying me dinner for helping you move or what?" Ian asks, stretching his long arms out.

"I can't even enjoy the bean bag for five seconds?"

"Nope. And bring your credit card. I'm maxing you out today, Kaufman."

9

GRACE

MIDWAY THROUGH THE WEEK, the team finally gets to meet our client: Mr. Arnold Feldman. He's the head of an architecture firm that's been around for decades, but they're trying to revamp their image to keep up with modern trends and bring in the clients like us: Start-ups with open floor plans and shameless hipster vibes.

When Mr. Feldman presents his ideas, you can tell he desperately needs Treasuries Inc.'s expertise and he's not afraid to ask for it. He may be older—with a bit of a hunch and balding with the grace of an eagle—but he still holds the confidence of a man ready to make the changes necessary to keep his company alive. You can tell he means business by the way he paces the front of the conference room.

Cameron is at the front as well, hands behind his back, looking more attentive—and attractive—than I've ever seen him. He decided to wear a suit today and he may as well be running for president because he looks like he's ready to deliver speeches and kiss babies. It's a navy-blue suit, so even though it's trimmed exactly to his figure, at least the color lends itself to be a bit more casual. Though, that doesn't fix how impossibly distracting it all is. I can tell his black eye is covered with some type of concealer. But in typical man fashion, he was clearly clueless on how to apply the makeup evenly. Weirdly enough, it still doesn't detract from his overall look of "God I need to jump him now" hotness.

I shift in my seat as I watch him scan the room. It's like he has this aura of heat bounding off his body and soaking into me. It's intoxicating. I have to tug myself away from looking at him.

Focus on the presentation, Grace. This is why you're here. Art. Design. Innovation. And you know what you're not here to do? Admire the boss.

I settle into the presentation again, looking at examples of what Mr. Feldman's company is looking for. Once he clicks to the next slide, I'm immediately excited. They're going for an 80s revamp look. This is right up my alley.

If John Hughes had a number one fan, it would be me. *Pretty in Pink, Breakfast Club, Some Kind of Wonderful...* Ramona has almost thrown a DVD case at me for suggesting we watch those just one more time. And don't get me started on listening to glam rock.

"This is definitely something we'll be able to tackle," Cameron says, as Mr. Feldman finishes up the final slide. "It looks like you're going for something a bit more dated, but that is the idea, isn't it?" He says with a laugh. They good-naturedly shake hands.

Dated? This is a classic gold, Billboard top 100, door-banging hit of a design. How can he not see that?

"Yes and no, Mr. Kaufman," Mr. Feldman says. "I'm not looking for some gimmicky mess of colors. We shall see."

This guy gets it.

He's starting to pack up, looking a bit off-put by Cameron's comment. *Uh-oh.*

Wait—are we done? Are we not going to discuss design

options? What was even the point of this meeting? To simply introduce the client? None of us have even said two words to him, and Cameron doesn't exactly look *unhappy* about it. Maybe he just needs someone to speak up and help him out, and maybe everyone is just a bit too shy. But I refuse to be just "everyone."

New job, new Grace.

I shoot my hand up toward the ceiling. Everyone looks at me in confusion. Even Gary, who almost always looks perplexed by life, appears even more concerned as he pauses mid-gummy bear.

Cameron's eyebrows rise up almost as high as my hand. Mr. Feldman stops mid-suitcase snap and points at me. "Yes, Miss…?"

"Holmes. Grace Holmes," I say, totally channeling my James Bond vibes. "I had a few suggestions on design, actually. I don't think you're looking for something dated."

He tilts his head to the side and Cameron's head cocks as well. They both look so much like Hank it's laughable. Though, contrasting Mr. Feldman's genuine smile that's beginning to form, Cameron's face holds an unmistakable scowl.

What the heck is his problem? Am I not allowed to have opinions here? Doesn't he want a go-getter? I kind of thought he would appreciate this. Do I want him to appreciate me?

"Go on…" Mr. Feldman says, knocking my eyes away from Cameron's glaring ones.

"Yes, absolutely!" I spout out color schemes that flow through my head: Bright purples, pinks, and yellows that perfectly capture the spirit of the 80s without ever actually stating what he wants is the 80s because I can guarantee you that a man has no idea what he's looking for until he sees it.

And suddenly we're all discussing it. One of the designers is raising his hand. Gary's speaking up, sliding his snacks to the side, and pulling out a pen. Cameron is at the white board, scribbling down every thought we have.

As another team member, Karoline, stands to illustrate her idea on the presentation board, I look over to steal a glance at Cameron only to see that he's already looking over at me. We lock eyes for only a moment, but for those few seconds, my stomach sinks into my gut and it feels like my mind is drowning underwater. He is *seething*.

Maybe I should have listened to his advice and kept my mouth shut? I'm starting productive conversation, though!

I just keep pushing forward and his glare gets deeper and deeper.

10

CAMERON

Who the hell does Grace fucking Holmes think she is?

I leave the meeting as tactfully as I can, but inside, I'm fuming.

She stepped over the line by undermining me in front of our new client—*my* new client. This is my first project as creative director of this team and I need to put my best foot forward. But not like she would know or care about that. She's just a budding designer and I'm willing to bet she'll take down anyone who stands in the way of her career advancement.

Generally, at these kick-off meetings, we hear out the client, establish some takeaway items, and reconvene as a team later to discuss. It's a bit unconventional for what you would expect from a start-up type of culture, but we like maintaining a unified front at Treasuries Inc. If all designers can be on the same page, we have a better chance at convincing the client our ideas will work. We've been doing it for years and it's effective. But the new girl apparently decided that wasn't good enough and started a brainstorming session right then and there.

These types of new junior designers come and go. I've been one—the kind that says, "Look at me, I'm a gift to the design world!" But you quickly realize that you're not and you're only pissing off those around you that are much smarter and much more talented. Unless a new designer learns how to navigate this hierarchy fast, they won't last long. Somewhere along the line, somebody will need to put Grace in her place. And I'm happy to be the man to do so.

"You have a great team lead in there," Mr. Feldman says, walking in to my office with his briefcase by his side. He's the picture of a classic businessman, all the way down to his combed mustache and the grizzled strands of balding hair. It's not what I strive to be, but shit if I don't respect the man. He's the head of an architecture firm I was eyeballing back in college. A few of my cohorts went to go work for him, while I went on to design instead. Which makes his comment sting that much more.

I straighten my tie, trying to form some semblance of order in my life that will make me appear less flustered by Grace's insubordination. Mr. Feldman doesn't seem to notice. And if he does, he doesn't address it.

"Who?" I ask, trying to mask my snappy voice with a bit more of a professional tone. But I know exactly who he's talking about.

"Miss Holmes."

I find myself laughing a bit, but he doesn't seem to get the joke.

"She actually just started last week," I say. "I'm the creative director and team lead. We're a small group."

He stops packing and laughs as well. "Then you've got yourself a keeper in this group. I'd listen to her."

Listen to her?

Is he trying to give me an aneurysm? I can feel my heart pumping faster and it's taking everything I have to not close my eyes and scream.

I nod in response. "We'll keep our eyes on her."

I keep reliving the memory of that ridiculous girl with her freckled arm sprouting into the air... A confident smile plastered on her face as if this was just old hat for her, as if she knew what she was about to say was not only a slight against me, but exactly what the client wanted to hear.

She's too confident for her own good.

He places his briefcase on the couch and clicks it open. "Do you have a hard copy of the prospective timeline?" he asks. "I have to get going, but you said first drafts will be in two weeks?" It's more of a statement than a question, but I answer anyway.

"Yes sir."

Mr. Feldman smiles, taking the schedule from me and placing it in his briefcase. He snaps the handles closed, clicks the dials on the combination, and reaches out to shake my hand, both of us squeezing just hard enough to establish equal authority.

"I expect great things from this team."

"So do I," I respond with a smile.

He nods and takes his exit. But it's not even a few seconds later until another man, of a more familiar towering stature, barrels into my office with one kick of the door.

"Food. Now. My treat today," Ian says throwing his wallet on my desk, causing a couple of my papers to crumple.

I grab the wallet and toss it back to him. "Not the time," I say, letting my suppressed irritation spew out.

"It's always the time for food," he says, pocketing his wallet back with an arched eyebrow. "What has you in such an awful mood?"

I run my hands through my hair. "The new girl. Grace Holmes. Did you say you knew her?"

He laughs and it feels like he's mocking me, the bastard. "Yeah, she's my sister's best friend. Always been a little firecracker but, you know, I kinda like that about her," he muses.

I roll my eyes. He's not the one having to manage her.

"Why? What did she do?" he asks.

"She decided to be a designer," I exhale, patting my pockets for my wallet and phone. On second thought, food is exactly what I need right now.

"Good lord, she's doing her job?" he gasps. "Call in HR."

"I mean, who does she think she is?" I ask, shutting off the light and walking into the hall.

I can't stop picturing her. The bright red hair that's way too smooth-looking, her stunning blue eyes—and then there's her cocky personality, and that pretty much ruins the whole package.

"Don't talk to me about having a shit day," Ian scoffs, shoving his hands in his pockets. "I've had three potential lawsuits from accounting—each one claiming harassment to some degree, and they're really fucking up my vibe."

"Your vibe?"

"Isn't that what the cool kids say now?" he asks, and I shrug. "Whatever, I need hamburgers."

My stomach rumbles at the thought of food. I guess I must have skipped breakfast and went straight to coffee this morning.

"Yeah, give me a burger covered in chili and cheese," I say and my stomach grumbles again. *Did I skip lunch, too?* "With fries. Lots of fries." I'll work it off at the gym tomorrow or something.

By the time we get back, my stomach is in knots from both the chili-doused hamburger and Ian's manic driving. In short, he should not own a sports car.

I am far from excited to be heading back to the office to catch up on work, so I jump into my car and drive a short distance to my apartment, take Buddy out for a quick walk, and then return to the office with a little less of a stomach ache and my dog in tow.

In case you're wondering... Are dogs allowed at the offices? No. Do I do it anyway?

You bet.

After five or six o'clock, people generally start to leave and, while I normally sneak Buddy discreetly into my office, he seemed so relaxed in the new place and I didn't have the heart to put a leash on him. I guess I'll have to party until sundown by myself. And by partying, I mean bury myself in paperwork. You would think creative directors get more skin in the game design-wise, but you would be wrong. Just paperwork.

The good old days of constant designing are gone; management days have arrived. The only positive change is that I can allocate the creative side of my brain entirely to architecture now. The piles of sketches are starting to build up next to my home desk, and I couldn't be happier about that. But it came at a cost. They say you can't buy happiness with money, and they're right. My promotion came with a hefty raise I was hoping I could use for travel, but so far I haven't taken any vacation and I'm almost ready to burn all this paperwork to the ground for that amount of "happiness" it's given me.

When I get back to the office—Buddy at home with a movie on—I notice the parking lot is only occupied by the cars of one or two managers in other departments and, in the back corner of the lot, a tiny yellow Volkswagen.

Whose car is that?

My questions are answered the instant I sneak back to what I expected would be an empty design studio but is instead occupied by a single light: The tiny desk lamp on the back corner. Grace Holmes beneath it, head buried into her tablet, so close that she may as well be burning her eyes out.

Of course she is.

It's clear she must not have seen me walk in because my appearance breaks her concentration. She jumps in her seat, swinging her hand out and knocking her coffee all over her.

"Damn it!" she yells.

"Shit," I say, adding to the chorus of expletives. "Let me get some paper towels. I'll be right back." I hastily jog to the break room and return. Grace stares back at me with zero amusement.

She's clutching the neckline of her shirt and wringing out part of the coffee back into the cup. I hand over the wad of towels I have in my hand.

"Maybe you should pay more attention," I snort.

Sure, I should be more empathetic, but I'm still a bit raw from this afternoon. I only feel a little bad. Just a little. But when I see her begin to pat her shirt, any feelings close to irritation disappear. The shirt she's wearing *was* completely white. Now, it's also see-through.

Fuck me.

"Is this your clever way of kicking me out so you can have the office to yourself?" she asks, raising an eyebrow. She tosses away the paper towels and begins to gather her things.

I wait a bit too long to avert my eyes from her top, but she doesn't seem to notice. Even if she does, I'm so turned on that I forget proper office etiquette for a good five seconds, like the fact that you shouldn't be staring at your employee's tits.

"I didn't knock over your cup, you did," I clarify, blinking myself back to the here and now.

"And you didn't scare me on purpose to make me spill it?" she asks. She crosses her arms, remembers her shirt is soaking wet, then uncrosses them with a small curse and wipes at the coffee residue on her arms. My gaze slides down, almost against my will, to a sliver of cleavage where the wet part of her blouse is stuck to the rest of her shirt. I pull myself back together with some effort and clear my throat.

"Absolutely not," I say.

Although if I could have done it on purpose knowing I

would see her wet blouse, I know I would have. What the hell is wrong with me?

"Very likely story."

She stumbles a bit as she hefts her large bag, and without thinking, I hold my hand out to steady her, taking gentle hold of her forearm.

Her skin is soft beneath my fingertips; it's been too long since I've felt the smooth skin of a woman—felt how it practically slides beneath my hands. I sit on Gary's desk and cross my ankle over my knee. My blood has rushed south and that's the last thing she needs to see.

I don't feel guilty being attracted to Grace. I'd be blind if I wasn't. Even without a see-through top to keep me entertained, the large slit along the side of her long black skirt exposed most of her upper thigh when she was sitting down.

But the fact remains that she's number one on my shit list right now. The reminder helps clear my head.

"Let's have a chat real quick." I say, as she walks by me toward the main lobby area.

She turns to face me. She's not happy, I can tell, but I also sense some sort of mental obligation to pay attention to me since I'm her boss.

Good.

"In the first meetings with clients, we listen," I say. "Pitching ideas without prior input from the team is presumptuous and not exactly the rules we follow here."

Her posture falters a bit. "And why don't we pitch ideas?" she asks, a genuine tone of confusion in her voice. It barely masks the layer of defiance lurking beneath.

"Because we're a team," I say. "This isn't a one-woman show, Grace."

"I wanted to get the ball rolling," she says with a small shrug.

"And speaking out against me was the way to do it?"

She pauses, inhaling a shaky breath but exhaling with more determination. "That was out of line. I'm sorry. I'm still learning the ropes."

"You're damn right you are." Probably a bit too much force on that one, but my temper is rising and it's like I'm in that conference room all over again looking at her cocky smirk, her silly hand arced toward the sky.

Her chin trembles as she considers words, but her eyes show no sign of potential tears. I can tell she wants to snap at me, but I'm her boss and that isn't happening tonight.

"Well, good night, Cameron," she says, moving her shoulders back to raise her head a bit higher.

"Most people call me Cam," I correct.

At this point, I'm honestly just looking for things to be right about. I want her to know who is in charge here. What I say goes and I'm not having some chick with zero experience coming in here to say otherwise.

But then she opens her damn mouth.

"I prefer Cameron," she says, shrugging once more, then turning on her heel to leave.

I'm going to lose my mind, and she's only a couple weeks in.

11

GRACE

I'll admit it: I'm not at all comfortable that Cameron stays just as late as I do. It's like the second I see his devilish smile, I know it's my cue to leave or else I'll inevitably make some snarky comment that digs my hole even deeper... or I'll just end up with a see-through shirt by accident.

Ugh.

Even as infuriating as he is, it's the sarcasm, the charm, the blazers, the rolled-up sleeves, and the dimples that keep me longing for his approval. It's like a constant battle between forcing him to see that my design decisions are inarguably the correct ones and the tick-tock of my dry spell timer wanting nothing more than to have him push me up against a wall.

Can I seriously not control my hormones? Am I thirteen again?

The only solace I have is getting work done through my lunch hour. I make sure to pack my sandwich before I head out the door for work and thankfully, getting to my desk early also grants me another hour of free work time. Sure, I see Cameron come in with his swagger of a walk and his leather computer bag slung over his shoulder, but I try my best to bury my nose in work so he doesn't catch me waiting for him to come in every morning.

I *hate* how attractive he is.

By the time Friday rolls around, I'm more than ready to follow Saria's ever faithful lead over to the warehouse where I can already hear the popping sound of plastic balls on the beer pong tables. I make my way over to the crowded bar and shove through enough people to find a free stool. Geez, this is worse than a normal bar.

I check my phone for the first time in hours and find a text from the only devil worse than Cameron: Joe. I've been so distracted by my hot, infuriating boss I forgot Joe and I had upcoming dinner plans.

Joe: How is this Sunday night? I got a reservation at that cute Italian place. Your favorite :)

Of course he picks the fanciest restaurant in town, and of course he's already made a reservation without even confirming whether or not I'll be going. What is he—my mom? And yes, it *is* the one restaurant we frequented every year for our anniversary. He didn't take me this year. He said he was busy with work, so I just stayed in. Joe's going on full date mode, and I refuse to be naïve enough to think he doesn't know what he's doing. This is about more than selling the house. If I want to bail I could—and should.

Grace: Sure, I'll see you then.

Apparently I'm not that smart.

Joe: Want me to pick you up?

No. Absolutely not. I don't even need him knowing where I

live now. Not that Joe has ever been a creepy kind of guy, but the last thing I need is for his texts to graduate into waiting outside my window with a boombox at three in the morning.

I really need to lay off the 80s movies.

Grace: No, I can meet you there.
Joe: Always the ever-independent Grace. Sexy.

I would say I have butterflies for Joe, but they're more like those gross moths. Flesh eating moths. Do those exist?

I'm not going to lie: I need sex *so* bad. I've been starved for too long, and the idea of someone calling me sexy is so appetizing. I find myself thinking of his naked body—tight abs under his white shirt, thick arms wound around me.

No. I can daydream elsewhere and of someone else.

Grace: I will cancel right now if you keep that up.

His only answer is another winking emoji, which doesn't make me feel better. I shove the phone in my pocket.

I don't know what I'm doing and I feel stupid for having even agreed to go in the first place. If I'm being honest with myself, I'm not sure what I want. I wouldn't have been in a relationship with him for three years if I didn't think at some point he was the last man I would ever date, but now things are so messy. Can we even go back to how we were before we drifted apart?

Do I even want to?

My phone vibrates again. I reluctantly pull it out of my pocket, hoping maybe it's Mom, Ramona, or hell, even junk mail begging me to purchase more expensive clothes, but it's not.

Joe: I'll see you then :)

I let out a low groan and toss my phone on the counter in front of me.

"What can I get you?"

I know that voice.

Lo and behold, there he is, the second devil in my life: Mother-flipping Cameron. He looks like he's having an internal struggle between being both very tired and very desperate to drink the alcohol he's serving. I notice the bruise under his eye is beginning to heal up, but it still looks a little swollen. If anything, if gives him a bad boy vibe, like maybe someone I shouldn't be bringing home to Momma.

No; stop those thoughts, Grace.

He takes a glass from underneath the counter and fills it up beneath the closest draft handle. He places a pint of dark brown beer in front of me, the head of it foaming almost an inch before reaching the top. I can smell the hops of a very bitter IPA drifting up into my nose and I'm instantly repelled. But instead of denying it, I stubbornly pick the glass up and take a swig. It settles in my chest and I can practically feel my tongue tingling at the strong taste. I hate IPAs.

He leans his elbows on the counter, holding one fist in the other. His eyes are the deepest brown with little flecks of green sprinkled throughout. They're captivating and I have to shake off my urge to stare longer.

"I expected a bartender to have better taste," I say.

"I'm not a bartender," he snaps back.

"And yet you're behind a bar."

He barks out a laugh. "Does the title 'creative director' mean nothing to you?"

I open my mouth to speak, close it, then narrow my eyes and flash the least genuine smile I can muster. "Yes sir."

He's infuriating and at the same time my willingness to say "sir" in his presence is oddly turning me on.

"Why does it feel like you're mocking me?" he asks, tilting his head to the side.

"I'm simply expressing my opinion." I snap my fingers. "Oh, right, but you hate it when employees do that."

He shakes his head. "You know I can write you up, don't you?"

I don't. In fact, I frequently forget he's my boss; I'm too busy staring at his ass when he turns to write on the whiteboard during meetings. But then I'll make a suggestion on using a different typeface, he'll override with some twisted logic that somehow makes my idea sound like trash, and we continue on with the meeting as if it never happened.

I want nothing more than to strangle the guy.

I lean in. "You know my ideas are good. You wouldn't put me on the bench."

He pushes his arms on the counter to lean closer to me as well. "Try me," he growls.

I can smell his campfire scent again and my desire to slap him across the face quickly turns into a burning lust to grab his collar and kiss him. Thankfully, my unruly sexual impulses are pushed to the side when Ian shows up.

"Figured you could use some company," Ian says, plopping himself on a stool beside me. I think he's talking to me, but then Cameron leans back and groans.

"Please," he begs. "This is basically jail."

"Glad to see my company is such a joy," I say, regrettably taking another swig from my glass. I cough. I forgot what was in there.

Cameron lifts an eyebrow and smirks.

"It's your last night, Cam." Nia says, quiet as a cat while she approaches. "I'm not trying to punish you."

Jesus Christ where did she come from?

When Cameron offers her a beer, she simply raises her hand in protest. "No, not for me."

No wonder she's able to maintain her figure. Lack of beer will do wonders. I could probably learn a thing or two, I think as I'm swallowing another mouthful of beer I hate. My face contorts in disgust.

"So, how are you guys enjoying tonight?" Nia asks, a smile crossing her face. She's friendly enough—at least as friendly as someone who needs to be familiar with her co-workers is.

"I'm doing good," I reply, and Cameron nods in agreement.

Ian moves forward to catch Nia's eye on the other side of me. And even though it's painfully obvious, she's definitely trying her best to ignore him. If I know anything about Ian, it's that he's persistent.

"I'm doing good as well," Ian calls down to her, giving a slight wave.

"Didn't ask you, Ian," she replies.

"Come on, Polly," Ian coos. "Don't be like that." *Polly?*

She exhales and glares at him. "I've told you not to call me that."

"Well, you also didn't like it when I called you Apollo, so I figure I'll try something else out for a while."

"Just Nia is fine."

"You never come to Beer Fridays," Cameron says, as if trying to change the subject away from... whatever *this* is.

"And now I remember why," she shoots back, meeting Ian's eyes with so much contempt and focus that I wonder if either of them would even notice if I left right now.

Tension radiates off her and I get nosy, mentally begging to know context behind this interaction. Instinctually, my eyes flick to the one other person present who's not involved in this awkward exchange and find that he's staring right back at me—eyes wide open and cringing as well.

At least Cameron and I can agree about something.

"Polly," Ian croons. "don't be that way."

"You are ridiculous," Nia groans.

I watch her stomp off and Ian shakes his head with a grimace, but the determination doesn't leave his face.

"Do you always do that?" I turn to face him, leaning my head in my hand.

"Do what?" Ian says, still looking at the spot where Nia was. "Try to get to know her?"

"No," I say. "Do you always get on her nerves like that?"

"Not always," Ian says, taking a sip of the water glass Cameron discreetly set in front of him.

"But that was silly."

"Best not to insult HR, Grace," Ian says, lifting an eyebrow.

Cameron snorts and I shoot him a glare.

"She's never gonna like you if you keep that up," I say, but my comment is mostly pointed to Cameron. At least in my head it's because, well: Who does he think he is, laughing at me?

"Seven years, Grace," Ian laments. "Seven years, and I still think she'll break one day."

"Ian thinks he's invincible," Cameron says. "Kind of like some other person we know." He lifts an eyebrow at me. I grumble.

"She hasn't written you up yet?" I ask. "I thought that was common around here." I try my best not to meet Cameron's eyes. He doesn't deserve the satisfaction of snarking back at me.

"No, she has not," Ian straightens his back and points between the both of us. "And why do you think that is?"

"Because you wouldn't listen anyway?" Cameron asks, causing Ian to laugh.

"Because," he explains, lowering his voice in the way some people would share deep secrets. "I don't think she really minds me all that much." Ian taps the side of his head with his index finger in a knowing kind of gesture as if to say, "Didn't think of that, did ya?"

Cameron smiles at Ian and leaves to fill another beer for a

passing employee who's frantically waving him down. Ian and I don't exchange words. He's staring off in the distance, and I imagine he's still replaying the interaction with Nia. I don't interrupt his thoughts. Cameron returns to us moments later, his arms crossed as if contemplating whether to say something or not. The silence kills me, so I blurt out the first thing I can think of.

"So, how'd you get that bruise, Cameron?"

His eyebrows tug to the middle and he takes more than a comfortable amount of time to answer.

"Yes, Mr. Cameron, how did you get that bruise?" Ian asks, coming out of his thoughts and batting his eyes.

Cameron shoots him an eat-shit look, but then exhales. "How do you think I got it?" he asks me, avoiding the question.

Dick.

"Well," I muse, "I'm thinking you went to the zoo and had a fight with a bear. It's the only logical answer."

"Oh really?" he says, barely amused at my clearly super clever response.

This man does not know humor.

"Hell, how about a dragon if we're playing that game?" Ian says, tipping his water to his lip as if bored.

He seems less than impressed that Cameron isn't sharing the true story with me. Which means that Ian totally knows. And I want to find out even more now.

"Both of you are mistaken," Cameron says matter-of-factly. "It was a lion."

"Not a hippo?" I gasp. "I hear they're nasty."

"If only. That'd be quite the story."

"And lions aren't?"

"Nope. Any old schmoe can fight a lion," Cameron says, exhaling dramatically. "Alas, I'm just another story."

"Oh, woe," Ian mumbles.

"Boo," I say, throwing my thumb down in protest. "I demand better stories."

"I don't have time for that. I'm volunteering, remember?" he says.

He shoots me one last glare before walking away to serve another employee. The crowd is picking up once more, and I don't expect him to return.

"So, Grace," Ian starts, swiveling on his bar stool to angle himself toward me. "It's not like I'm the lawyer or anything, but eventually Cameron's manager side might come out. Maybe you should tone down the whole kickass red-head act before you piss him off."

"Oh Ian," I sigh. "You know me better than that."

He laughs, "Unfortunately, I do. But you're an employee now. Don't forget that. Plus, I vouched for you." He pokes my shoulder. "Don't make me look bad, all right?"

"No promises," I grin.

He rolls his eyes.

No promises.

12

GRACE

"I've got it, I've got it!" my mom sing-songs, her head rocking from side to side, her low red ponytail swinging with it.

Ramona jumps up and down on the balls of her bare feet in excitement. Her fresh hot pink toenails match both mine and my mother's, and the bottle of polish is resting on the paper towel with smears of paint blotted on it every couple inches. I notice Hank is starting to get curious and shove his old dog snout against the bottle, so I pick the polish up and place it on the coffee table.

"There's no way you already know it," I groan.

My mom likes the game *Clue*. My mom is good at the game *Clue*. My mom. Never. Loses. *Clue*. But the end result is always fascinating to Ramona. I don't know how Mom can always guess within the first few rounds what the winning answer to the game will be, but her guess of, "Professor Plum. With a rope. In the kitchen." is identical to the three cards hidden in the middle of the board, eliciting a roar of applause from Ramona and signifying the end of the game. My mom is the victor once more.

I laugh and try not to be bitter about her winning *again*. In all honesty, it's less about losing and more about the fact that I unsuccessfully tried to distract myself from my pseudo-dinner date with Joe tomorrow night.

I don't expect anything to come from it. It's not like I'm begging to get back with him. I have two simple motives.

Number one: Get my piece of the house pie. I put enough work into remodeling that place to get my fair share.

Number two: Do what my mom told me to do by giving him a piece of my mind.

I still haven't exactly practiced what I will say. "You convinced me I wasn't good enough?" or "You downloaded a dating app while we were still dating?" I don't know. It's still a work in progress, but something needs to be said. And it will be anything other than, "I need sex really bad, so please get back with me." I'm stronger than that.

"Ooh, Professor Plum," Ramona shimmies her shoulders to me. "So naughty."

"Professor Plum seems like a fine gentleman," Mom says, picking up the cards and stacking them back together.

"A fine gentleman with a rope," Ramona replies, arching an eyebrow.

Mom shakes her head and chuckles. "What happened to just plain sex?" she says, stopping to look up as if reminiscing. "Why do we need to throw in all this... this"—she throws her hands around—"stuff? Like rope and... vibrators, or whatever."

I cover my ears and groan, curling into a tight ball on the floor. "Mom! I don't want to hear about your sex life!" Hank trots over to lick my face and check on me. I pet him to signal that these words aren't actually killing me—although they could.

"Aww, you're making little Gracie all embarrassed!" Ramona coos, patting my exposed head. I swat her away.

"Sorry *not* sorry that I don't want to hear about my mother in compromising positions," I say, sitting up and smoothing back my ponytail. "Or compromising material in said positions."

My mom innocently laughs. "Well, I just said I didn't do that, though."

"Nope!" I interrupt my mom and throw my hands in the air. "Nope! We're done with this!"

The two horrible women laugh together. Bunch of bullies.

We clean up the remnants of tiny plastic toy murder weapons and various cards while my mom climbs off the floor, dusts her flower-print pants off that are probably straight from the 70s, and walks back to the kitchen.

"What new recipe are you learning now?" Ramona asks, crawling onto the couch. I'm fairly sure that corner of the L-shaped couch has a dent exactly the same shape as her tiny butt given the number of years she's claimed that specific spot as her own.

"I'm trying out avocados, I think," my Mom says, hands on her hips with determination. I now notice the pile of three avocados next to her on the kitchen island, ready to be cut.

"Isn't that a bit... bland?" Ramona asks, her lip curling up as she looks to me for some type of backup.

"Oh, you ain't getting my support on that, Ray," I say. For real though: Bring on the avocado.

"Well, hang on," Mom protests, "you can make... guacamole. And... well, lots of things. There're recipes everywhere." She throws her hands in the air and grabs her apron off the hook on the pantry.

When she slips it over her head and begins to tie the string, I recognize this as yet another glorious, Ramona screen-print creation. She gave it to my mom for Mother's Day last year. The apron says *"Cooking Mama,"* but underneath is a bear wearing a chef's hat with a frying pan in one hand and a fish in the other.

Very typical Ramona. It's almost as bad as the crop top she's wearing now that has a hippo with the phrase *"#Hungry"* above it. I'm assuming she thought this board game night would end with a different game.

"Oh, let me look up some recipes!" Ramona says, leaning back to lift herself from the cushions and pull the phone out from her back pocket.

Ramona will be the first person to pounce on research. She's smart like that. Give her a task to look into and she'll show up at your house with marked-up encyclopedias and a binder full of tabbed pages indicating every detail you hadn't considered.

Flicking through her phone, Ramona laughs, leaning forward and shoving the screen in my face. "Wait, look what Wes just sent to me!"

It's a picture of a golden retriever, tongue out, cheesing up the camera like all adorable goldens do. He's wearing goggles and sitting behind a black-top science table with the words "*I have no idea what I'm doing,*" written under it. We both laugh.

"Thought you'd like that," Ramona giggles, plopping back into the corner of the couch and tapping her fingers over the screen.

I pull out my own phone, take a deep breath, and prepare to be not at all surprised when the screen lights up displaying no new messages. For a second, there is a red bubble indicating I have one email, but I remember it is just a glitch in the app that didn't process the last time I refreshed it. It's sad I know that glitch even exists.

Then, like clockwork, as if the universe was answering my prayers for some form of human connection, there's a new text.

Joe: Can we reschedule for Monday?

Okay, you didn't have to be such a jerk, universe.

I can't parse through my emotions fast enough to know whether I'm relieved that I have more time to brainstorm how

I'm actually going to handle this dinner, or if I'm depressed that I can't just get it over with.

Why couldn't Joe ever send me pictures of some golden retriever wearing goggles? Am I crazy for wanting that type of companionship? Maybe I'm just not the marrying type. Maybe I'm the date-for-three-years-and-realize-I-made-a-mistake-but-I'm-still-gonna-reschedule-our-reconciliation-dinner type of girl.

"Ew, are you texting that dickbag Joe?" Ramona asks from behind me.

I feel the couch move against me and she's leaning forward with her leg hanging off the side, squinting to look at my screen.

"Language!" my mom calls from the kitchen.

"Nosy!" I say to Ramona, moving the phone down to cover it with Hank's unwilling paw.

"Hank, you release that phone right now!" Ramona demands, holding out her hand.

Hank blinks and moves his paw so he can get up and browse the kitchen—no doubt hoping Grandma Holmes will toss something down to him. *Deceit!*

Before I can react quick enough to grab the phone off the floor, Ramona barrels forward and snatches it, reading the open message and shaking her head in disbelief.

"Why didn't you tell me you had a date with Joe?" she asks, lowering the phone and sounding hurt.

"Shame on you for not telling Ramona!" my mom yells from the kitchen.

"Thanks, Mrs. Holmes!" Ramona yells back as I'm sure they no doubt mentally high five.

"I'm just going to see what he wants," I say. Do I sound innocent? I hope I sound innocent. "Plus, he's rescheduling anyway so he's obviously not much of a stand-up guy." I lean my head side to side. "No changes there, I guess."

"Well, I think he's already made it clear he's a dickbag," Ramona scoffs.

"Language, Ramona!" Mom calls from the kitchen over the sound of a hard knife on cutting board.

"Sorry, Mrs. Holmes," she groans, still looking at me.

"It means nothing," I say.

Am I forcing confidence in this situation again? Because honestly, I don't even know anymore. It makes me sick to think of him, so why am I even agreeing to meet up with him only to have my heart broken again?

"If it means nothing," Ramona says, uncrossing her legs and reaching for the nail polish on the coffee table. "Then why are you going?"

"To give him a piece of my mind," I say. "Right, Mom?"

"Sure, honey!" she calls, ever the supportive figure.

Ramona is clearly not convinced. "There have got to be hotter guys in your life than Joe the dick—I mean, dirtbag." She looks over to the kitchen and sighs a breath of relief. My mom is too distracted to notice the third slip-up.

"Sure, there's... well..." My phone buzzes and I swear if it's another text from Joe... But instead, it's a meeting invite from Cameron.

"My boss," I say.

Ramona's eyes widen and she grins. "Your boss?"

"Grace Holmes!" Mom drops her knife on the counter and storms over to where we're sitting.

She listens now...

You'd have thought I just said I screwed Cameron silly in the break room. "I don't think I need to tell you that making arrangements of any kind with your boss is a horrible idea, right?" my mom says. Looks like she's coming out arms swinging. "You are twenty-seven. This is a new career path and you're just going to—"

"Hi, Mom. I love you too," I interrupt, letting her take an

inhale of air before continuing. No mercy, this woman. "But I thought you taught me to be friendly and approachable."

"Ooh, how friendly?" Ramona winks, sitting up with her feet folded beneath her.

"He can fire you," my mom says, exasperated.

"You know, technically, I'm not sure he can," I say, holding my index finger up. "That's like, HR or something."

My mom huffs in response, but Ramona is playing the devil on the other shoulder.

"I don't want to condone workplace sexual harassment, but girl, you harass that man."

"Ray!" I almost knock over the nail polish bottle but catch it just in time. A little drop falls on the carpet. I groan and get up for a paper towel.

"I'm serious!" Ramona says. "An office romance, can you imagine!" The day dreaming in her voice sounds wistful.

Can I imagine it? What kind of question is that? Of course I can. I picture his large hands around my waist, taking me in the breakroom, on his desk, on the copier…

"Oh yes, I've imagined it," I say, almost just as day-dreamy and wistful as she said it, and then I'm back to reality. "But I'm not about to act on it."

"Good girl," my mom says with a defiant nod of her head.

"Why not?" Ramona asks, almost offended by the notion of me not risking my career. "I never got the chance to sneak around and get nasty in an office." She emphasizes the word "nasty" with a thick twang to make it seem like the word itself is a sexual act. "Let me live vicariously through you, Gracie! Describe him for me!"

"Don't you own an office space with your husband?" my mom asks, eyebrows raised at her.

"Mrs. Holmes, it's not the same." Ramona places a hand on my mom's arm as if physically communicating the "bless your heart" that's oozing through her expression of pity.

Mom exhales. "Just don't be stupid," she says, slapping my arm with back of her hand.

I'm not stupid. Or maybe I am. I'm still agreeing to go on a pseudo-date with my ex while I'm day-dreaming about my hot boss that can't stand me.

Way to go, me.

13
GRACE

I'M OVERDRESSED, but I know I wouldn't have enough time to go home and change after work before my not-date date with Joe, so now I am doomed to wear my cocktail dress to an office environment that is, generally speaking, very casual.

I tried to dress the look down a bit with a cardigan but there was no hiding the way the dress hugs my curves. My main goal for today is to remain at my corner desk so as not to draw more attention to myself than necessary.

The only time I leave the corner is to attend our Monday meeting. The moment I walk in, Cameron is already leering at me, but then there's a second where he eyes me up and down and... is it contempt, or is he checking me out? My face flushes pink, which is hard to hide given my fair complexion. I find a place at the conference table, unlock my tablet, and look over my notes.

Five o'clock rolls around and I'm still here. And, of course, so is Cameron.

He walks through the designers' room like he owns the damn place which I guess as creative director, he pretty much does. He's adjusted his business casual attire to a more relaxed look. The sleeves of his denim button-up are rolled up to his elbows, exposing toned forearms and displaying the obvious work he puts in at the gym. He's unbuttoned his shirt twice to reveal the crisp, white undershirt beneath.

No. Go away. Git. Scram. I can't handle this today.

As if reading my mind, he walks to his office and shuts the door behind him.

Good riddance.

I continue sketching on my tablet and notice I can't seem to get a straight line in. Then I notice it's because my hands are shaking. I wonder if it's the sight of Cameron, or maybe the fact that I'm about to meet up with my ex-boyfriend (because apparently, I love testing my own sanity), but then my stomach rumbles.

Right; I forgot to eat lunch again.

I wonder if the vending machines in the breakroom have decent snacks, but once I get there, I'm disappointed to find the machines out of everything edible with the exception of sunflower seeds, and yeah, no thanks.

My stomach grumbles again and I groan.

"Hush, you," I hiss to it.

I turn to the doorway feeling dejected and desperately hungry when Cameron walks in, eyebrow raised.

"Who are you talking to?" he asks, irritation in his tone.

"My stomach," I say, covering it with my hands. "It's loud and obnoxious."

Immediately I hear a growl come from his stomach, too. He reaches to cover it just as I did. I feel some odd satisfaction at his discomfort.

He looks past me to the vending machines and a frown falls on his face, but he switches from sad to determined and immediately makes his way to the fridge, swinging it open and squinting to see everything inside.

I'm hoping he brought food and that he's in some

wonderful mood to maybe share, but I know better than to think he's willing to be nice to me for one moment.

I exaggerate a slumped posture over to the fridge and lean over the door to look inside.

"I didn't bring anything if that's what you're wondering," he says.

Is he actually a mind reader?

"But"—he picks up some Tupperware and examines the top with a name scrawled in black sharpie ink—"it looks like Saria did."

Through the transparent sides, I can see a turkey sandwich cut in half, a spinach side salad, and some grapes. It looks beautiful and like everything I need in the world right now. Normally, I would balk at the idea of stealing food, and instinct tells me to knock it out of his hand and insist he put it back immediately, but Cameron opens the lid and the smell of Caesar dressing and oregano rises out.

"She won't miss it," I say, forgetting all ladylike sensibilities and snatching it from his hands to place it down on the nearest table. Cameron has already shut the fridge and is now rifling through the cabinets to find plates.

"Who said I was sharing?" I ask.

"Don't be a jerk," he responds. "Finders keepers, anyway. It's technically mine."

"No, I think it's technically Saria's."

We sit across from each other with one half of the sandwich and bits of the salad haphazardly thrown on our plates in our joint effort to get this food in our mouths as soon as possible.

We begin eating and I try to maintain a polite approach, but Saria's sandwich skills far surpass my own and before I know it, I'm scarfing down the sweet tastes of honey mustard, swiss cheese, and pickles like a girl that hasn't eaten in months.

"So how was your day?" I ask between bites, trying to be as

nice as I can. We did agree to share a stolen sandwich after all. This counts as breaking bread with your enemy.

He swallows his chewed food. "Better now that I have Saria's overlooked leftovers." A sly smile follows, and he takes another bite, making sure to finish it before continuing. "Hey, throw me one of those, will ya?"

I pick up a grape and he opens his mouth wide. Is he seriously wanting me to throw it in there? I toss the grape up and he moves his head toward the line of trajectory just in time for it to fall in his mouth.

"Well, there lies your true talents," I say. "Catching grapes."

"I don't have any more talents?" he asks.

"You're sure not good at management," I laugh, but his sense of humor is barely present.

"God, you're irritating," he says, forking salad into his mouth. "Were you this much of a pain at your last job? Did you get fired? Because I'm having a hard time believing you can be this rude to someone directly above you."

I stiffen. The mention of being fired brings me back to reality. My mom is right. I shouldn't be doing anything to jeopardize this job. It's been my dream and I'm sitting here insulting my boss over some grapes. I've gotten too comfortable too quickly, but where the heck do we go from here? I've already set the tone.

"I think I could put 'world record for the most times I've burnt soup' as one of my talents," I say.

Well that's one way to lighten the mood, I guess.

He shakes his fork at me. "That's a mouthful... How does one burn soup, anyway?"

"With talent," I say. "But also forgetfulness. It stays on the stove too long, then the bottom part of the pot has a layer of black, burnt soup." I run my palm horizontal to the ground to indicate the underside of a pot and he nods in understanding.

"Delicious," he responds, yet with a little less contempt than two seconds ago.

I'll take it.

We finish our thieved food with Cameron placing the now empty Tupperware in the very back of the fridge so as to conceal our horrible deed, then we return to the designer den, where I'm feeling very full and not at all prepared to be thinking about stupid dinner with Joe.

"What's wrong?" he asks. I turn to look at him and shake my head.

"Uh, we stole food," I say, avoiding the truth. "Doesn't that bother you?"

"You're the one who ultimately took the food out of the fridge," he says, shaking his head. "Don't drag me into this."

"You're gonna rat on me, aren't you?"

I think he's starting to smile when he starts fumbling in his pockets. He pulls out his phone and stares at the caller ID for a second, a look of dread falling over his face before saying, "I gotta take this."

I quickly wave my hand in dismissal. "Go, go. Take your call. I've gotta run anyway."

He doesn't even raise his head to look at me when he walks away, stopping for a second mid-movement as if considering something else, then enters the office and closes the door.

His leave reminds me that I, too, have a commitment in the form of apocalyptic doomsday. I take a deep breath, pack my things, go to my car where I take one last look at myself in the rearview mirror, try to come to terms with the fact that I definitely overdressed for this asshole, then drive off to dinner with Joe.

14

CAMERON

"Why did you talk to Abby, you idiot?"

I have an entire spread of tacos, Buddy's head on my lap, and the words I need to hear coming straight from Ian's mouth. This is the second time he's been in my new apartment scorning me about my life, and it's beginning to feel like I'm just destined to sit in this beanbag chair with my sorrow forever.

I wonder if I'm drawing Ian away from a much better way to spend his nights. He'd probably be reading tons of books, like the smart man that he is, or picking up chicks at bars like the very single man that he is.

However, he hasn't complained about spending his time here, so I'm not going to be the one to call him out. It might be selfish, but I need his presence about now.

I called him right after I hung up the phone with my ex-girlfriend. I was stunned to even see her number pop up to begin with. But she had me hook, line, and sinker the second I answered. She sounded sad, and I felt guilty.

"I don't know." I groan, letting my head hit the back of my

beanbag chair. Buddy raises his head in concern, sees that I haven't hurt myself, then lays back on my lap.

"You're a sad sack of a man, you know that?" Ian says.

"Yes, I'm fully aware," I mumble. "Throw me some chips?"

He ignores me.

"What did she say?" he asks, his tone a bit more consoling —at least as consoling as it can get given our mutual agreement that I am a very stupid man.

"I don't know… she tried justifying everything. She said that she'd gotten bored, we changed into different people… she wanted more, and I couldn't give it to her…"

"Does she want you back?" Ian asks, crouching down to my level.

I pause for a moment, thinking back to the conversation. It had ended up just being one hit after another toward me. She's a master at insulting someone and making it seem like they weren't actually insults. Apparently, the breakup was all my fault, and she listed every instance in which I didn't try to make the relationship work. I couldn't tell if she was right or if I was feeling sorry for myself, but I just accepted it as truth. But regardless, it didn't matter; she wasn't calling to apologize for her own actions or the naked man that grabbed my dog.

"No," I say, looking at him in the eyes. "She doesn't want me back."

Not every man wants marriage. Not every man wants a baby. And, to be honest, not every person loves someone deep enough to makes those type of commitments. I'm not sure I'm capable of doing so.

"You know what you need?" Ian says, slapping his legs and standing up in one smooth motion. His spider limbs lend to such agile movements. "You need to get laid."

"What a cliché response, Ian," I say. "This isn't some movie where the best friend pushes the guy to go to some club where he acts as a pickup artist to help him overcome his depression."

"You really think I could be a pickup artist? What is this, the early 2000s? No, I'm asking you to get some release out. You need to toss your memory of Abby to the curb and carry on with your life. You know what? It doesn't matter that she doesn't want you. Because you don't want her. Or else you would have married her."

He isn't wrong, but my gut still feels like it's being punched.

"I don't know…" I can't seem to get out of my beanbag chair long enough to even put on something other than unwashed gym shorts and an old band tee from '03. Bars are out of the question.

I start a new sentence before he interrupts with, "Are you even listening to me, Cam?" He crouches down again and puts a hand on my shoulder. "You need. To get laid."

I lean back and groan once more.

"How about we go to a skating rink?" he suggests, wiggling his eyebrows.

"A skating rink?" I ask. "Why the hell would we do that?"

"You can put on the roller blades and zoom around. Let the wind hit your face, let your hair down."

"And?"

"Did you not hear me say roller blades?" he says. "Plus, the women at skating rinks on a weekday…"

"Yep, there it is."

"Cam, regular skaters are there on weekdays. Regular skaters have thighs more muscular than mine and they can just"—his hands move through the air in wild motions—"they wrap around you and show you a good time. It's a wonderland of possibilities and adventure."

"Ookay, Ian. I'm calling it a night. Scratch the roller blades idea. The sun is going down, my tacos are getting cold, and I need to get some work done."

"You know what other tacos are getting cold?"

"Stop," I warn.

"Just think about it, bud." He shoots me a wink.

"Yeah, yeah," I motion to the door. "Now get out, you heathen."

"You're welcome for the tacos," he calls back.

"Thank you!" I yell seconds before he closes the door.

He really is a good friend.

I BURIED myself in work at my desk for hours. I'm not doing actual day job work, but instead finding solace in the blueprint sketches of the hotel I've been working on for months. It's calming me down enough to focus on something other than Abby or the sinking depression mixed with boiling anger in my gut. It's a lot of emotions I'm not equipped to handle.

So, I focus on architecture and zone out.

My phone buzzes and I have a good feeling I know who it is. I look at the name and there she is again: Abby. And to think, I had just begun to enjoy the Monday night she initially ruined.

I decide that I won't answer the phone and she can deal with it.

"Hey." *Damn it, how did this phone get to my ear?*

"Hi," she says. A few seconds pass and there's no sounds between either of us, but I decide not to let this continue. With her silence eventually comes the tears, and I can't bear to listen to that.

"Why did you call?" I spit out. It's a bit more aggressive than I would like, but what else did she expect? A soft sort of kindness? She said her piece earlier, and I'm not sure what else can be said at this point.

"I just needed to hear your voice," she says. Her voice quivers and there's a small sniff. "I'm sorry, Cam. I'm so sorry. You know I didn't mean to hurt you."

I feel the heat rise in me. Is she fucking kidding right now?

"I know this doesn't accomplish anything and I'm not even sure what I wanted to say but talking to you earlier really felt nice."

It felt *nice?*

"Tell me something. Tell me about your week."

I shake my head even though she can't see me. "Come on, Abby, really? We just got off the phone and the last thing you mentioned was that I spent too much time at work and that I'm ridiculous for not wanting marriage... I mean, what do you want from me?"

She coughs and lets out a quick sob before going back to silence.

"Is that what you think of me?" she asks, after a few moments pass.

"As a woman who cheated on me? Absolutely." I'm turning to irritation and righteousness. How dare she call wanting to talk? Didn't *she* break up with *me*? What insanity is even happening here?

"Fine. I'm sorry for calling you and bringing myself back into your life. I'm sorry I exist." Her voice is determined and I'm feeling the familiar sense of being manipulated and torn in multiple directions. They're harsh words and she's putting them in my mouth, knowing full well this isn't how I feel. She's hoping I'll stay on the phone a bit longer and tell her how I'm happy she does exist. No, I'm done playing these games.

"I gotta go, Abby," I say, and before she can respond, I hang up.

I wait a few minutes, pacing my apartment, wondering if she'll call back. But she doesn't call back. And suddenly, I know I need a drink.

I tear off my sweatpants, throw on jeans, slip on my black leather loafers, and head out the door to walk to the nearest bar.

15

GRACE

I should not have met with Joe.

I knew it was a bad idea from the start. I wanted to stand him up. I wanted to abandon him. Unfortunately for me, my mom encouraged me to go and also tried to convince me that this was the perfect time to let him have it. "He needs to see how strong you are, and how you're achieving your dreams every day! Without him!"

Thanks, Mom.

A few minutes later, I'm standing in front of the little Italian place we used to call our own. There are too many memories here. Our first date, our anniversary, and even that one time we snuck into the bathroom for, *ahem*, other activities. Hey, I'm not proud of it!

I reach for the handle of one of the double doors but pull back. *I can do this. I can do this.* I stretch out my palm and shake my fingers out. Looking at my reflection in the window, I tug down my tight dress that has already bunched near my thighs. *Okay, let's do this.*

I attempt the door again, but then a scent of the spice

washes over me and a hand touches my waist. Another reaches from behind me to open the door.

I twirl around to see Joe. Looking at him is like seeing a ghost. I barely recognize him. His chest is broader than it had been three months ago, and I can tell his arms are toned by no doubt a constant repetition of the heavy weight barbell. He always could lift me above his head, but now I wonder what else he could do. And why did he start going to the gym *after* our breakup?

"Hey, beautiful."

A try to smile, but it only tugs at one side of my mouth. "Hey, Joe." *Yep, I'm not ready for this.*

We go inside and are escorted to our table. He tries to put his hand on the small of my back to guide me and I shimmy out of his grip. When he tries it again one second later, I try to make conversation with the hostess.

"Wow, crazy night, huh?"

"Ma'am, we're always this busy."

Wow, excuse me.

Joe and I sit across from each other and I stare intently at my menu, but I've been here a thousand times and the saltimbocca special will probably be just as good as it always is. The only thing different here is who *we* are.

"Are you going to look at me, or are you changing your regular order of capellini?" His tone is deep yet still playful. It urges me to look up with only a few words.

Joe has always been a sight for sore eyes, but the gym has clearly increased everything about him. He's trimmed down and his suit fits every new muscle he's worked for. His jawline is more prominent, as is his Adam's apple, and even his deep brown hair looks softer and clean cut.

I mean—does he have a glow about him now, or am I crazy?

"Don't hate on the tomatoes here," I say with a gulp.

It doesn't feel right throwing sarcastic comments his way. I don't feel like he deserves witty banter and a good time. I'm here to give him a bad time by spewing all my revenge curses at him. Like a witch with a voodoo doll, except my real-life doll is right in front of him. With every word, I want a new wound in his chest.

"I hear they added some type of soup." I lift the menu over my eyes. *Oh yeah, really wounding him here, Grace. He's going to feel that sting for sure.*

He chuckles, a low, rumbling sound. His chest rises and falls. I can smell his fresh toothpaste across the table. I used to know that toothpaste. It used to kiss my lips every night before bed. At least until a couple months ago.

"You're still just as funny as ever," he remarks.

Bullshit. I didn't say anything funny, you liar.

"I've been going to the gym," he says. He puts down his menu and leans forward to steeple his hands.

"Good for you," I say, lifting an eyebrow. "I'm a designer now."

"Oh really? We got a new designer at the office recently. He's a pretty cool dude. He goes golfing with me from time to time. He told this funny joke the other day—you would have loved it, Grace."

And then he goes on to tell me some stupid joke from some guy I've never, and will never, meet. The punchline is predictable, but Joe still laughs afterward like it's the funniest thing he's ever heard. He even wipes his eyes with the cloth napkin beside him.

"Yeah, he's hilarious. Terrible golfer, though."

"God forbid," I say.

This gives Joe pause, but only long enough to flash me another grin. "So, tell me what you're up to now, Grace."

I wish he would stop calling me by my name. Like, sure, I know it's my *name* and all, but it feels oddly impersonal. He reads a lot of self-motivational books which I am admittedly a fan of as well, but he reads the ones that are less about self-improvement and more about manipulating others to your will. I'm absolutely positive he read somewhere that calling someone by their name makes conversations that much more intimate. If wanting to barf all over his freshly cut Armani suit is intimate, then I've been doing love all wrong these past few years.

"I moved into an apartment," I say. "Hank is adjusting well."

"He's old, though," Joe interrupts. "How picky can the dog be?"

"He still has preferences, Joe." *Yeah, how do you like it when I call you by* your *name, dickbag?*

"Remember when we went to the shelter and tried to get a new dog?" he asks.

"You wanted a new dog," I clarify. "You said Hank was getting old."

"His white hair isn't getting any more golden," he laughs.

I don't get the joke, but I still laugh anyway. I hate myself for it.

"There's that smile." He reaches across the table to stroke my hand. His touch is impossibly soft and warm.

My heart leaps into my throat and I suddenly feel dirty—and not the good kind. Goosebumps rise up my forearms. His touch feels like a violation. I pull away and lean against the back of my chair before he can rub his thumb across mine again. It was good timing too, because they were going to be clammy in T minus three seconds. Maybe I should have kept them there so he could feel disgusting, too. My clammy hands are no joke.

I clear my throat and pat the napkin in my lap. "I really like the company I work for. It's Treasuries, Inc."

"That's great," he says. "Never heard of them."

You liar. You big, filthy liar. Who in the modern world hasn't heard of my company? But I say nothing. I just let myself smile cordially and nod.

"I got a promotion."

"Oh yeah?" I ask. I don't really care but if it will keep the conversation moving then I'll be happy.

My gaze drifts toward the door in any effort not to lock onto his dark brown eyes—a warm, chocolatey color. The color of comfort.

"A lot of hard work. A lot of golfing, if you know what I mean."

"Schmoozing?" I ask. Why am I smiling?

"You get it, darling. You've always gotten me."

My eyes dart to the door again. Do I want to run or am I just hoping somebody, anybody, will walk in and save me? My heart is racing, and this napkin is doing nothing to quell my shaking hands.

"Listen, Grace, I'm a changed man."

"I don't want to hear..."

"Listen."

I look back at him. His eyebrows are cinched in the middle as if pleading for me to hear him out. And, silly me, I give him my undivided attention.

"Okay, go." I direct, exhaling a shaky breath.

"I've changed. When you left, I... I felt lost. Like I'm missing a shoe."

"A shoe?"

"A *limb*," he corrects, stretching the word so I can feel the weight of it. "I want you to pursue your dreams of art and design. I got a promotion for you. They told me I was the best employee they've had for years. That I'm a prodigy. I have my own office now."

It's weird; the words coming out of his mouth don't seem to match the expression on his face which is still full of remorse.

"I've been hitting the gym again," he continues. "I can deadlift almost two hundred pounds now. I lost ten pounds. I would have lost more, but I think it's all muscle. I quit the dating app. I didn't need it anymore. I only need you. I was getting hit after hit after hit, but it all means nothing. Even the models. Nothing compared to you, Grace."

"That... sounds rough, Joe."

"It's been a fucking nightmare."

I don't respond, but instead find the nearest server and order their most expensive bottle of wine. I'd have to remember to tell my mom that my integrity went out the window completely.

We continue exchanging pleasantries. I barely mention the details of my company before he's diving into how his personal office has floor to ceiling windows. The chairs are leather ("*Leather,* Grace!") and his desk is mahogany. I'm relieved when the meal arrives and I shovel it into my mouth. I don't have much of an appetite, but anything to wash down the horrible taste from this sorry conversation.

Was he always like this? Have I been blind to who Joe is? As I shovel half of the pasta in my mouth, letting it flop around the haphazardly twirled fork, I try to recall when we started dating. We met at a club. Ramona pushed me there against my will and even threw me in one of her bodycon dresses that fit me like a boa constrictor ready to swallow me whole. Little did I know I would be meeting a snake that very night.

His first line to me was: "Can I buy you a drink?" and the rest is history. That was all it took for me before I become a snack that took him two years to digest.

"I have to admit something," he says after the fiftieth golf story of the night.

I know more about this new designer than Joe himself, which is saying something given how proud Joe is of his new biceps that require exactly four sets of twenty repetitions. Per arm.

"You'll laugh when you hear this," he says, setting his fork and knife down on either side of his plate, barely touched. I want to protest, but he continues before I can. And it is the last statement I would expect from this dinner. "But I'm actually seeing someone."

I sit there in stunned silence. I can suddenly feel the weight of the steak, heavy in my stomach. I want to ask so many questions. The one on the tip of my tongue is, "Who is she?" And I voice the question before I can stop myself.

"I met her at the gym." There it is. I now know his new, stellar life with some new chick that can run a mile on a treadmill without stopping and do that whole pull-up machine and probably all the while giving Joe those *come-fuck-me-while-I-call-you-Papa* eyes.

"I need you, Grace," he says. "I can't live without you, and I would end it with her faster than you could come back to my house and stay the night."

"Are you fucking kidding me?" I whisper.

I blink over and over to try and make the world appear high definition again. So far, I've been floating above my body just looking down on this situation. I see myself with my hands folded over each other, my posture so fitting of a bright young woman. But what bright woman goes on a date with this kind of man?

"Are you seriously motherfucking kidding me?" I repeat in a whisper. But then I repeat it again. And again. And again. Louder and louder until I'm finally yelling it through the restaurant. The waiter briskly walks over and asks if there's a problem, asks me to lower my voice when I shout back, but he doesn't understand. He doesn't know what man—what demon —is sitting across me. If he did, I'm sure he would be screaming, too. Which I am, while simultaneously throwing cherry tomatoes at Joe's face.

"For the record, your eyes don't look like chocolate!" I yell, tossing my food bit by bit with every piece bouncing off his stupidly perfect cheeks. "They look like poop!"

"Gracie, calm down!" Joe demands, holding his arms out like Chris Pratt trying to calm the velociraptors in *Jurassic World*.

"Fuck you!" I shout, standing to my feet.

"Ma'am, that's inappropriate language—" the waiter starts, but I interrupt him with a swift come back.

"*You're* an inappropriate language!"

Nailed it.

Before he can demand that I leave—I can tell by how tightly his arms are crossed—I snatch my purse and storm off.

"She means nothing!" Joe yells after me. I hear the squeak of his chair moving as well.

The hostess, oblivious to what happened inside the dining area, smiles at me as I stalk past her.

"Have a good night, miss—"

I snarl wordlessly at her. Because I'm a crazy person.

Joe follows me outside yelling things like, "I need you!" and "It's not attractive when you yell!" But I storm off in my car, zipping out of the parking lot with a wheel spin that could rival *The Fast & the Furious*. And boy am I furious.

I drive until I find my way to my apartment and, might I add, it was without the help of a GPS for the pure sake of letting myself get lost so I could drive more and cool off. When I finally park, I break down. I grip the steering wheel and sob like it's the end of the world—like nothing else can heal this moment. I even put on some Coldplay because wallowing in my own self-pity seems like the logical thing to do.

What was he thinking? I can only imagine that poor girl. All she wanted to do was build a nice ass with some squats and this douchebag comes into her life with his big arms and toned abs and ruins it all in one fell swoop. And she doesn't even know it yet.

I need a bar.

I get out of the car and slam the door behind me before making my way to the gate of my apartment complex, blasting it open and letting it bang shut behind me. I whip out my phone and dial the one person I can hopefully blame for this mess, and after three rings, she finally answers.

"That was a horrible idea, Mom." I'm such a wonderful daughter. "He's an asshole, a cheat, and doesn't deserve any words from me—insult or not." I spit out words. I don't even know what I'm saying at this point. I'm just spouting out sentence after sentence, throwing out language I would never dream of saying around my mom.

After a bit, I feel guilty and make a point of saying that none of it is directed toward her, but then my disdain and pure rage toward Joe continues once more, unrestrained and uncensored.

"Honey, slow down, slow down," she says, finally getting some words in while I'm in the middle of a deep breath. "I'm sorry I told you to go. I'm sorry he's such a horrible man. And I'm sorry, so sorry, that you have to go through this."

"Men are trash," I say. "Men are garbage that don't understand how the world works. This isn't their world where they can play games with whomever they choose—"

"I know, darling. I know."

I stop walking for a second. My heartbeat slows and I take a deep breath, letting the cool night breeze blow through my hair. I close my eyes and continue walking with a bit more decency. "Mom, I can't do this."

We let the silence drift between us over the line and it's almost soothing to hear nothing except the crickets in the night.

"Listen," she says. "I'm going to make a pact with you, okay? For just a few months, don't date, and neither will I. Your father was one of the good ones. Not all men are bad. But maybe let's take a bit to realize that."

My mom rarely discusses my dad. I hold my breath wondering if there will be more. But of course there never is. I pale in comparison to Mom's level of denial about Dad's passing.

"Yeah, you're right," I finally say. "I don't need anyone. Plus, love is a joke." I stop myself from saying more, hoping I haven't already offended her. Love doesn't exist for me and probably never will at this rate. But my mom and dad's love was so powerful that it probably sucked all the love out of the rest of the potential couples in the world.

"Don't let Joe take your progress and make it worth nothing," she says, not rattled by my cynicism. "Do we have a deal, Gracie? No men for just a couple months."

"I like it. Let's do it." I say.

Up ahead is my trusty neighborhood bar. It's a borderline biker bar with way too much haze for my taste, and I already know I'll have to do laundry immediately after getting home just to get the smell of smoke out of my clothes, but it seems friendly enough.

"So, tell me about work," she says. "How's the project coming along? Anything interesting?" I can hear her rummaging through the kitchen, no doubt making some late-night healthy muffins for tomorrow morning or something. I wonder if she's using avocado again.

I open the door and walk down the rickety bar stairs thinking about projects at work. The only thing that strikes me as interesting, however, is Cameron. I think about how he adjusts his mess of hair, how he bites his tip of his pen while he's thinking, and how he looks at me with those eyes—the brown and green that strike through to your soul.

"Yeah, a couple things," I say, smiling to myself without

even thinking about it. Compared to my night with Joe, thinking of Cameron actually cheers me up to a small degree.

I make my way to the bar, sliding through a couple people and apologizing as I pass. It's the opposite of the nice Italian restaurant I just came from and I soak it all in. The floorboards are sticky from night upon night of booze tipping over clutched glasses. There's a raised platform where a band is probably supposed to be, but is instead now a stage for the drunkest individuals of the night. The bar on the opposite side of the entrance is occupied by people who you just get the sense are probably regulars. They're holding drinks and chatting with the bartender.

There's a low hum of talk and the scent of smoke in the air. It's not glamorous and I'm very overdressed, but it's exactly what I need right now.

Mom says, "Honey, where are you?"

Before I can answer, I see a mess of hair on a man hunched over the counter on the last bar stool at the end. The very man who happens to be on my mind.

What the absolute heck is Cameron doing here on a Monday night?

There are a couple empty stools between him and the crowd, and it looks like he's avoiding the world. I have never connected to him more.

"Mom, I'm gonna have to let you go," I say.

She quickly gets in her goodbyes and we exchange an "I love you" before hanging up. I slide my phone into my crossbody purse and walk toward my boss.

Once I get closer, it's easy to see that he's a total wreck. He's wearing a ratty black t-shirt with various holes in on the side and near the hem. His fitted jeans flatter his muscular thighs, and he's sporting nice leather loafers, but his eyes look heavy and his hair is more disheveled than I've ever seen it.

He lacks any signs of energy at the moment, loosely holding

an almost-empty tumbler. He stares at some unknown spot behind the bar, eyes glazed over.

"Cameron?" I ask, tilting my head to the side and trying to get a better look at his face.

He comes out of his thoughts and blinks at me as though seeing me for the first time.

"Oh," he says, "h-hello." He struggles to get the word out and, by the smell of the alcohol drifting from him, I can tell he's been drinking for a while.

"Mind if I sit?" I feel weird voluntarily joining him for drinks, but it'd be even weirder to leave now.

"Be my guest," he grumbles, patting the seat of the stool next to him. I place myself down, and the full force of his whiskey-scented self passes my way.

Oof, he's definitely not sober.

"Is everything okay?" I ask.

I expect no long-winded answer from Cameron. So far, he hasn't been one for being emotionally transparent in this off-kilter relationship of ours. He breathes in then exhales slowly, letting his eyes drift over to meet mine. He nods his head to consider his next few words.

"No. No it is not, Holmes," he says, bitterness oozing out in his tone. "And I'll tell you why. My girlfriend... well"—he thinks for a moment and continues—"my *ex*-girlfriend thinks I'm a pretty big piece of shit. So big, in fact, she thought it would be a good idea to pick useless arguments, give me blue balls for months, and, oh right, let some other man sit naked on my couch—*naked*—and rub his wrinkly balls all over it."

Welp, didn't expect that.

"He was... rubbing his balls on your couch?" I ask.

"Probably," he answers. "With balls like those, I'm sure they flopped around all over the damn couch without him even trying."

I smile and try to suppress my laughter. The idea of free-flowing balls definitely improves the state of my mood.

"So, what did you do?" I ask.

"I punched the guy," he deadpans. "He touched my dog."

"Is... that a... euphemism?"

"No, he was touching my actual dog."

"Well then that definitely crosses the line," I agree, putting my hands on my hips.

He looks me up and down before tipping his drink to me and whispering, "Exactly."

My back straightens and my face flushes. This dress suddenly feels much too tight. He finishes the rest of his glass in one gulp and taps the bar to alert the bartender—or anyone who's paying attention—that he needs a refill.

"So, I'm guessing that's how you got the black eye, huh?" I say, raising two fingers to the bartender to indicate we'll need another of the same. "He punched you back?"

"No, that was from the lions, remember?" he says, side-eyeing me.

"The call you got yesterday," I continue, ignoring his jab. "Was that her?" I hope I'm not crossing a line, but I guess he's already mentioned blue balls, so I think my question isn't invasive.

"Bingo," he says, exhaling once more. He looks over to the bartender and then to me. "You're ordering whiskey?" he asks as the bartender places the glasses in front of us. I mouth a quick "thank you."

"I figured I'd jump in the party," I say, lifting my glass to Cameron. "Seems like you have the right idea."

He raises his glass as well. I notice his hand swaying, the drink sloshing around. A bit drops over the side. "What are we toasting to?"

I think for a second then clink my glass to his. "Bad relationships."

He nods back and yells, "To bad relationships!"

I look around to see if anyone notices, but the thought of Joe hits me once more.

"To bad relationships!" I yell.

A wide smile spreads on his face and my heart races, hoping the scream wasn't too loud.

He clinks my glass again and raises the drink to his mouth, but quickly puts it back down on the counter before it can reach his lips.

"Wait." He closes his eyes, trying to center himself once more.

I'm sure his brain is moving too fast for his reflexes to catch up. It's kind of cute and it gives me some extra time to scan over his body while he isn't looking. It's only a quick glance, but it's hard not to notice that, even though his shirt has at least three holes in it, his torso fills it well; his large arms pull the sleeves taut. I've never seen him in a t-shirt long enough to notice, but I could definitely live life in a state of bliss if it involved more of Cameron Kaufman in black t-shirts.

"Wait, so..." He gathers his thoughts slowly but surely. "Bad relationship... are you? Did you...? How is that going for you?"

I laugh. "I just had dinner with my ex."

He stares at me for a couple seconds before spitting out, "Why?"

It's incredulous, to the point, and honestly it makes me feel like an idiot because "why" is a very good question. Why did I want dinner with Joe? Was it to talk about our potential future? Did I expect him to compliment the way I dressed, or give me some chaste kiss at the end of the night?

"He wanted to talk about our house," I say. It's a truth, but maybe not the whole truth. "He's going to sell it."

"Were you married?" Cameron asks, taking a small sip of his drink but not breaking eye contact with me for even a moment.

"No, he didn't really want to. Said he didn't want kids, so what was the point of marriage?"

Cameron is quiet for a moment. He narrows his eyes at me, trying to decipher what to say next, or maybe he's expecting me to keep talking. But after a few seconds, I continue.

"I'm pretty impartial toward kids so it wasn't much of a concern for me," I lie. I'm sure coming off as the lovesick puppy desperate for a family isn't a good look in front of your boss. "Eventually, we just drifted apart, I guess. Found our own hobbies, stopping hanging out, and now I'm twenty-seven and living the apartment life just like I did in college."

"Woah, don't diss the apartment life!" he says, hands in the air with palms out in front of him. "Pump the breaks on that kind of talk! I like mine."

I smile and take another drink. "Well, that makes one of us."

We both stare at our glasses, and I glance over at the bartender to gesture for one more drink. Cameron raises his hand to signal for one as well, but I touch his arm and lower it down. The bartender's mouth twitches up in a sly smile.

"I have a question," Cameron says, moving his glass on the counter, letting the condensation glide it from side to side. "You're twenty-seven, and you just started at the company as a junior designer. Why is that? That's an entry level position."

Yes, I made a complete career change a bit later in my twenties than some people would. Some of my friends from art school are now museum curators, art teachers, or even creative leads like Cameron is. And I'm just a junior designer.

"I was working in collections," I admit with a small shrug. "I never wanted to work in a corporate environment. I went to art school, but I had to get a job out of college. I didn't feel like I was talented enough to pursue art, so there I was: At a desk, in a cubicle, calling people all day about bills they didn't want to pay."

"You didn't think you were talented?" he interrupts.

I clear my throat in embarrassment. "I had a lot of work to do on the whole 'confidence' thing."

"Don't have a problem with that now," he slurs with small smirk, taking large gulps of his drink. "So, go on..."

"Oh, well, when Joe and I—the ex, I mean—broke up, I decided I wasn't happy. I wasn't doing anything I loved anymore. I went to work, then yoga, and spent the rest of the night having my so-called boyfriend sit on his phone and avoid me. Found out later he was browsing dating apps, so that's a fun tidbit." Cameron cringes for me and I appreciate the gesture. "In short, 'college Grace' would be really disappointed in the 'present Grace.' So, I decided to make a change. And here I am."

He smiles for the first time tonight. It's a small, barely visible smile, but I can see the indention in his cheek where his deep dimples would be were he grinning.

"Sounds to me like the breakup really only did you a favor," he says.

"Yeah," I smile, "Yeah, I guess it did."

"And what do you think of Treasuries?" he asks, slinging his tumbler around. "Is it everything you thought it would be?"

"Sort of," I laugh. "I have a boss that is absolutely off-putting so there's that."

"Sounds like a nightmare," he says, his eyebrow cinched in as if apologizing. At least I think he might be. I notice he's drifting closer to the bar, having a hard time holding himself up. The more his head dips down, the closer his elbow gets to mine.

"I don't think he's too bad," I say, tilting my head to admire him. Even at his current state, he's still weirdly adorable.

Yep. And there he goes. His head lowers to the counter, but a sly smile drifts onto his face.

His head rolls over to the side and he gets a good look at

me. He stares into my eyes, not moving an inch, as if taking me in. My face gets warm and my muscles tighten.

"You think we could be friends?" he asks. "I don't really have a lot of those."

Friends?

The words stop me. Cameron Kaufman just wants a *friend*? I'm almost wondering if it's a trap. Is this some part of his game where he continues to insult me? Is he just gonna pull out some finger guns and shoot them in my direction yelling, "Gotcha?!"

I look at him, sitting there staring at me with borderline puppy dog eyes. He just seems like a lost child, begging for scraps of comfort. I've never seen him like this, so desperate for a response. But what would we even do as friends? I've never just been friends with a guy. Doesn't the whole "I'm attracted to you" thing get in the way of this? Cause I'll be honest, I've never been so attracted to a guy in my life. Not even Joe the asshole.

Added note: This would not *just* be friendship with a man. This would be a friendship with my boss. Intimate friends where we maybe talk about exes, vent about work, and I sit next to him while he's drunk.

Well, I guess we're doing that anyway. And who can deny those eyes?

Let's take the plunge.

"Sure, Cameron," I say. "I don't see why not."

He smiles at me with dazed, heavy-lidded eyes, and it's like I'm a genie granting him a wish.

"Good," he says, slapping his leg as if it were a gavel and we just declared this friendship law.

Yep, he's had enough to drink. I touch the top part of the glass he isn't holding and try to take it from him. He loosens his grip and whether that's from a current lack of sober strength or if he's conceding, I still think he must know it's about time to call it a night.

"But I'm still your boss," he says, almost as if it's a warning, shaking his finger in my direction. Not like I needed the warning, but I think both of us—even him in his drunken state—know this is not solid ground.

"Of course you are," I say. "Nobody needs to know you don't entirely hate me."

"Good," he says again, a quick nod following as he looks down at his hand. "Now where's my drink?"

I lift up his stolen glass in my hand and toast to him. "I got you covered, friend."

He squints and shakes his finger once more. "You know what, Holmes? I like you."

I laugh, but it's more of an uncomfortable, "What are you even saying, please stop," laugh. I like this nice Cameron, but I'm also a bit afraid of where this may go. I've been around drunk people and they say the darndest things.

"You're drunk," I tease, grinning.

"Hell yeah I am," he says, his speech getting slower and less deliberate. "But I still like you."

"That's very nice, Cameron," I smile, trying not to let myself get overwhelmed by the amount of eye contact he's sharing with me. He won't look away, and I feel like he's that snake from *Jungle Book* just pulling me in to his entrancing gaze.

"How are you planning on getting home?" I ask, changing the subject.

He wiggles his eyebrows at me. "Why?" he growls. "Are you coming with me?"

Oh good lord, I've died. I'm reeling into heaven with my wings flapping because I am dead. Or maybe I'm diving deep into hell with little horns because I want nothing more than to say, "You bet your ass I'm coming home with you."

It's hard not to picture us in his house. It's most likely a nice, modern home with stylish furniture and sleek countertops. I can imagine him lifting me on top of them, his hands traveling all over my body, my stomach, my breasts. He would take my nipples between his fingers while his hand travels down to...

Shake it off, Grace.

"Cameron, let's both forget you said that," I say. "You'll thank me on Monday."

I could easily believe he blacked out the second he said that because his eyes glaze over and focus on a spot over my shoulder. He probably won't remember *any* of this. I ask for his credit card, which he hands over. I call the bartender over, telling him it's probably best if we leave soon, and thankfully he's quick to process the bill. I make sure to tip him well. It's not my card, anyway. And if I have to babysit my boss, he's paying for it.

"Let's go, Holmes!" Cameron exclaims, getting a surge of energy and pocketing his wallet. "To the streets! I'll be your Watson! We can solve mysteries like the classic mystery duo we are."

I let out a restrained laugh, trying to cover it with my mouth. "Well, I walked here, so we may have to call you a ride."

"Not a problem," he slurs, lifting his arm and placing it around my shoulders. My breathing hitches until I realize he's just doing it to help himself off of his stool. I let it stay once he's up. I tell myself he probably needs the support anyway. "I can walk home, too. It's only a few minutes."

Knowing he lives close enough to walk as well makes my heart jump to my throat. But that's nothing compared to the actual walk.

He spends the entire time trying to gain footing, tripping over his own legs, and gripping my shoulder every time he almost falls. His hand on my arm sends shivers down my spine. They're large, slightly rough on the inside of his thumb and index finger from what I imagine are countless hours of gripping drafting pencils.

He directs me toward his home, and we travel the same way

to his place as we would to mine, taking the same sidewalks and passing the same empty parking lots and scattered trees. It's beginning to get eerie and I start to consider... Do we live in the same complex?

No that's silly. Of course not.

But what if we did?

And, of course, my suspicions are confirmed once we stop in front of the iron gate to my apartment complex and he mumbles, "This is me."

He lives in my complex. He is mere steps away from me at all times. Is the universe playing some practical joke? Because this is the least funny prank I've ever seen.

"You're gonna have to be more specific than that, Cameron," I say. Not the second floor on the right. Not the second floor on the right.

"Left... I think."

Whew.

"Okay, I can work with that," I say, almost more to myself than him.

He's beginning to groan, and I can tell if I don't drop him off soon, he'll be leaning over the bushes having a horrible time. I have sick empathy too, so let's not even go there.

"Third floor," he mumbles. "316."

Is it a question or an answer? I genuinely don't know, but I have no other leads to determine if he's correct so I apartment 316 it is.

"All right, let's get moving." He leans on me a bit more, and I find it difficult to hold his weight. Given my height, I'm still fairly thin at 120 pounds, but he's at least fifty pounds heavier and all muscle.

We move up the path and my shoulders start to hurt, but if we can just make it to the stairs, maybe I'll have better luck at maneuvering him around. How naive of me. The second we make it to the stairs, he walks up one, maybe two, steps and then lays down right on the third. His head rests on the step above and he curls into a fetal position. I'm admittedly a bit amazed at his efforts to find some place to sleep.

"Cameron, you have to get up, okay?" I say, putting on my sweet voice that I only reserve for Hank when he's begging for food.

You ever tried to deny a dog chocolate? If it wouldn't kill the poor guy, I would have caved years ago.

Cameron groans, lifting himself off the stairs in a single push-up (oh my God) and takes them one step at a time. I jog up a few steps ahead of him and reach out my hand for support should he choose to fall again. He instead grabs the railing and hoists himself up the stairs on his own. Only a tiny bit of disappointment washes over me as I am denied my chance at feeling his rough hands once again.

We climb two more flights of stairs with a bit more ease when he finally discovers the human power of lifting his feet. By the time we're on the third floor, he knows exactly where his apartment is—thank you, heavens above—and he pulls out his key to turn the lock.

Once the door pulls open, I'm bombarded by his dog. It's a golden retriever just like Hank, but with noticeably less white and gray fur. He's as golden as this breed can get and just as wild.

"Oh, hi there!" I say, bending down to pet him. He's already feverishly licking my hands and arms. Definitely a friendly boy. I'm not used to such an excited dog, as Hank mellowed out years ago, but I will take all the precious dog love I get.

"Buddy, no," Cameron groans, barely getting out the words. He's clearly unable to control the happy beast, so I assist by grabbing the dog's collar and taking wide steps to corral him back into the apartment.

"He's all right," I say between laughs as Buddy's tail whacks

Cameron while he tries to side-step through the narrow foyer. "I like dogs."

Once we're in and the doors are closed, I look around and realize my expectations for his nice apartment looked very different from the reality of it.

A lone bean bag chair is the centerpiece of the apartment and, from the way it's displayed, seems almost like it could be some Indiana Jones booby trap. A few steps away is a giant dog bed that is noticeably nicer than the Temple of Doom beanbag. And then there's a desk in the corner. This seems to have much more activity surrounding it. Pencils, papers, and a small stack of books adorn the top. The laptop computer is slightly open, and the wireless mouse is drifting a bit too close to the edge for my tastes. It looks as if it had been pushed aside in a hurry.

But the items that stick out the most are the blueprints push-pinned to the wall above the desk. They look like a layout of a home, maybe a restaurant, or even a lobby to a hotel. The lines are crisp and artfully crafted like pure love was poured into each one. Surrounding each draft is a heavy dose of sticky notes with Cameron's handwriting scrawled across each of them.

"Did you do these?" I ask in awe, walking over and running my hands across the papers, feeling the indentions of the lines.

"Oh, yeah." He sounds like than enthused. "But, they're just... drafts. Just messes."

Messes? They're beautiful.

"I need to lay down," he says, taking a seat in the bean bag chair. It depresses under his weight and instantly, his dog is next to him, sitting straight as statue with only his tail giving away the excitement he's trying to hold back. If there was anything nearby other than the chair, his wagging rear-end would knock it over without a care in the world.

"I didn't know you loved architecture," I say.

"It's nothing," he groans.

I turn to find his head in his hands. Oh right, I almost forgot that he's not doing well.

"Do you want me to get you anything?" I ask. "Water? Something for a headache?"

He shakes his head.

"No, but you're great," he says. I can tell it's a struggle to get the words out. I've been there before where any drunken, slurred word could potentially cause your stomach to churn. But despite his pained response, I feel something resembling butterflies run through my chest. Not moths like with Joe. Straight up butterflies.

"I'll say this: You sure hit the jackpot with friendships, boss," I joke, taking my own keys out of my pocket and twirling them around. *Play it cool, Grace. You can be smooth.*

He looks up at me, staring me dead in the eyes. "You're beautiful."

My mouth opens, but nothing comes out. My tongue is dry, and my throat feels like it's constricting.

"And your ideas are good, you know," he says. "You're damn pushy, but you're smart."

I can't help but smile. "You're just drunk."

"Nah," he says, waving his hand in mock dismissal, but a smile creeps up the side of his face and I'm surprised we're even joking around like we are.

I laugh. "Let's get you into bed."

His smile deepens enough to show his dimples and I throw my hand out to cover it before he can say anything else. His eyebrows waggle up and down suggestively, and I shake my head.

"No more compliments, Cameron. I don't think I can handle you being so nice."

"You're so nice," he mumbles under my hand and I roll my eyes.

"Bed, now," I demand.

I reach my hands out for him to take and together we lift him off the beanbag chair. I escort him to his bedroom and let him flop down. I roll him on his side just in case. I'm too paranoid to let a drunk person lay on their back. I've heard too many horror stories.

I make my way to his kitchen and find the cups to pour him some water. When I return to the bedroom, he's already passed out. A light snore exits his mouth and it's almost like watching a puppy breathe heavily in its sleep. It's endearing.

I go back to the living room and grab the beanbag chair to drag it into his bedroom. I'll stay for just a bit. There's no point in leaving a drunk man by himself. His dog follows me and places a toy by my side. I throw it for his pleasure, and we spend a while having him run out and back with it covered in drool.

Once he starts to get tired, I whip out my phone between toy tosses and scroll through my texts. I have quite a few from Joe, but I scroll past them.

Even babysitting a drunk person that's been kind of an asshole to me up until now beats talking to Joe.

Cameron's dog barks, and he shifts around a bit, but doesn't wake. His head lolls over the side of the bed and I see every etching in his face, the slight remnants of the bruise under his eye, and his soft lips parted slightly as he snoozes.

Yeah, I've definitely had bad nights, but this isn't one of them.

16

CAMERON

Ian's ticking wall clock is like a bomb counting down to an explosion that's about to detonate at every passing second. Who puts a ticking clock in their office anyway? He may as well have a tall grandfather clock in here. I don't know which would be louder.

"You went drinking without me?"

"Voice lower, please," I beg, bringing my fingers up to my temples and rubbing as hard as I can to make the buzzing go away. "On a scale of one to ten, my hangover is a solid fifty."

It's been a little over six hours since I made a show of pounding drinks in that bar, and I'm no spring chicken anymore. This type of hangover should have been reserved for weekends when I can lay on the floor groaning in a pit of misery all day—not for Tuesday mornings at work.

"No, you do not deserve my sympathy," Ian shoots back, his volume rising a bit. I cringe at the vibrations in my head. "You got drunk. You, a man that has never gotten blackout drunk, got blackout drunk and can't remember a thing."

"Geez, Ian, it's a burden I must bear."

That is a lie I told him for my own sake. The truth is that I've never been blackout drunk, and this time is no exception.

The burden does not lie with not remembering anything, but instead with being able to recall every fucking detail. I know every single word I said to Grace, and I have spent the majority of my morning reliving it over and over until I forced myself to take a small nap in my office so I could try not to think about it.

The most exhausting thing were the dreams I had last night. It's like I couldn't escape her. At one point, she was in my bedroom doorway, leaning against the frame naked with her foxy red hair falling in front of her tits, denying me a look. In another dream, she was wearing a crop top with the bottom of her breasts slightly exposed, but not enough to see it all. My imagination made Grace a damn tease.

"You disgust me," Ian says, and I'm jolted out of my reverie. If only he knew. "What happened to the skating rink? I thought you didn't want to go out."

I can only think of Grace and I realize it would be very risky to stand up at this point with the way my erection is pressing into my zipper.

"So, do you feel better, Cam?" Ian says with sarcasm that makes me almost want to punch him in the face. He lifts himself to sit on the corner of his desk even though his feet still touch the ground. Lanky mother fucker. "You did the whole depression breakup thing, so let's move on."

I close my eyes. Ian's giving me tough love and I hate it, but it's definitely what I need. So, I decide he's right and I need to do the only thing I truly know how to do: Distract myself with work. "Mr. Feldman needs designs by Friday. I'll just focus on that."

He rolls his eyes and I'm willing to bet he wasn't surprised to hear that answer.

"I'm honestly not even surprised."

Told you.

"Yeah, yeah, yeah," I mumble.

"Well, hop to it then," he says. "I'm actually busy for once."

I laugh a little, but it hurts my head. "And I was starting to think your job was just hanging out in my office."

I brush off my pants, finally able to stand without embarrassing myself, and roll my neck before opening the door and walking down the hall back to my office.

I haven't seen Grace this morning. I don't know how long she stayed at my house last night, but I remember waking up for a short moment of lucidity and seeing her on the floor curled up with Buddy. It was the cutest damned thing I'd ever seen. At the time, I'd wondered what life could be like with that kind of sight every morning—except she hopefully wouldn't be on the floor. Abby took care of Buddy like it was a chore. She would walk him because he needed to do business. She would play with him because, if we didn't, he was unruly. But I never once saw her cuddle with him like Grace did last night.

As fate, or whatever otherworldly being, would have it, I round the corner and knock over someone connected to tangle of red hair.

Fantastic.

"Wow, way to go, boss." Grace says with a joking smirk. She crouches down to start picking up her papers, and I'm given a clear line of sight down her shirt. She's wearing a black bra and, in the center, right between her cleavage, is a tiny, red bow. If I weren't so stunned at the sheer irony of this, I would have said, "I'm sorry."

I attempt to bend down and help her pick up the dropped papers, but instead my body yields to the hangover once more and I clutch my head in my hand, hoping to hold myself together. I almost forgot that my brain is in hell.

"Don't worry, I got it," she says.

"No, it was fault," I say, pulling myself together just enough to bend down to help her. But this is mostly in an effort to avert my eyes from her neckline.

We both stand up and I hand her back whatever sheets I could grab. She quickly shuffles them in her hands and hugs them to her chest. She smiles at me, and even though I feel too uncomfortable to talk, she gets out the words for the both of us.

"How are you feeling?"

"Stellar," I lie, my hand instinctively going to my head again.

She laughs a bit, and I feel like it's a knowing laugh. A mocking laugh. A laugh that makes my stomach churn. I'm honestly unsure if it's the hangover or the dread of knowing what transpired.

I told her about Abby. I hit on her. And I touched her. A lot. Her hands, arms, her shoulders, her waist... it's all so blurry and yet so clear in my mind. I can barely picture how she looked, but the feel of it all under my fingertips... my erection threatens to return. I shove my hands in my pockets.

I know that we need to talk about it. This isn't the first uncomfortable conversation I've had in my life, and it sure won't be the last. If my job has taught me anything, it's that awkwardness shouldn't exist for a manager. You should always be calm and collected, so like a switch on the wall, I trip it on and bring in the much-needed light to this conversation.

"Do you want to meet for lunch today?" I ask.

A slow smile spreads over Grace's full, pink lips. "Sure. Whatever works for you."

It feels sensual, but I'm honestly too overwhelmed by my imminent nausea and pounding headache to think about it too much. If I do, it will only make me sicker.

"I'll meet you out front at noon," I say.

"Absolutely." She nods and walks past me.

We can take lunch to talk through things and maybe clear up some misunderstandings. There's no reason our relationship can't return to normal. Maybe we'll even go back to hating each other if I'm lucky. It would probably be for the best.

I count a few seconds then turn around and spend a bit too much time admiring the way her dark jeans fit her body.

I might hate myself, but I definitely don't hate her for that.

For lunch, we decide on a quick taco joint within walking distance of the building. Thankfully, by the time noon rolls around, I have a lot of my appetite back and I've popped enough Ibuprofen to be at around seventy-percent functioning capacity. Even though we don't address any events from last night during our walk, I think it's heavily implied this lunch time is for discussion away from the office, and for some type of fattening, greasy food to keep a potential worsening hangover at bay.

I pick a high top for us to sit at after we order, and she hops up on the stool and rests her chin between both hands. She's giving me some goofy smile. I know what she wants, so I take a deep breath and jump in.

"I'm sorry," I say, exhaling. The admission makes me cringe.

She raises an eyebrow in mock confusion. "About what?" She's pressing me to be more specific, and I'm both irritated and oddly a bit turned on at her pushiness.

"About last night," I clarify, to which she nods in some act of clear understanding. "I'm not proud of it."

"You remember?" she asks, letting her elbows slide forward on the table.

"I've never been one to blackout," I grumble. "Unfortunately."

She giggles. "Oh no, I'm definitely feeling like this is a fortunate circumstance."

"And why is that?" I ask.

She's absolutely loving this shit. She loves being in control of me for once—holding me hostage with potential blackmail and what I'm sure she's hoping is guilt.

"I think we have some kind of connection now," she says, straightening her posture and holding her head higher, almost haughty.

The heat rises in my face. "That's funny, because I'm under the impression I'm your *boss*."

"And yet, you want to be my friend."

My chest sinks as the air rushes out. "Oh God, I said that."

"Yes, you did," she responds with a laugh.

I glare and I feel my heart beating fast, my veins pumping in my arms. I'm seething at her, yet her expression doesn't falter. She believes she has me in a bind. She's much too cocky for her own good.

"I'm not here to play games," I say. "I just feel like this needed to be addressed."

"So, let's address it."

"Are we not?"

"No," she says, leaning back with her arms crossed. A smirk tugs at the edge of her lips and it crinkles her nose. It's fucking adorable, but I try to wipe the thought from my mind. "Let's talk about your apartment."

"Sure," I concede, dragging out the word and narrowing my eyes at her.

What did she notice? I can't remember if my apartment was clean or messy. Were my clothes hanging around the laundry, dishes piled in the sink? It's a crapshoot most weeks, and given that Abby decided to call me out of the blue yesterday, I could've easily let the apartment go to pot fast.

"Your desk," she says. "There was a lot of architecture type stuff. It looked really good."

Oh, right. The drafting table. It's not exactly a sore subject, but trying to tell someone that you tried at something and failed isn't exactly a fun conversation to have over lunch.

"Thanks. Yeah, I majored in architecture in college. I liked it, but it just wasn't my thing," I lie. It was my thing, but I let that thing go.

"Hey, I majored in art and ended up getting back into it." She waves her fork at me. "Maybe you can go back to architecture."

I grimace. No, I can't.

"It's a just a hobby." I shrug.

"I'm sure design was at one point too," she says. "Now look at you!"

Yes, look at me: I'm thirty-three and have the word "director" in my title at a very successful marketing firm. I would be an idiot to upend my life right now. Most people my age are getting married, having kids, or have already accomplished both by now and looking forward to retirement. I'm not stumbling into a bigger life altering mess than the one I'm already in. A breakup and apartment life? I need to keep at least *some* of my stability intact.

"Let's talk about something else, huh?" I suggest.

"Fine. Well, what else do friends talk about, Mr. Kaufman?" she asks.

My muscles tense at the formality of hearing Grace call me by my surname. It brings something in the forefront of my mind, and it sure isn't friendship.

"Work. Because we're boss and employee—not friends," I emphasize, lifting an eyebrow.

She arches hers in return, testing my patience. "Friends help friends home when they're almost blackout drunk."

"I didn't black out."

"Friends spend the night at each other's houses to make sure they don't die in their sleep."

"I could have handled myself."

"And friends go out to lunch together, have some tacos, and share intimate stories about their true passions. Like architecture."

I want to argue. I want to tell her that my true passion isn't architecture and that it doesn't matter anyway because going out to lunch and having this conversation is inappropriate. Our little adventure was unacceptable. And she is my employee—an employee with an amazing ass—but my employee nevertheless. But then her smile gets me. The sun shines in the window, illuminating her freckles and her bright blue eyes and they stare into me, seeping through me.

It's ridiculous. She doesn't know the first thing about me past whatever drafting junk she saw on my apartment wall, but I decide to bite on the hook. She can reel me in anyway.

"Tell me what you think friends talk about," I say.

"They could talk about why they're such an asshole to their employee designer."

Fair.

"Who, Gary?" I ask. She throws a small piece of lettuce my way, dragging a laugh out of me.

"No—me," she clarifies, joking but with a hint of a seriousness to her voice as well. "Why me, Cameron?"

"Because you're just such a pain in my ass," I say, letting a smirk pass across my face.

I can't help it. It's the way she's simultaneously glaring at me and letting her tongue trace the inside of her lips that drives me wild and makes it impossible to think straight. Like she's been presented with a challenge she's trying to figure out. Does she even know she's doing it?

Then I notice a small thing on her purse. A pin in the shape of a golden retriever. On its fur are the words "Life is Golden".

"Oh, do you like dogs?" I ask.

"Yeah," she says with a smile. It's soft, as if she's recalling a close sibling or a child. "My dog is a golden."

Of course she would love dogs.

I clear my throat. "You've got great ideas, Grace, I'll give you that," I say, and it kills me to admit that while sober. "But you're adamant about them. You push and push without considering the team first."

"Doesn't the client want good ideas?" she asks, genuine.

"Yes, but they want good ideas from Treasuries—not just Grace Holmes."

"Well, that's harsh. You're not exactly a team player either!" she snaps, almost as if it's a "if you're snitching, I'm snitching" kind of thing.

"How so?" I ask. The balls on this woman continue to surprise me.

"You're a manager that doesn't accept ideas," she starts. "You shoot down everything I suggest, you don't accept criticism well, and you've never just walked around and seen what everyone is working on."

"I'm not going to micromanage," I say.

"Well, you could at least try to *manage* at all and stop being so... so huffy!"

Her comment hits me in the gut. I didn't realize this was what I had become. I used to speak to everyone. I was the social guy—the guy that shared all of my ideas and brainstormed with the team. Now all I do is sit in my office and review paperwork, pass along the team's ideas, and veto any that don't meet my personal standards.

"I'm sorry," she says after we're both quiet for a moment.

"Don't be," I say. "*I'm* sorry."

Well, aren't we just a couple of cute kids.

She narrows her eyes at me. Is she still judging me, or is she thinking about something? Women are a fucking mystery and it drives me insane.

"Fine." Her voice is sharp and to the point. "Fine then. I have an idea, mister boss man."

"Shoot."

"You'll teach me to toe the line, but in exchange, you'll pay attention to what I have to say."

"That seems one-sided," I say. "And who says I don't pay attention already?"

"I do," she laughs. "You purposefully ignore me."

The last thing I do is ignore her. It's impossible not to notice her. The curve of her hips, the fierce red of her hair, the way the tip of her freckled nose tips slightly up. Plus, there's that incredibly annoying fact that her ideas *are* actually good. She understands design principles and knows how to bend the rules to her will. I definitely don't ignore her, but maybe I'm a bit dismissive.

What do I know about this whole management thing? I was promoted because I'd been here the longest; the guy before me was retiring, and I was fairly charismatic around the office. Not sure what happened to that guy, but maybe I do need a few lessons on how to act.

"How about instead of bending to your every whim," I start, and she can't help but give a satisfied smirk. "I get you to toe the line and you teach me how to be a decent manager."

It's not the dumbest idea I've ever had, but for some reason, it tugs at me like a necessary evil. If I'm going to succeed at this job—this one thing I have going for me right now—then maybe I need to employ the help of someone who isn't afraid to tell me like it is.

"All of that, plus you consider my ideas," she says. "And you need to be nice to me."

"No," I deadpan.

"Not even some of the time?"

"Absolutely not."

"What was that whole thing about friendship?" she says. "Didn't you say you wanted that?"

She gives me this look that looks like she's internally celebrating her victory. Goddamn she's manipulative. Maybe not a complete nutcase like Abby, but just enough to get me riled up. I can't tell if I like it or hate it.

"Are you threatening me?" I ask.

"No, I'm simply using the leverage I have." She leans forward on the table, curling her finger toward me in a "come here" motion, and before I have any sense to resist, I'm peering at her much closer than before. "I won't tell anyone that my manager hit on me while drunk if you can resist being an asshole to me for just two months."

I suddenly hate her and yet I also think I could love this woman on some level.

"Two weeks," I say.

"One month."

"Three weeks."

"Done." Satisfied, she backs away, and already I miss the smell of her flowery shampoo. It makes my blood boil to even think I could admire her after she just pulled that stunt.

I huff out a breath I didn't even know I was holding, and in response she leans on the table and holds out her hand with a pinky straight out.

"What are you doing?" I ask, but I know full well what's she doing.

It's cute, sure, but ridiculous. I am not pinky swearing on this. I could force an honest handshake, but I draw the line at pinky swears.

"It's a pact," she says. "This is what you do."

"Is that a rule?"

"It's a rule," she insists.

It's not a business handshake with an implied knowledge

that a contract will follow like I'm used to with clients, and it's not Ian making a bet that the other has to pay for a dinner buffet if they're wrong. It's a simple pinky swear, and I guess I can swing that.

With both our arms on the table, we wrap our pinkies around each other and seal the deal.

17

GRACE

Cameron and I finish up with lunch and return to the office building. I feel like it was a highly productive lunch, and although he flashes me a slight knowing smirk before heading off to his closed off office, I'm still reeling from my cleverness.

However, when I get to my desk, it's in that moment that every detail from lunch sinks in and I whip out my phone, busting out texts to my mom faster I thought my fingers were capable of.

Grace: I think I'm friends with my boss.
Grace: The hot one.
Grace: I also think I just blackmailed him. Whoops.

I lock my phone and toss it into my purse, not even wanting to confront the shame that is waiting for me once it rings, which it does in less than five seconds. I flip it over to see my mom calling and I send it to voicemail.

A few minutes later, I'm finally too curious to not listen to it. I regret this immediately because she pulls every mom card she can muster. *How could you risk your job?* She says this is an important role and I'm being far too cavalier about taking it seriously. Apparently, I need to get my priorities in order and rethink the friendships I form at work. Before she can get more worked up, the voicemail service cuts her off. The last thing I hear is something about our pact to not get involved with boys.

I'm not sure it was necessary for her to mention our "no boy" pact. It's not like I'm going to hop on Cameron's desk and pull up my skirt anytime soon. Although the thought is, admittedly, intriguing. And yes, I do feel a bit guilty the second the image crosses my head. And not because I wouldn't want it.

No, it's because I *do*.

ONLY TEN MINUTES into work and I already got called into Cameron's office. That must be some kind of record. I fully intended on getting here early to plan for the week, as I spent far too much time worrying over Cameron and our awkward situation yesterday to focus on any form of work. His email was titled, "I need to see you at 8:30," and guaranteed I wouldn't be getting anything productive done this morning, either.

I head to the breakroom, prep my coffee (which I will undoubtedly need if I'm having to see Cameron's usual uniform of well-fitted chinos and blazers) and make my way to his office.

I knock at his door. He's scribbling across a notepad, but looks up and waves me in with—*is that a smile*? I guess that's what happens when you drunkenly hit on your employee and are now being held in a stand-off of wills.

Not that I'm complaining.

"Mr. Feldman's coming back on site a bit earlier than we anticipated. I was hoping the rest of the team would get here early too for a quick pow-wow, but it's not like they can read my mind."

"Or maybe they overlooked your early email," I say, taking a seat on the couch and sipping at my coffee, hoping I'm pulling off some type of cool vibe.

"Nah, I just felt like bothering you," he says, smirking.

"You're doing really well with this whole 'kindness' thing. You know nobody is watching, right?"

"Don't push your luck," he chuckles.

"So, if nobody else is here, why did you call me in?"

"I saw you walk in and took advantage."

I let out a snort of laughter, spitting into my coffee. "Too early for that kind of talk."

His smile widens, then fades, and he clears his throat and shuffles papers around on his desk. The air in the room changes and I wonder if maybe the vents turned on, but mostly I have a sinking feeling he isn't in a joking mood this morning. Even though he was two seconds ago.

Wait, am I hallucinating?

"I think we need some rules for being at work," he says, and I feel like I'm getting reprimanded by a teacher, but I follow along anyway. "I just don't think that..."

"No, I get it," I interrupt, hoping to end this awkward conversation as soon as I can. "Amendment number one to our agreement: Maybe friendship-type of talk is outside of working hours only."

He gives me a lopsided smile and nods. "You got it. But, hey, still friends."

"Of course," I say, sticking out my pinky. If someone breaks a pinky promise, I'm not sure I'd ever trust them again. I trust these more than handshakes any day.

"Seriously?" He raises one eyebrow.

"I'm gonna need some solid evidence of friendship," I say, shifting my eyes from his face down to my pinky and back couple a few times. "I promise I'll be only your employee during the day. Let's go, Cameron, bring it on in."

He stands from behind his desk, walks to me, and wraps his pinky around mine.

"Is this the moment when we spit?"

"Ew, what?" I ask, scrunching up my face.

"In classic movies," he says, blinking at me. "Come on, they always spit after promising. It's their secret handshake."

"Yeah, I'm gonna have to pass."

"Your loss," he says.

It's then that I notice our pinkies are still entwined, so I break it off. He smiles at me for a moment, then heads back behind his desk.

"Lesson number one on management," I say. "Don't tell your employee you want to spit on her."

He laughs. "Lesson number one on being a super star employee: Maybe don't accuse your boss of wanting to spit on you when it was just a movie reference."

I grin and he returns the gesture. "Lesson number two for management: Be in a better mood first thing in the morning."

"Lesson number two for employees: Pick your battles wisely."

We stare at each other, exchanging glances. Even though there's a small silence, it's filled with this... electricity. We're like fire and ice; with each interaction, more steam erupts.

"Cam, Cam, the man!" Ian busts in the room full-on sitcom style, pushing the door wide open with his foot as he claps his hands together. Does this man have no off switch? "I have the perfect plan for—"

Ian sees me and laughs. "Oh, whoops. Did I interrupt a meeting or something?" he asks, pointing between the two of us.

"No, absolutely not," Cameron says, a fake optimistic ring to his voice makes me giggle behind my mug. "We're just counting our blessings that our favorite star Ian showed up."

"Well, count me in!" Ian says, grabbing the chair on the

other side of Cameron's desk and stepping over the side to straddle the seat, letting his arms hang over the back. "So, I'm thinking about Nia, right? And I think maybe for Easter I could get her cat a little bunny headband or—"

"Sorry," I interrupt, holding my hand up to stop him midsentence. Funnily enough, he doesn't seem the least bit offended. "Should I be hearing this?"

Ian's eyes pass from mine to Cameron's and then back and he shrugs. "Why, do you have something against bunny headbands or human resources?" he asks.

"I... well, no, neither." I say.

"Ian, I was just telling Grace here that *professionalism* is key in the office," Cameron says, his eyes just wide enough that I can see the clear signal for Ian to stop acting like this in front of me. But Ian's casual nature and the way he shrugs again makes it seem like this is old hat for him.

"Who's going to sue the lawyer?" he asks, grinning.

"Nia would," Cameron says. A smirk teases at the edge of his lips, sending a shiver through me that I try to conceal behind my mug.

"Cam, you're a piece of shit," Ian says, pointing his finger accusingly.

"And yet, you keep me around." Cameron laughs, giving the most boyish grin he can muster, straightening his back proud and tall. His shirt tightens against his chest when he stretches, accentuating his broad shoulders.

I blow on my coffee to mask my swoon. It's fun watching him joke around with Ian. I've only seen his sense of humor a handful of times, and I revel in seeing it more.

"Holmes, you know nothing leaves this room, right?" Cameron says, smirking to me.

I swear he gives me a barely noticeable wink as well, but maybe it's just me being hopeful. Or maybe he had something in his eye.

"Sure thing," I say.

If this information does leave the room due to my own negligence, and I guarantee it won't, maybe I'll get another reprimand from Cameron. We'll settle this in a duel of words and petty insults. Is it weird that he's a little hot when he gets irritated by my big mouth? Shame on me for wanting to see just how irritated he can be. And shame on me again for wishing he would take it out on me. Preferably on top of a desk.

18

GRACE

Ramona: Good morning! Don't drool too much at work.
Grace: I don't need your sass this morning.
Ramona: I bet Mr. Cameron Kaufman would want some off your sass.

I DON'T TEXT her back for a second, and inevitably get another message.

Ramona: Are you ignoring me?

I flip my phone down on my desk and get back to drafting up some designs. I made the mistake of telling her about mine and Cameron's "arrangement." She had completely the opposite reaction to my mom, which was unsurprising. However, what *was* surprising was she tried to stalk him on social media to gather more info, but was unable to find him anywhere.

"I've never seen someone be so invisible," she'd told me, her panic practically tangible over the phone. "I mean, how can I not find him?" She's the queen of researching people on the internet. To have not found anything was a difficult feat. But it would be Cameron who eludes her; He eludes me as well.

I get so involved in work that I don't notice it's noon until my stomach lets out a loud growl. I look around, hoping nobody heard that, and thankfully the rest of the office is either wearing their headphones or out for lunch just like I should be. I take out my turkey sandwich and unzip the baggie.

Before I can take a bite, I hear someone one say, "Grace, do you have an hour for subs?"

The voice is unmistakable. It's tenor-like with a slight edge. When I look up, Cameron's smiling over at me, smirk peeking through the scruff of his beard. Behind him towers Ian, hands in his pockets, a smile on his face. I'm unsure if this is even a good idea. Didn't he want to maintain professionalism during the day? Plus, I already have a sandwich. Why spend money to go buy another? But who would I be to deny a lunch out with my boss and the freaking lawyer?

I zip my sandwich back in its bag, put it away, and grab my purse.

We pile into Ian's car. It's a two-door Audi and Cameron has to lean the front seat forward to let me squish myself into the back. I have a small frame, but I'm taller than I would like, so my legs wind up accordioned to my chest after Cameron crawls in the front. Thankfully, he scoots his chair forward to give me a bit of extra room, but it doesn't go far. His legs are even longer than mine.

"Nice clown car," I comment.

"I can still kick you out of it," Ian says.

I look through the middle console and see a smile tugging at the edge of Cameron's lips.

The car revs and we're off. It doesn't take long before I'm gripping my seatbelt in sheer terror. Ian's driving is borderline manic. He switches lanes like a bat out of hell. I'm doing everything I can to grip the back of Cameron's seat and hold on for dear life.

"Nice to see your driving hasn't changed," I say. The words are strained. He responds with a cackle. *Damn you, Ian.*

Cameron and Ian are talking about God knows what, because I'm definitely not comprehending anything except panic. One of them asks me a question, but all I can say is "Uh-huh," and go back to focusing on keeping the contents of my stomach down. Ian laughs, and the obvious mocking doesn't even bother me. I'm about one more sharp turn from ruining the inside of his beautiful car.

The sub shop isn't too far away, so by the time my motion sickness starts to really kick in, we swing into a parking spot and I squeeze myself out of the back seat once more.

"Geez, were you trying to kill us?" I ask, gripping my head and walking toward the restaurant like a dizzy zombie.

All I get in return is a chuckle from Cameron. Ian opens the door and the bell above it dings as we enter.

Whoop de doo. Glad he finds it so dang funny.

I would take time to admire how cute the shop is, but car sickness overtakes me. I focus on the ground and notice the cafeteria-style floors. Small tables scattered around the room almost make it resemble an old diner. It's a mismatch of different eras, as if they couldn't decide on the one they liked most.

I walk up and get in line, then order whatever's on the top of the menu and find one of the diner-style booths to slide into. By the time Cameron and Ian are done telling the cashier what they want, my vision has stopped looking hazy like I'm underwater.

"So, Grace," Ian says as he slides into the seat across from me. "I'll put it all out there: You're eating at your desk and it's sad. Ray would be disappointed."

"Don't insult her sad life." Cameron joins us, drink in hand, as he sits down in the booth next to me. I take in his cologne, the close up look I can get of his stubble—which seems to have grown a bit longer than usual—and the deep brown of his eyes with just that secret hint of green.

He's not of this world.

"No, she needs to hear it, Cam," Ian insists. He looks across the table at me with an exaggerated frown. "It *is* sad, and you've got to stop."

"I like to think I'm being a star employee," I say, puffing out my chest and flashing a side smile to Cameron, who rolls his eyes with a half-concealed grin.

"You'll grow out of it," Cameron drawls, already finished with his drink and slurping up the empty remains in his cup in several loud spurts.

"Well *you* didn't," I tease, making Ian let out a bark of a laugh.

"There's a reason I'm a manager," Cameron argues, giving me a slight shove with his elbow. I can't tell if he's flirting or genuinely upset. I guess the shove would have been more deliberate if it were irritation.

"Yeah, because the last guy quit and I'm sure they had nobody else," I quip. "Who were they going to pick? Gary?"

"Hey now," Cameron says. "Gary is a very nice man."

Ian rolls his eyes, shooting a thumb to Cameron. "Gary aside, this guy shouldn't be a manager. He once tried to outdrink almost everyone on Beer Friday. Drunk as a skunk all night. He wanted to carry me out to my car on his shoulders."

"You do remember Grace is my employee, right?" Cameron laughs. "What happened to respect?"

"Aren't you six-foot-four or something?" I ask Ian.

"Try six-foot-impossible," Ian corrects, and Cameron shoots him a finger gun in agreement.

"Good lord, why did you try to carry Ian the monster?" I ask, amazed but also not entirely surprised. I've seen Cameron drunk, and it *is* a spectacle.

"I wanted to be king of the world," Cameron laughs. At least he can find humor in his prior drunk escapades. At least more humor than the last one I witnessed.

"You said you were Leonardo DaVinci," Ian grins.

"Don't you mean DiCaprio?" I correct with hesitation.

Cameron shakes his head, "Nope. Definitely DaVinci. I wanted to be an artist on a boat. Or a ninja turtle. I actually couldn't decide."

"You still can't," Ian says, leaning back with a smirk.

"Hey, if I could fight crimes in sewers, I would."

"What's holding you back?" I ask, letting my arm fall over the side of the booth as I turn to him.

"Turtle power," he says with disappointment, slowly raising his fist and then lowering it and letting his head sag. "Damn turtle power."

They drop off our sandwiches on a round serving tray that looks like it's meant for a pizza, and I'm definitely questioning whether this place knows their niche or not.

The conversation continues to wind down the path of hypotheticals.

"If you could be a TV character who would you be?"

"Gordon Ramsay," I spout out, taking a large bite. It turns out the first thing on their menu is a turkey and bacon sandwich with ranch dripping over the sides.

"That's not a character, Holmes," Cameron protests through bites. "That's a real person."

"Says who?" I ask, swallowing my piece and putting down my sandwich.

"Says the definition of a human being in the dictionary. 'Fiction character' would not have a picture of the master chef next to it."

"I disagree."

"Fine." Cameron stands up and walks back to the counter. An employee approaches and probably asks Cameron how he can help him, but it's too far away for us to hear the words. Cameron makes a point to solve this issue by speaking louder. "Is Gordon Ramsay a character?"

The employee smiles and answers, but it's too low and far away.

"Say it a bit louder for the audience to hear!" Cameron yells, pointing to our booth. Ian waves to the employee who laughs in response and cups her hands over her mouth.

"No, he's a person!" she yells back.

Cameron turns and shakes her hand before coming back to the table with a winning look and a quick, "Yeah, you're wrong."

With our subs finished and my dreams of being a master chef ruined, we head back to the office. I make sure to keep my eyes closed the entire time while mumbling expletives under my breath as Ian revs the engine and slams the breaks with every chance he can get. Once we're back, they retreat into Cameron's office and I can hear their laughter continue while I trudge back to my corner desk and secretly wish I was in there with them.

I LOOK up at the clock on the wall. It's well past quittin' time, and yet here I sit. It's a habit I'm starting to develop, but one that I'm increasingly becoming comfortable with—especially since a couple hours past five o'clock always promises Cameron's arrival. It's not like I stay just to be around him. I'm genuinely enjoying the work, and I'm damn good at it. But seeing that man waltz in with his Rayban sunglasses with a total bad-boy, "I'm definitely the man your mother warned you about" vibe gives me shivers.

Not to mention my mother *did* actually warn me about him. Forbidden fruit in human form.

He appears from around the corner and spots me. "Staying late again?" he asks, his dimples deepening with every second I put off answering.

"Isn't that the sign of a good employee?"

"I never said you weren't a good employee," he says. "I just said you've got an attitude—which clearly hasn't improved."

"Oddly enough, neither has your management," I observe. "Funny how that works out."

He brushes it off and instead lowers his voice. It would be a whisper if his tone weren't so low and almost growling in tone.

"Ready for more bad management mischief then?" he asks, looking across the office to ensure nobody else is there. The rest of the department left hours ago.

Yes, I absolutely want anything that involves mischief with Cameron.

He lets out a low whistle and in barrels a familiar golden retriever, bounding down the aisle and jumping on me, sniffing with all the strength he can muster. Memories of having to wrangle this hyper creature come back to me and I try my best to both pet him with one hand and steady him with the other so the happy drool pouring out of his mouth doesn't start to dribble on to me.

"Hey, Buddy! Long time no see!" I scratch behind his ear as he twists his head in an attempt to keep licking any part of my arm his tongue can find. "Are we even allowed to have dogs here?" I ask, letting out a borderline nervous laugh.

"No," he says, shrugging and making his way down the aisle to me. "But I trust you well enough."

My chest beats like a bull behind closed gates. Cameron is

like some superhero with useless powers. By day, he's "working Cameron" with a sourpuss attitude and by night, he's a dreamboat with a cute dog that can melt panties at will.

I run my hands across Buddy's head as his tail wags dangerously close to the opposite desk's plants. They're goners.

Cameron hops onto the desk across from me to take a seat, and I wonder if Gary is aware that his boss's fine ass graces his desk almost every night. Cameron puts his hands beside him and leans back. The motion lifts his pants a bit above his ankle and exposes brightly colored toucans on his socks. I recall the corgi-patterned socks the first day I met him and smile.

"Do you always wear ridiculous socks?" I tease.

He looks down and grins. "Keeps me sane."

I can feel my body molding into my seat by the sheer weight of his gaze against me. I would probably become the chair itself if I wasn't nudged back into reality by Buddy's wet nose.

"So, five o'clock friends?" I ask. I'm not sure what compels me to say it, but I'm suddenly not scared to be a broken record.

His eyebrows raise and he looks to the floor, considering his answer before glancing back up at me. "It's just business."

His demeanor annoys me a little. He seems almost cheeky, and I want to hit the dumb, lopsided smile right off his face. His look seems to say, "deal with it."

"So, what do you want from me?" I ask, leaning back in my chair, raising my eyebrows and playing the same game. *I can be chill too, bud.*

He exhales and moves to rest his elbows on his knees, getting closer.

"I guess I just want you," he smiles devilishly. "As a five o'clock friend, of course."

Excuse me while I go pass out.

I know he means it in a purely platonic way. I know the

tone in his voice, though low and slightly seductive, wasn't intended to be taken how I want it to be. But boy if that sentence wasn't enough to make me squeeze my legs a bit closer together.

"Then what do you want to talk about?" I ask, exasperation in my voice.

"Let's have a real conversation," he says. "Friend to friend."

Buddy seems to like that answer because he gallops over to Cameron with a loud bark.

"Friend to friend?" I choke out a laugh.

"No professional Cameron or boss and employee weirdness. Just pals hanging out."

"Okay," I say, putting my hand on my chin. "What's your favorite color?"

"Ooh, getting real deep." He looks me up and down. I'm not sure he even expected me to see it, but afterward he stares at my hair then says, "Red."

Oh, you cheeky bastard.

"Favorite animal?" he asks back.

Without skipping a beat I say, "Giraffe. Hands down." Even if they're the scary ones Ramona drops off at my house.

"All right, very quick on the draw."

"Morning person or night person?" I ask.

His answer is immediate. "Definitely morning."

I await his next question, but he seems to be considering me. "Why didn't you get into the art field earlier?"

My heart drops and an awkward, surprised laugh pops out. Why? Because I felt untalented. I felt dumb. I felt like success wasn't for me. Revealing my low self-confidence was probably my downfall with Joe, but would it be the same with Cameron? He doesn't seem like a man capable of taking advantage of me, but I didn't think Joe was either. Sometimes, though, I just have to take risks and let other people in. *I'm growing, damn it.*

"I didn't think I was good enough," I admit. "I've always had a hard time with that. Confidence, I mean."

He nods, taking in my answer, and then smiles. "Wouldn't know it by looking at you."

My face gets warm, and I can't help but bite my lower lip to stop from blushing even more.

"And what about you?" I ask. "Why not architecture?"

"Same deal," he says with no elaboration. This feels very one-sided and I'm not above pressing further.

"It's not really the 'same deal' because you're still here not doing architecture," I say.

"Yeah, but it's mostly just for me. I think about buildings often, and the different ways things could be arranged. Better ways, really." He scoffs as if offended at the idea of horribly designed buildings.

"You could do it."

"I could," he says, but there's no conviction in his tone. "Yeah, maybe... So"—he takes in a deep breath and exhales—"what changed for you? Why'd you finally take the leap and apply here?"

"I figured it was about time I got some confidence and took hold of my life. I was just going through the motions with a guy who didn't even like me, and it's like I woke up and it hit me: I'm getting close to thirty and I haven't accomplished a damn thing."

He smiles. "Hey, no jokes about thirty."

I return the smile, but then a feeling of unrest washes over me. I don't want talk of careers. I want something more. This isn't interesting enough for me. I want more from Cameron. I want to know what makes him tick. And I want to see just how far I can push him.

"What happened with your ex?" I ask. If he wants a real conversation, I'm putting all the chips in. "Aside from blue balls of course." Shivers tear down my spine—both my surprise at even referencing that and the thought of picturing any part of his lower half.

Cameron lets out a laugh, then looks up in thought. Buddy comes up and rubs his nose against his hand, prompting him to pet his head. It's like the dog knows this isn't a fun conversation and assistance is needed.

"I didn't want marriage," he says. "Didn't want kids. None of the future she imagined."

My stomach clenches and I roll my eyes. His head rocks back in offense.

"What is it with guys not wanting marriage?" I shake my head. "Is this some universal guy thing? Wanting to be free and single?"

"It's not about being single or not." He squints in thought. "It just didn't seem right. Why would I want to eliminate a choice in my life? I think people who are okay with it are just lying to themselves or wanting to fit in or whatever. And she cheated on me, so I guess I was right in the end." He laughs half-heartedly, and then his smile turns to a look that almost begs for a change in conversation.

I want to be angry. I want to lump him in with Joe and every other guy that claims marriage isn't "for them." It's infuriating that commitment seems to be an ancient idea lost in this new age of millennials and avocado toast. Who doesn't want the companionship in marriage? The promise that no matter how bad things get, you'll always have that one constant in your life? Your rock?

I don't know what to think, but I know that following up with a discussion on the stupidity of modern society norms would be a bit ridiculous when he's just brought up his cheating ex.

"Well," I say, trying to put some pep in my voice. "Maybe you're just a total weirdo, mister ninja turtle."

I expect Cameron to balk at me or tell me to leave, but he

just chuckles. The chuckle turns into a full belly laugh so deep he doubles over and clutches his stomach.

He calms just enough to say, "I wish we could be friends before five o'clock, Holmes."

I wish that, too.

19
GRACE

ON MOST WEEKENDS, Hank and I go for long walks in the evening once the day has cooled off and the sun has gone down a bit. Today, I decide to take a walk a bit earlier in the day. I need a break from work.

I kept Hank cooped up on the back porch while I focused on preparing something new from the notes Mr. Feldman sent us. He was somewhat impressed by what the team produced at the end of the week, but it just didn't hit the mark. Cameron said indecision is normal with clients, but I'm determined to destroy any semblance of doubt in Mr. Feldman's mind. I don't want this project lasting longer than it needs to, because I'm confident the team knows what he wants. I'm so sure of this idea I spent all morning Saturday scribbling on my tablet with Hank patiently hoping for a walk.

I gather up his leash and look out the blinds. I've gotten in the habit of staking out the parking lot for Cameron. He still doesn't know we live in the same complex, and I have no intention of him finding out. Does peeking out the blinds to ensure he's not there make me paranoid? Do I seem crazy? Yes.

I do not need judgments on it, thank you very much.

Cameron and I are friends, and I like that. I want to remain friends. I mean, sure, I'd love to see his body without the work shirt, and I can imagine just what he'd look like in nothing but one of those cute pairs of socks, but that's beside the point. The knowledge that we live just one parking lot away is tempting enough.

I gather Hank's leash along with my keys and head outside. The coast is clear and all I have to do is bolt out of the complex and everything is smooth sailing from there. I lock the door behind me, and Hank leads the way, trotting down the stairs onto the sidewalk.

My phone vibrates in my pocket and I pull it out, looking down at the text notification and stopping in my tracks.

Joe: I left her. Can we please talk?

Of course it's him. I don't move for a second; my heart is racing. I don't miss him. Do I? He's a narcissist—but a gorgeous one—yet he told me point blank he was ready to leave his current relationship. How many girls did he say that to when he was with me? And how many believed him?

My thumbs hover over the screen for a moment as I think about what to respond. Hank circles back to me and nudges my hip to signal that he's ready to keep walking and that my text is clearly the least of his issues. And maybe he's right. This text is the least of *both* of our issues. I don't need to text back—especially right after he texts me. He doesn't deserve that courtesy.

I huff out a breath of resolve and pocket my phone once more.

I need to repeat the same mantras in my head: I am more than this. I am ready to take on life in front of me. I am—*oh my God*.

On the path in front of us is no other than my current worst nightmare. It's shirtless—*holy shit, abs*—Cameron. Did I not complete my stake out well enough? I'm disappointed in myself more than I am disappointed to see him jogging toward me. Whether he sees me yet or not, I'm not sure. But, breaking my eyes away from his body at this moment would be a sin.

Sweat runs down his broad shoulders. His abs constrict and release with each movement of his body and, good lord, is he glistening in the sun straight-up new age vampire style? His gym shorts rest loosely on his hips, directly above where the Adonis "V" of his hip bones curving in. His thick arms pump forward and back, a leash in hand, the unmistakable figure of his golden retriever, Buddy, running beside him at its end.

I want to curse Joe for texting me and distracting me just enough so that I run into Cameron, but then again, maybe I should thank him. Without that text, I would have continued sulking in the opposite direction and I might not have been blessed by this sight.

Cameron's eyes catch mine and I know I must look like a deer in the headlights by the way I'm staring. He slows from a jog to a light trot and waves over to me.

Shit. Shit. Shit.

He's walking closer. Don't check him out. Don't check him out.

Cameron is slightly out of breath when he reaches me, but Buddy lays down on the cool concrete shaded by the balcony in the apartment above. Hank goes over to him and sniffs with curiosity, and I would imagine that if Buddy weren't so tired, this would be a different situation. Thankfully for Hank, he doesn't have to be tackled by a dog more than half his age. My poor old boy couldn't take it.

"I didn't know you lived here," Cameron says, letting out steady, exhausted breaths and letting his headphones hang over his shoulders. I stare at his glistening neck for probably a moment too long then look up at him once more.

"I don't," I lie, giving a shrug and pointing down to Hank.

"Old Hank here likes the shade of this apartment complex, so we come in here for a detour."

"Oh, Hank, I don't think we've met," Cameron bends down and holds out his hand in a greeting to Hank, letting him sniff before he pets him.

"We should walk our dogs together sometime," he says.

"So now we're weekend friends?" I tease.

"I don't see an office space anywhere, do you?" he says, grinning.

I notice how long his facial hair has gotten. It's less like stubble and more of a well-groomed beard now. I wonder if his ex-girlfriend made him keep it trimmed short. I bet this is an act of defiance—a bachelor's beard. He looks at me, and even though I can barely see his dimples through the beard now, I know they're there. And could he have any straighter teeth?

My heart is beating so hard it's a wonder he can't see it like I'm some cartoon wolf with it literally pounding out of my chest.

"So, how long have you had this guy?" Cameron asks, turning his attention back to Hank.

Buddy gets a bit jealous. He also sits up and walks to Cameron, nudging his hands and begging for attention.

A shirtless man surrounded by dogs. I could faint right here and now. With him running his hands over both of their backs, I wish I could cry out, *Me next, me next!*

"I've had him going on eleven years," I say, looking down at Hank. He's still got the golden fur of a classic retriever, but his face is almost completely white. "He's a tough old bird."

"You should bring him in," Cameron says, ruffling both dogs' fur.

"Like, after work?" I ask with a laugh. "You may not have a fear of getting fired, but I'm not risking that."

"Nah, they won't fire us," he says, shrugging it off. "Well, at least not me."

I read those manuals on day one. Nia sat there while I signed each acknowledgement, and I can guarantee you "no animals in office" was written on page forty-two in bright red ink.

"This seems like bad management to me," I say. "Aren't I supposed to be policing that for you?"

"I bring Buddy, you bring Hank," he offers. "It'll be a party."

It's a combination of his sexy smile, his shirtless body, and the fact that he's great with animals that I just blurt out, "Sure, why not?"

"Great!" he says. "I'll see you again on Monday, big guy," he coos, patting Hank on the head one last time before looping Buddy's leash around his wrist. "See you on Monday, Holmes."

He holds eye contact for a second, maybe a minute, maybe an hour—I have no idea. All I can do is take in his smile, his eyes, and his floppy, sweaty hair. He is dripping sex, and I'm left feeling like I definitely need a cold shower.

———

"He was shirtless?" asks Ramona.

"Shirtless. So shirtless. No shirt. Just abs. Abs for days." I roll onto my stomach and prop the cellphone between my ear and shoulder, the spitting image of a teenage girl in an 80s romantic comedy. I may as well be twisting a corded phone through my fingers.

I can hear the bump of Ramona opening her dryer and moving clothes around.

"The fact that we're talking about your boss for the third or fourth time is alarming," she says. "But God, please tell me more."

My first action back inside the apartment was to call Ramona, babbling like an insane person until she pieced together what I was saying.

I've somehow paced my way into the kitchen, so I lay on the cold tile as my growing anxiety washes over me.

"He's gorgeous," I exhale.

Ramona pauses for a moment once more then says, "Do you want to touch his dick?"

"Ramona! Please!" She is clearly not grasping the severity of my emotions. I know I should have called my mom. I need a stern talking to. I need someone to tell me it's wrong to imagine all the horrible... vile... *wonderful* things I could be doing to Cameron. But all I get are Ramona's jokes.

"So, yes then, that answers my question. But you haven't, so I don't see the problem," she says. "Imagine to your heart's content." I can just picture her winking to her husband as if this is the most ridiculous conversation she's ever had but she's also highly enjoying it.

She drops her laundry basket to the floor with a sigh. It would be no surprise to find I'm most likely on speakerphone and Wes has been listening in the whole time.

"Hey Wes, you have any insight?" I ask.

Ramona laughs, "You're not on—"

"Hey, Grace. Yeah, so listen..." Wes gets closer to the phone and Ramona lets out an exasperated sigh in the background. "Everyone has office romance fantasies. Not a big deal. You admire from afar and move on."

"You do?" Ramona asks.

"Of course *I* don't, dearest," Wes coos. Ugh, they're so cute it's disgusting and yet also wonderful. "But I wouldn't worry about it, Grace."

"But I stared at him. With no shirt on. Doesn't that mean something?" I insist.

Wes laughs. "Look, *he's* not going to tell anyone."

Ramona barks out a laugh, but Wes continues, "He won't. Why would he want to lose his job, too?"

All three of us are silent, letting the realization of losing a job wash over us.

"Do you think I could lose my job?" I mumble.

Thankfully for my nerves, Ramona scoffs.

"Don't be silly," she says, "Repeat after me: Nothing. Happened. Plus, he's a dude. He's simple. He probably didn't even think about the fact that he was shirtless."

"Actually—I'm gonna stop you there, Ray," Wes interjects with a sense of immediate urgency. "He was definitely thinking about it. Let's all be honest with ourselves. We aren't that naïve, are we?"

My heart collapses in my chest. The idea that Cameron knew he was getting me flustered drives me up the wall. I was wearing clothes, but clearly sweating through them with the heat of my unadulterated lust, and he just kept talking like he wasn't some type of a Greek god standing in front of me.

I don't want to date my boss. Sure, he's hot as hell and he rocks a simple black t-shirt like no other man (Side-note: I definitely need to see him wear that band tee again), but doing anything past working on our project is a bad idea and, quite frankly, it's irresponsible. I'm putting my job at risk—a job with a fantastic company. I don't want to go back to being some collections agent at a call center. I want to keep designing. And I can tell you right now that writing "my boss snuck me into the IT closet and screwed my brains out against the server wall" on my resume won't help me out in the future.

However, that thought is *really* intriguing.

"Just tell me I'm being dumb," I say.

"You're being dumb," Ramona says. "But not for the reasons you think. You're just over-analyzing it."

They weren't there. They didn't feel the pure, animalistic, tension radiating between us. They didn't feel my urge to jump his bones.

"You're right," I lie. "I'm just overthinking it."

"Hey, you should come over this week," Wes says. "We'll get some wine, you guys can put on some stupid romcom like *The Notebook*, and I'll make snarky jokes the whole time. How's that sound?"

"Sure," I say. "I can do that." Maybe that's what I need: Some comfort time with Ray and Wes. Yes, just me and the cutest couple in the world. Thrilling.

"Good!" Ramona chimes in. "And Wes, I swear, if you say one single thing about Noah and Allie…"

"I know, I know! *The Notebook* is a gift to the world. No bad words about it," he says, then quickly mumbles, "…but the dude should have left a long time ago—"

"Out! Out, out, out!" Ramona yells, and I can hear his laugh fading away as he walks off.

We decide on Thursday and Ramona promises to make her homemade mac and cheese, which I definitely need in my life. As we're wrapping up and gabbing about other romcoms we definitely need to catch up on, my phone starts to vibrate, and I take it away from my ear to see my Mom on the caller ID.

"Hey, listen, I got to let you go," I tell Ramona. "Mom is calling."

"No!" she moans. "Just send her through! Let's all talk about your hot boss."

"I thought we were done with that?" I moan.

I would hate nothing more than to include my mom in this conversation, but with Ramona's pleas, I oblige and connect to a three-way call. Ramona answers for me with no introductions.

"She saw him without a shirt on, Mrs. Holmes."

"Oh, hi, Ramona," my Mom says, a little wary but still intrigued.

"Hi, Mrs. Holmes."

"So, who did my baby girl see without a shirt on?"

I rush in before Ramona can dig me a deeper hole. "Mom,

nothing happened. I saw my boss running outside and he wasn't wearing a shirt. Not a big deal."

"It was hot outside today, Lynnette," Ramona interjects quickly. "He was sweaty."

"No way," she breathes out in disbelief. I can't tell if she's mocking me or not. "You obviously took him back to your place, right?"

"Guys, stop." I groan.

"She's wishing she did," Ramona laughs.

"If I did, I wouldn't be on the phone with you," I say. Do I sound desperate? I sound desperate.

"You'd have a hot, sweaty man boning you, that's what you'd be doing," Ramona mumbles under her breath, eliciting a gasp from my mom followed by a good-natured laugh.

Whenever I make sexual jokes, my mom chastises me, but the second Ramona throws one in, it's a gas.

I groan. "Thank you, Ramona, for that."

"I just need you to know your options," she relents. "So, are you going to?"

"Going to what?" I ask.

"Hit on your boss," Ramona says.

I pull the phone away from my ear and shout into the receiver, enunciating every syllable, "*No, I am not going to hit on my boss!*"

When I bring it back to my ear, my mom is already saying, "Very good. I'm proud of you. That would be incredibly irresponsible."

Ramona scoffs, "Not as fun, though."

"Or as hot!" I hear Wes call from the other room through Ramona's speakerphone.

It's like I have an angel on one shoulder and devil on the other. My beautiful, innocent mother, and the spicy, no-nonsense best friend with her equally-as-irresponsible husband. It would do me well to be more like my mom, but I can't help leaning toward Ramona's reaction. It *would* be much more fun.

My phone vibrates again, and I wonder who else is calling me. Though, honestly, most of the people I talk to are on the phone at this moment. I check the screen: A text from Joe. I had forgotten to respond to him earlier, and I'm now thanking my horrible memory to have kept him waiting in agony.

Joe: Let's get dinner again.

I blink a couple times, hands hovering over the reply. I'm brought back by the sound of Ramona and my mom discussing recipes. I tap out of the text messages and lift the phone to my ear once more.

"Mom, what are you cooking now?" I need their comfort. I don't need Joe. I don't want Joe. I can't handle Joe right now.

"Still working on those avocados," my mom says, practically beaming through the phone.

How many things can she make with avocados? These are the true mysteries of the world. No, the true mysteries of the world would be more like, how am I avoiding Joe but slowly moving closer to an even more impossible man: My boss?

The world may never know.

20

CAMERON

If it weren't for the fact that I knew Grace and I would be hanging out after work, I don't think I could have handled Monday. But fast forward two new client calls and a meeting to plan even more meetings, and I'm rolling back in the office at seven o'clock, Buddy in tow.

There are only two cars in the parking lot—mine and Grace's yellow Volkswagen bug—which is lucky for me. It's one thing to have my own dog curl under my desk in my closed office, but I am definitely pushing my luck by allowing Grace to bring her golden, too. Thankfully, with nobody here, and the fact that her dog is older and significantly less hyper than Buddy, we shouldn't have any issues.

I round the corner into the designer bullpen and see the familiar light on Grace's desk lamp, creating a halo around her red hair and giving it an oddly angelic glow. Ridiculous trick of the light.

Buddy trots past me, not entirely running, but just enough to take Grace away from her work and realize we both walked in.

"About time," she says, reaching both hands up to the

ceiling to stretch. I look in the floor area around her desk as if trying to find her dog in hiding, but it's really just a way that I can avoid looking at her chest while she arches her back.

"So demanding," I respond, and she gives me a slight smile. "So where is the old boy?" I walk down the row of desks and crouch to find Hank resting in a large dog bed placed inconspicuously in the corner of her L-shaped desk where it can be hidden from the rest of the office. "Very smart."

"Yeah, I figured the hard concrete would hurt him," she says, spinning in her chair to look at him and smile. "He's got creaky old man bones, don'tcha, boy?"

"Wow, you seem very sensitive to his disabilities," I tease.

She shoots me a glare that carries no actual threat when paired with a badly concealed smirk.

"He is old and wise," she responds with her chin raised in defiance. "If he needs a fancy bed, I'll get him a fancy bed."

"Hank is clearly pampered rotten," I say, oozing sarcasm as I rise up from my crouch to hop on the desk across from her.

"Oh? And where does Buddy stay when he's here?" she asks, crossing her arms.

"He likes the couch."

She laughs and shoves her finger in Buddy's direction. "Check your privilege, dog."

Buddy looks to me in confusion and I just shake my head in return.

When I look at her tablet, I notice her sketches and lean forward to take a better look. Her face flushes pink, hiding her freckles in the process.

"It's just a mock up," she says. "But it's definitely going to be a winner."

She starts her statements with such modesty, and then she keeps talking and it turns into the cocky mouth of hers I'm quite averse to.

"Have you consulted with the rest of the team?" I ask.

She rolls her eyes. "Please. Like I need to."

"Have you learned nothing?" I balk, tension in my stomach rising each second. It's like the more upset she gets, the more my blood pressure rises.

"Clearly not." She shrugs.

I would do anything to cover that mouth of hers with mine and let nothing else come out. She knows which buttons to press, and I'm not sure she even knows she's doing it.

I look down to her mock-up again and wave my fingers toward it. "You're going for the 80s look?"

"That's what they want," she says matter-of-factly.

"No, that's what they implied," I reply. "We take their ideas and make it something new."

"I beg to differ."

We're stuck in the same pattern as usual. My struggle for some form of management power, and her placing her foot in the metaphorical corporate door to stop me. We're in a classic Western showdown of wits, and I'm not about ready to give up. She's the first to break eye contact and huff out a breath of air, and I'm surprised but willing to accept the win.

She focuses on the work in front of her, but then shifts to my feet hanging off the edge of the desk. After a second of eyeing them, she laughs. And it's light, yet still hearty and meaningful. There's no taunting behind it or even condescension.

"Are those Christmas trees?" she asks, pointing to my socks. "It's not even Christmas, Cameron."

"I celebrate Christmas in the summer."

"Are you planning on wooing someone with those socks of yours?" she jokes.

Now why would she say that? I realize I'm taking way too long to answer since she caught me off-guard, but I'm too distracted at the sight of her to gather my thoughts. The red hair, the freckles on the bridge of her nose scattering across her cheeks... The little black top she's wearing under her flannel that looks better than *any* black top Abby ever wore.

My erection isn't going anywhere, and I'm both trying to conceal it and will myself not to imagine what we could be doing in this empty office. "I've got ideas," I say. "I'm sure women are bound to love the Christmas spirit in July."

"Surely," she agrees. "Although I bet it works best when you're only wearing the socks."

The words leave her mouth, and though it sounded like she said every word with absolute purpose, guilt spreads across my body like someone just cracked an egg on my head and let the yoke run down my neck. Grace bites her lip and raises a curious eyebrow.

Is she imagining me in just my socks?

I laugh a bit, trying to play it off as a joke. She's laughing as well, but I think it's just one of those, "Wow I can't believe you thought I was serious and now I'm uncomfortable" laughs.

"Now what would HR say if she heard this conversation?" I tease.

Grace lets out a single, forced laugh to punctuate the end of our flirting and the guilt continues to roll down onto my shoulders.

What the absolute hell am I doing? This is irresponsible, stupid, and not to mention risky for both of us. I'm being reckless because I haven't gotten laid in months. That's got to be the reason. And now I feel like I'm abusing my power over her, too.

This is not me. I cannot keep this going.

I change the subject back to the project as if our little conversation detour didn't even happen. I'm grateful that Grace allows that talk to just slip into the vault of things we may never discuss again. Just our little secret.

At least... I hope she's the type of girl that can keep a secret.

21

GRACE

I pick up a tennis ball and toss it over the line of desks beside me and off shoots Buddy, tripping over himself to find it. Hank simply looks up, sees that getting there first would be an impossibility, and goes back to sleep.

"I can't imagine a life where a dog doesn't almost kill himself trying to go get a tennis ball," Cameron says, bending down to pet Hank, whose tail wags lightly behind him.

"Hank is old," I answer.

It feels like Cameron is attempting to walk on eggshells. I made a comment that was way too bold and inappropriate. For someone who says I really want to keep my position at this company, I'm doing a bang-up job maintaining that. But for some reason, his apprehension makes me feel like I can get away with it. If he's just laughing and I'm not fired yet, have I really done anything *too* wrong?

I will say that my flirting game is totally off. Not that I should be having game anyway.

Socks? Bet you look good in them and only them.

Yeah, I'm a real smart cookie.

He changes the subject from work to dogs. I think it's just

because he saw Hank lying there and needed something to talk about. *Let's talk about... dogs! There is dog! Words can be dog! Dog!*

"He was my graduation gift from high school," I continue, trying not to laugh at the internal vision of Cameron panicking inside my head. "I attended a local college, so I demanded some type of responsibility since all of my friends were moving away and being real adults."

"Demanded?" Cameron chuckles.

"Oh yes, I demanded it," I say. "I was snotty teen."

"You're still snotty." He smiles and it's that wonderful, mysterious half-smile that deepens a single dimple.

Is he admiring? Is he judging? Do I even care which one it is?

"Anyway," I press on with a drawl added in for emphasis. "Hank has been with me through everything. Finally moving out of my parent's house, then moving in with my ex, and now here. He's a trooper."

Cameron nods in understanding but says nothing. I wonder if the mention of Joe bothers him a bit. No, I'm definitely giving myself too much credit. He couldn't care less about my ex.

"How long have you had Buddy?" I ask right when a flash of golden fur turns the corner and runs straight for us. Cameron's dog screeches to a halt, nails scratching the concrete beneath him, and he drops the slobbery ball right at my feet. He sits, paws trembling with anticipation until I throw it again. Off he dashes to find it once more.

"About five years," Cameron laughs.

Buddy attempts to roll the ball toward himself with one paw, but it instead shoots past him with the same amount of excitability he put into retrieving it. This dog clearly doesn't grasp the concept of Newton's Laws of Motion. He runs to another side of the desk in search of the ever-elusive ball.

"He never really grew up," Cameron says, clearing his

throat before continuing. "I got him right before Abby and I started dating."

"Oh, Abby... Your ex?" I say as casually as I can, but it still ends up sounding so forced and nosy I wonder why I tried to hide that it was. I want to stop the words right when I say them, but there's not much I can do at this point.

"Ha, yeah," he says. Oh, he totally picked up what I was putting down. "She was something else. Never really liked Buddy."

I try not to focus on what he may have meant by, "something else."

"One time," he says with a smirk on his face. "She bought a brand-new coat—I'm talking high-class shit. I don't even know the name of the maker and I don't even think I could pronounce it if I did. But she brings it home because she didn't trust leaving it in the car. It's got this limited edition, fancy ass tag that said 'finely stitched' with whatever other key words they could throw on there. So, we drop it off at the house and then we head out for lunch"—he pauses and chokes out a laugh—"and we get back, and this damn dog has ripped the coat to pieces except for the words 'fine tit' leftover on the tag."

Cameron laughs, trying to continue the story but unable to get the words out. "He"—laugh—"he's just sitting"—laugh—"there with the biggest fucking grin on his little face."

As if on cue, Buddy returns and lets the ball drop out of his mouth, his tongue lolling out like he's waiting to receive praise for the world's most impressive trick.

"You amazing idiot," he says, ruffling the fur on top of Buddy's head and tossing the ball once more.

There's something about a man and his dog that really gets me. It's the way he still loves Buddy even after he destroyed something that must have cost Abby more than a month's salary—well, at least for *my* paygrade. It's the way he gets up, runs across the room, and starts playing with the dog. It's the way he hugs Buddy, then looks up and smiles at me, like he wants me to know that even with all of Buddy's faults, he's still the best damn dog in the world.

My heart is melting, and I really wish it would stop.

22

CAMERON

I TEND to keep my office blinds open so I can peer out into the designer's bullpen. It's definitely not to look at Grace when, as usual, she's the only designer left. She sits in her secluded corner, just the glow of her lamp and only a small sliver of Hank's tail poking out from under her desk. I don't know when she left to get him and bring him back. I've been too focused on work.

It's the first night we haven't hung out, which is probably for the best. I'm loaded down with papers and I can tell she's feeling the pressure, too. At our meeting today, she jotted down notes and only stopped to turn the page to another blank sheet. Her nose is practically touching the screen of her tablet as she swoops the pen across it.

I take a look at my watch. 8:00 p.m. Maybe it wouldn't hurt to take a small break.

Buddy and I stroll out of my office (okay, Buddy bolts over to Hank) and I go down the aisle of desks toward Grace. She looks up, her eyebrows contracted in the middle, exhaustion showing on her face.

"You're going to ruin your vision if you get any closer to that screen," I say.

"I like to think I'm paying attention to detail," she says.

Ever the rebel.

"Socks?" she asks, glancing down at my feet.

I prop myself against Gary's desk and lift my pant legs up a bit to reveal my sock of choice: White anchors on plain navy blue.

"Boring," she yawns, exaggerating the movement by placing her hand over her mouth and stretching.

"You're getting very judgy on my sock choice," I say, and she smirks.

"I expect only perfection from the boss."

"I could say the same. Let me see what you've got so far." I make my way around her desk and lean over the back of her chair, breathing in the sweet aroma of her perfume. It smells like flowers and fresh laundry and I can't help but breathe a little deeper.

She straightens a bit as I lean in to see her sketches. This is the closest we've ever been, and I don't feel the need to move if she doesn't want me to.

"Could use some work," I joke. She juts her elbow back and it hits me in the side. When I chuckle, she leans back in her chair and the base of her neck rubs up against my hand. But she doesn't shy away from it. She stays right where she is.

Goddamn.

I'm doing everything in my power not to move an inch. I can't risk her moving away. I cherish the feel of her smooth skin, and I'm resisting every urge to stroke where her hairline ends and her neckline begins.

"Let's practice some management one-oh-one," she says. I can't see her expression, but I feel like she's grinning. "Give me some actual pointers instead of insulting me."

"You first."

She huffs out a breath, then pinches both fingers in to zoom out on the tablet and spreads them apart to zoom in to a different detail of the logo. I take a chance and lean back in. I move my free hand that isn't frozen to her neck and place it on the desk, my chest hovering just over her shoulder and still I feel the need to be closer. We're separated by merely inches; my blood pressure is rising. Well, maybe falling. ...Down to where I definitely don't want her to notice.

"This looks messy," she says with irritation. "Pointers?" I have no fucking clue what she's trying to show me, because I don't care about a single thing except my fingertips against her skin and feeling every single motion she makes.

"You could just make it... not messy."

My suggestion is stupid, but I'm trying with every fiber of my being to not move a muscle. Her arm hovers over mine as she plays with the side panel to trigger layers off and on in the program.

I've never noticed her hands. They're small, and I'd kill to see them playing with something else other than just her silly tablet.

She clears her throat softly, and it hits me once again that we're riding on thin ice.

I straighten myself up, move a step back and say, "Yeah, go with that."

She swivels around in her chair a look of both confusion and tension in her eyes. Her chest moves up and down, as if she's controlling every breath. I realize I'm doing the same.

"No suggestions? Seriously?" she asks, not changing her blank expression but forcing sarcasm in her tone.

It's not real. She's trying to bring us back to our dynamic. The "I insult you, but you insult me back, remember?" kind of deal. I can't reciprocate.

"Not a one," I respond. I exhale, crack my knuckles, and walk away. "I have a lot to do. I'll see you tomorrow." I don't even turn around to wave goodbye because I know if I try to meet her eyes, I'd feel some type of regret about the smartest decision I've probably ever made.

Buddy follows me back in my office and when I close the door, I have to fight every urge in my body to not go home and give myself some form of release. The smell of her still lingers on my clothes. I look out the blinds, but she's packing her stuff up. She nods to Hank, who follows her out.

I'm left sitting in my chair, staring into blank space and wondering how awkward I just made things between us.

23

CAMERON

Grace arrives at work the next morning with her ever-dependable, chipper attitude, a coffee mug in one hand and bag in the other. You would think absolutely nothing happened, and I guess honestly, that's the truth.

I keep reminding myself that everything is exactly the same. I only looked at her designs. Sure, my hand somehow ended up on her neck, but what co-worker hasn't accidentally been in some awkward position from time to time? I think I saw that new guy in IT reach past Nia to get something from the printer and his arm grazed her boob. Granted, she shot him a horrible look afterward that would shrink any man's balls, but it's proof that accidents happen.

"Hey, did you see that new guy in IT?" asks Ian, waltzing in to my office and plopping down on the couch, his feet dangling over the edge as per usual.

"Can you read my mind?" I narrow my eyes.

He narrows his eyes back at me. Probably not—I bet he just put in too many IT requests.

"Why, are you thinking about how I've sent in three IT

requests since yesterday and I'm still not receiving any new emails?"

What the hell?

"You're a genius. And"—I snap my fingers as if I've just had an epiphany—"maybe you're not getting emails because people just don't like you."

"I'm a lawyer," Ian deadpans, resting one of his arms across the back of the sofa. "I deal with people who don't like other people."

"Good point," I say. "Then yeah, let's go kick that IT guy's ass."

"That's more like it." He reaches in his pocket and pulls out his phone. He swipes down a couple times before exhaling and lolling his head back on the couch in defeat. "Let's go out Friday night. Karaoke and wings."

"But it's Beer Friday," I groan.

Selfishly, I had hoped Beer Friday would be my excuse to see Grace again on a semi-casual basis before the weekend. There was always the chance of seeing her tonight, but I think working solo would be the best choice after what happened—*or didn't*, I remind myself—yesterday. She doesn't seem to be showing any signs of discomfort, but I also haven't spoken to her yet.

"Every Friday is Beer Friday," he says, still browsing his phone. "Let's make it some other Friday for once. Maybe Karaoke Friday." He snaps his fingers. "Yes! Let's make Karaoke Friday happen!"

"Fermented Drink Friday?"

"That makes it sound disgusting. And it still heavily implies beer."

"What can I say?" I toss my hands up. "I'm a creature of habit."

"Be unpredictable for once, man," he says. "Kar-ao-ke Friday. Kar-ao-ke Friday." He starts patting his legs to the chant.

Maybe going out wouldn't be such a bad idea. After last night, I bet even one more after-hours session with Grace would result in something much worse. Maybe Ian's reading my mind again and planning for the outcome that doesn't wind up with me getting fired.

"Fine, fine," I relent, sighing. "Let's go with Rum Friday instead, though."

"Call it whatever Friday you like. Let's just get out of here and spend a Friday as men for once."

"Are Beer Fridays not manly?" I ask.

"Well, I can get laid at a bar," he says. "But I can't get laid at work, so you tell me."

I smile in agreement, but a tinge of... *something* runs through me and I can't exactly pinpoint why.

AT FIVE O'CLOCK, I head out to grab Buddy. I feel a weird sense of giddiness as I toss my keys in the air and catch them. Maybe it's that I know it'll be another night working late with Grace. I don't expect anything, but then again...

As luck would have it, on my way out, I see Grace sliding her tablet in her bookbag and zipping it closed. I can't help but stop in my tracks.

Oh no. I must have really screwed up last night if she doesn't even want to stay late with me anymore. What the hell have I done?

"You heading out early today?" I ask, trying to hide my obvious disappointment by tucking my phone into my pocket and twirling my keys.

"Looks like you are, too," she says, gesturing to my keys.

"No, just going home to get Buddy."

She nods. "Right, that makes sense."

"Are you picking up Hank a bit earlier than usual?" I ask.

That's got to be it. She's just getting a head start on the night. Smart girl.

"No," she admits, swinging her bag over her shoulder and grabbing her cellphone off her desk.

We both begin walking the same direction out the door and toward the exit. Each step feels odd, like things have changed.

"I'm actually having a girl's night tonight," she says. "Me and my friend haven't had one in a while, so it's long overdue."

"Even in my thirties, I still don't even know what girls do at those things."

"Oh, the usual: Paint our nails, talk about boys, and end with a pillow fight." Grace blushes a little when she says this, and I smile.

Okay, so things aren't weird? Come on, woman. Make up your mind.

"Oh really?" I ask, opening the front door for her as she exits out. "I'd always wondered."

"It's our little-known, super-secret not-secret."

"Scandalous," I respond.

We stop mid-parking lot because I see her car across the lot. She must also see that we'll be walking in opposite directions soon.

"I'll see you tomorrow, though. You going to Beer Friday?" she asks.

I can sense the excitement behind her voice and I internally curse Ian for his stupid Karaoke Friday event. Or Rum Friday? Whatever.

"No, it's a dude's night, actually." The sentence itself makes me cringe. *Dude's night? What the hell.*

Her eyes widen. "A dude's night? And what does that entail?"

"Oh, the usual: Paint our nails, talk about boys, and end with a pillow fight." I smirk.

"Knew it."

24

GRACE

Thursday night is less of a romantic comedy kind of night and more of Ramona just fishing for more information on Cameron. At first, I felt weird about it, but then I realize I want to talk about him just as much as she wants to know about him.

I want to tell her all about the night before and how he touched me and I let him, but it all seemed so trivial the more I considered it. Nothing happened. We leaned in, he critiqued my art, we were mean to each other... pretty much the usual. But Ramona wants every detail of every day. I only give her the highlights and I try to emphasize my love for my job because in the grand scheme of things, *that* is the most important factor. And I do—I absolutely love my job.

I look forward to staying after hours, getting lost in my ideas, and falling prey to yet another late night.

"This is everything I wanted; everything I dreamed it would be," I tell her.

As any good friend, she swoons almost as much as she would be if I were talking about some boy.

"I like seeing you this happy," she says, taking a sip of her red wine. "You're one us now: The dreamers."

"Baby, the three of us are living the life," Wes says, leaning back on the recliner and taking a large gulp of his own wine.

I throw myself on the couch and let my head fall in Ramona's lap. She strokes it in the motherliest way possible. I surround myself with caring, doting figures, and I firmly believe everyone in life should have a Ramona and Wes.

"I'm afraid something is going to ruin this," I admit. "When things are this good, you can only go down from there, right?"

"Nah, don't think like that," Wes says.

I can't help but think of Cameron again. Our touch, the feeling of a forbidden rush, the knowledge that if I wanted to ruin my life, he would be the way to go. And yet, I'm so entranced by him. He's the one thing I can't have right now; the one thing I desperately want. What type of trouble could I get in? What type of trouble might be exciting enough to be worth it?

"What are you thinking about?" Ramona asks, braiding my hair as Wes turns on the TV and finds a romcom for our approval.

"The eventual destruction of my life," I say, and she laughs.

"Debbie Downer. Hey, Wes, are you going to sleep?"

He's fully reclined on the couch and his eyes are closed. "No, just resting my eyes. You guys keep talking."

"I swear he's becoming an old man every day," Ramona groans. She goes back to braiding and I look up in time to see her stick her tongue out at him. The annoyance isn't real. It's an expression she gets when she's trying to play the role of nagging wife, but it's just a game. She adores him.

I close my eyes and picture Cameron's face, his smile, his arms, the feeling of his breath on my neck as I tried to play with the tablet like I knew what I was doing or what I even wanted to show him. My hands go to the braid in my hair and I unravel it bit by bit, strand by strand, imagining just how slowly his hands could do this as well and just how sensual it would be. And just how fast they could travel under my shirt.

I probably need to stay late at work again just as much as I need a nail in the head.

25

CAMERON

IAN SINGS along with whichever self-proclaimed karaoke superstar is up on stage, and I'm at the bar sipping my dark liquor of choice, picking at the free peanuts. It doesn't take long before he puts in karaoke requests and gallivants on the stage, making eyes at various women in the audience who're swooning back at him.

I tell you: His charm is absolute magic. I'm not sure where it comes from or how he can seduce several women at once by just glancing over to them from behind a microphone, but it's working. I know I'll be riding home alone tonight.

After his second rendition of, *Big Girls Don't Cry*, he moseys his way back to the stool next to me and knocks on the bar for another water, which the bartender brings over. I think I've only seen Ian get drunk once or twice. The guy just likes to karaoke sober.

"You see that blonde over there?" he asks me, gesturing to a woman at a high top near the door. Said woman waves coyly at Ian.

"She's pretty," I say, giving her a simple one-motion wave back.

It's hard to deny that she's almost a perfect doppelgänger for Nia, but with shorter hair. She looks quite a bit friendlier, too.

"I think I'm going to talk to her," he says. He takes a swig of his water and gives her a smoldering look.

That was his way of saying, "We'll probably have mind-blowing sex where I can proudly say she made sounds resembling animal noises."

He says that, but I'm honestly not sure how true it is. I don't really want to know.

"Well, good luck, bud."

Ian places a hand on my shoulder. "Thank you for believing in me."

I return the gesture, giving a neutral expression. "You are absolutely welcome."

And with that, he gets up and approaches the Nia look-alike with all the confidence of classic James Dean. It's admirable, but I see truly just how similar she looks to our Human Resources manager; I can't help but feel a bit sad for him. Does he even know he's subconsciously pursuing the one thing he can't have? Which gets me thinking about Grace.

No. Stop it.

I can't be having these thoughts. I need to shove them from my mind. Maybe I should even go back to being "Professional Cameron." But then we wouldn't have our nightly work sessions. And I wouldn't have been so close to doing something more than Professional Cameron has any right to do.

I'm going too far. I'm pushing my limits, and it's getting beyond my control. *No, I am in control of my life. I am a man having a dude's night with heavy liquor and my bro.*

And yet it looks like Ian just left and I'm alone with a drink.

Surely, I'm in control.

26

GRACE

"This is missing something, and we all know it," Cameron says, tapping his pencil in the palm of his hand in irritation.

He paces the front of the conference room, and nobody on the team speaks. If they do, it's just mumbling. We've come so far, and yet we're still so not close to the solution.

"What if we moved that element slightly to the left?" I suggest without raising my hand.

He doesn't make eye contact with me, but instead paces to the laptop and clicks to adjust it. The change is projected on the screen. The design looks worse.

I don't even know what I'm saying. I just want excuse to talk to him, but we haven't spoken since Thursday, and I'm dying inside. It doesn't help that he's getting more serious, which is totally hot and driving me insane. I'm just a helpless fool trying my best to focus on the project at hand.

"I like it," Mr. Feldman says from the corner, looking up from his laptop before shooting his eyes back down.

He never comes in the office, but it's getting to crunch time and everyone can feel it. I almost feel like he's supervising us. It makes me uneasy; sometimes he looks at me, then types faster.

Once the meeting's over, I return to my desk. But now it's eight o'clock, and I'm hunched over my tablet trying to parse through my thoughts. I feel brain-dead, and trying not to glance at Cameron in his office is taking more attention than I'd like. I've been doing pretty good for a bit when a paper ball hits me on my head, bouncing off my haphazard bun.

I lean to the side to look around the monitor—which I'd purposefully placed in front of me to resist looking toward Cameron's office—and find the man himself walking down the aisle, a steaming mug in each hand.

He takes a sip from one and places the other on my desk.

"Well aren't you nice," I say.

I can feel the electricity running between us. It's almost palpable, and I'm unsure if coffee is something I should even be touching at this point. I take a sip and instantly know I'm right. That caffeine is no laughing matter.

"Wow," I laugh, smacking my lips and taking in the bitter taste. "Expecting me to stay late?"

What an unfortunate question; he smirks when I say it.

"I know your work ethic. Why, are you planning on leaving soon?" he asks, gesturing toward my desk with his mug.

It's littered with... well, everything. There are drafts of various design elements on loose sheets of paper, my tablet and its partnering pen, a desktop, a laptop connected to it, blue pens, black pens, purple pens, a mug with more pens, and a chewed-up tennis ball. I've been so buried in work I don't even remember Hank bringing that back.

I sigh. "Probably not."

Cameron hops up on the empty desk across from me, cupping both hands around his mug and smiling. The cuffs of his black pants rise up to expose his socks with a small pattern: They're giraffes.

"Hey, my favorite," I say, pointing to them. I try to remain casual about it, but I'm hiding the fact that I'm hoping he did this for me. He must have. "Those are the best socks so far."

Cameron looks down and chuckles. "Last week you said the toucans were your favorites."

"I think I was just craving fruity cereal then," I say, staring up at the ceiling to give off the impression of wistful daydreaming. "Oh, sugary cereal… wherefore art thou, sugary cereal?"

Hank settles his head on my lap with a small whine. I look up at Cameron and let out an exhausted sigh. "Hey, you think we might be able to go for a walk? Hank seems restless."

I am, too.

He smiles. "I don't see why not." He lets out a swift whistle and around the corner comes Buddy, his nails tapping on the concrete as he bowls into Cameron's legs and almost knocks him off balance.

"Oof! Watch it, Bud!" he says, scratching the dog's ears and shuffling past him to grab the leash from his office.

I catch a glance of him walking away and lord; those pants fit snug against his toned ass and… I need to pull it together tonight.

I clip Hank's leash on his collar and walk him through the back door while Cameron tries to get Buddy to calm down long enough to clip his.

"Sit, Buddy!" The dog's entire behind continues to wag until Cameron says again, "Sit!"

This time it's got some force behind it, and the dog's butt slams on the ground faster than Cameron can even finish the word. The new tone in his voice prickles my skin. I open the door and feel a rush of the wind. Yes, please bring on the fresh air.

Cameron catches up to me and Buddy attempts to take the lead. Cameron runs his free hand across his chin, combing out his small beard.

"Is it getting too long?" he asks.

"The beard? Nah—but are you going for the Sasquatch look?"

"Haha. Funny," he mocks, knocking into me with his arm.

He's only teasing, and it barely nudges my shoulder, but with biceps like his, I know he's capable of pushing much harder. I wonder if he would be able to push me up against a wall...

The dogs guide us around the building to the open sidewalks that form a circuit around the office space.

"So, how's the hotel going?" I ask.

"What hotel?" he asks, looking straight forward at the sidewalk.

"Come on, the hotel!" I say, emphasizing the term as if it's the only hotel that could possibly exist in this world. "With the parking lot and the lobby and all that junk." I wave my hands around motioning to an invisible building, pointing at each part. "Please tell me you're working on it. I'd love to see it."

He winces. "It's not simple. I can't just make a hotel pop out of thin air."

"You can do whatever you want to do," I say with a definitive nod. Hank gallops to me with a stick in his mouth for me to throw and I grin. "See? Hank is twelve, and if he can get up and start the day with a stick in his mouth, then why can't you?"

"I don't want to wake up with anything long in my mouth."

Goddamn you, Cameron.

"That's not the point," I wave my hand around, washing away the cloud of the potential hotel from the blank area in front of us as well as my dirty thoughts. "You could do it if you want to. We work for a marketing firm. With clients. And connections."

"Yeah, that's called breaking the non-compete agreement we all signed on our first day," he says, his arm tightening up a bit to hold Buddy back once he eyes a squirrel in a tree on the opposite sidewalk.

"No, it's not," I say. I may not know much, but I was given nothing but the new hire paperwork for my first two days, and I didn't have much else to do. "You haven't read it in years. I read it two months ago. You're not selling marketing secrets or starting your own marketing firm." I nudge him on the arm. "You're an architect."

"I'm a designer," he emphasizes, nudging me back.

"A designer of buildings," I say.

Cameron just rolls his eyes with a smile and keeps walking.

"Listen, I partied, lost my connections I'd built through college, and transitioned into graphic design instead. I gave up and I know it." He shrugs. "I can't go back."

After a moment of silence, he turns his attention to Buddy and begins running, making sure to distract the dog with some play. And no doubt to avoid this conversation.

I didn't know he lost connections. Is that what's holding him back? He's embarrassed about his old days? If I've learned anything these couple months, it's to stop living in the past because the future is all we have. There's no point in being unhappy with what you have. And yet, I can't bring myself to say this to Cameron. It seems as if the memories alone pain him.

They both fall on a grassy knoll nearby and Cameron wrestles with him a bit before Buddy gets exhausted and falls next to him. I click my tongue toward Hank and we both settle in beside the two of them.

We're in a section that's technically behind the office building, but still facing another complex. The buildings are close but still far away enough to create some grassy medians to lay in. Lucky us, however, we catch the sunset.

Wow, how romantic. I can't handle this.

The sky is full of pinks and purples, radiating through the

clouds. They're wispy, stretched thin and transparent, letting what's left of the sun shine through. We sit there long enough to have the sun disappear behind the building. But when we stand to go back in, there's enough light that we can make it back before the streetlights turn on.

I brush off my dress, getting the last of the grass off my behind and the back of my legs. When I finish, I look over and Cameron's watching me with a grin.

"What?" I ask.

"Nothing," he says.

I take a deep breath and secretly let out an exhale. If he wants to look at me like that, then I'm a goner.

We make our way back to the office and I let Hank off the leash as soon as we're back inside. He trots back to the comfort of his bed under my desk and Buddy joins him, finally tuckered out from the walk.

"Oh!" Cameron says, making me jump.

"Yes?" I laugh.

"I need to show you something," he exclaims. He walks to his office and I follow.

By the time I get there, he's already at his desk, sifting through the papers and presenting a design to me.

It's my design, but slightly improved: Completely vectorized with striking colors I had yet to add and a couple additional features that make it pop more. I take the paper from him slowly.

"This is wonderful," I breathe.

He'd put in the extra work to make it stand out, and it's even more beautiful than I could have done on my own; it's a combination of both our talents.

He walks around the desk and stands beside me. Our shoulders are touching, but neither of us breaks contact. I look up at him, our noses inches apart. His deep brown eyes stare back at me. My gaze darts to his lips.

It's tension that we've never explored. We've brushed against one another and the touches have lingered more and more, but the leap into crossing that line—the decision to break the barrier between boss and employee is something we're both scared to do. If we move forward just an inch, if I welcome him to me and feel the warmth of his breath, it will change everything.

Cameron doesn't move. I get the sense that he wants this to be my decision. He doesn't want to be the boss that takes advantage of an employee, and that makes me respect him more. It's more attractive; more... forbidden.

I want to lean closer, so I find that I do. I can feel the heat from him, the energy between us, the passion we need to release. I turn my head to the side, our faces only inches apart. Then we hear a bark. Two barks.

Oh no.

Our eyes widen and we pull away. I grab a stack of papers on the desk and start to shuffle. What the hell else looks totally natural?

Cameron walks out of his office as if this is just another day, another late-night working. And definitely not a mistake we almost made.

"Hello?" he calls. It's a few seconds before he speaks once more and I hear him say, "Oh, I'm so sorry."

Then there's another voice, much shakier and older. I can't hear what he's saying so I exit the office as well and turn the corner to find a hunched, elderly man in a navy jumpsuit holding a vacuum. I'm fairly sure it's the only thing keeping him standing.

"Not a problem, Mr. Kaufman. Not a problem," he says, getting the words out with a struggle. "It's been a while since I've seen you this late."

He seems good-natured enough. Not the kind of man to suspect anything. God, I hope not.

"Oh!" he says, finally noticing me.

I get the feeling his vision isn't 20/20, or maybe I'm just praying he doesn't see how obviously flustered I am. Is it selfish to wish the man's vision is failing him?

Come on, man. Why now? I think, but I should probably be thanking him.

"It's a big project," Cameron says, his tone unwavering. "There's been a lot of people staying later. I guess we just lost track of time."

I look down to my watch and my eyes widen. Nine o'clock. It makes sense that the cleaning crew would come once they were sure everyone was gone. I notice the man now eyeing Hank and Buddy, who are standing in the doorway behind me, their tails wagging.

"That explains the chewed desk legs," the old man chortles and Cameron good-naturedly laughs back. I even throw in a laugh for good measure. *Probably a bit too much.*

"We were just heading out," Cameron says.

The man nods. He must know Cameron quite well, because the boyish smile satisfies his curiosity just fine. He walks away into the accounting department and we start gathering our things, packing our bags, putting the dogs on leashes, all while not saying a single word to each other. The tension is still there, but it's waning. I can feel my own heartbeat start to normalize and I can think straight once again. We head out into the parking lot and stop for a moment to look at each other.

What do we even say? He's looking just as flustered as I am, but he runs his hands through his hair to mess it up and my mind is clouded once more with thoughts of how much I need to take him back to my apartment.

He begins walking toward me. I want nothing else than to continue what we started, but...

One time a year ago, I came home from work, exhausted from delivering one cold call after another. All I wanted was to lay next to Joe, exchange massages, and end the night with our clothes off and me yelling passionate profanities. But Joe wasn't having it. He said he'd an even busier day than I could even begin to understand, so the last thing he wanted was sex. I wonder if he ever regrets that day, considering it was the last time we even discussed sex.

And I wonder if I'll regret my decision to do exactly the same now.

"I should go," I say, and he almost skids to a halt right in front of me.

I'm making the right choice, so why does it feel so wrong?

Cameron stares at me for a moment, looks to the ground and nods, then smiles at me. "That's a good call. I'll see you tomorrow, Holmes."

I get into my car and get Hank settled in the back. He lays down to fall back asleep, and I stare out at the parking lot and watch Cameron drive off. My heart is pounding and my legs feel like noodles, like I could be standing solid while also falling. Just noodley limbs attached to meat. What is this—*Cloudy with a Chance of Meatballs?*

An accurate description of my life.

Who even am I?

I'm becoming a crazy person, that's who. I almost kissed my boss tonight. What was I thinking?

Hank and I make it back to the apartment after I took way too much time to find a parking spot in the back of my complex's lot so my bright yellow bug wouldn't be noticeable. My mind won't stop racing, and the only thing that distracts me is Hank, looking miserable while he tries to settle in again. He's an old dog, but he's not normally *this* morose. I bend down to pet him. He seems all right, but then I remember what I told Ramona: Things can only go downhill from here.

I hope I'm wrong.

27

CAMERON

From: gholmes@treasuriesinc.com
To: ckaufman@treasuriesinc.com
Subject: Day Off
Cameron,

I won't be in today. I'm taking Hank to the vet. I should be in tomorrow, or at least working remotely. I'll keep you updated should anything change.
Thank you,

Grace Holmes

I LOOK over the email a couple times, dumbfounded. My immediate internal debate is whether I can believe that Hank actually has an appointment, or if she's instead using that an excuse to avoid me. And if she is, can I blame her?

But no, she wouldn't lie about her dog going to the vet. What heartless person would do that? Plus, Grace is straightforward. If last night was an issue, she would be the first person to tell me, "Hey asshole, that was almost uncalled for." Almost. Because ultimately nothing happened.

I start typing out a reply, but then I notice a tiny thing right below her name and just above her job title in the email signature: A phone number. I don't remember a phone number ever being in her signature, as most of us just get our email through our phones anyway. I look up a previous email she sent regarding design approvals. Just her name and job title. No number.

Does she want me to text her? Or am I just being crazy?

I copy the number from her signature and paste it into my contacts. I type out a message asking if Hank is okay, then shove my phone back in my pocket. There. Simple. Done.

"Let's talk about Grace."

I look up and Mr. Feldman is on my couch, peering over his laptop with one eyebrow raised. How long has he been talking?

"Okay," I say, picking up a pencil and scribbling on a paper, putting nothing of value there.

"I think she should be a team lead."

"A what?" I say, dropping the useless pencil.

"She's the only one on your team with enough gumption to do anything," he says. He's not trying to be rude, but *is he trying to be rude?*

My leg begins twitching in anxiety. My tic probably looks obvious to him, and I can tell he's just as comfortable as I am to be having this conversation, which is to say not at all.

"She's just a junior designer," I say this and realize it feels odd that even came out of my mouth.

Here I am, unable to stop thinking about the red-headed wonder, and I'm still trying to sabotage her future. No—not sabotage. I just have a hard time losing a grudge. She's still cocky and unruly and uncontrollable. She's a wildcard with disregard for rules and management.

And I want that in my life, bad.

"The project is almost over," I say. "But... I'll look into it."

"I would hope you do." Mr. Feldman smiles, and I return the gesture.

He sees her potential, and he isn't wrong. He goes back to his laptop and I go back to doing absolutely nothing on my own. I just click through tab after tab while my head swims.

My ridiculous grudge shouldn't be the thing to hold her back. She's got talent and the personality for my role. She could probably do it even better than I can.

Buzz.

I rip my hands into my pants pocket, trying not to appear too eager, but of course failing miserably as I lean the phone against my thigh in an attempt to conceal it.

Grace: Hank is fine. Normal appointment.

Well damn, I feel like a bigger ass.

Cam: What vet are you at? Let me know if you need me to drop off anything.

That's not weird, right? We've already crossed some line, so I'm sure having your creepy boss ask what vet you're at isn't too far-fetched is it?

Buzz.

Grace: Thanks, I should be fine though. But I do need a reward for my patience. This waiting room is garbage.
Cam: Most vet waiting rooms are. Is there some grumpy old woman with her cat yowling in a crate?
Grace: For the past twenty minutes.
Cam: At least one weird animal?
Grace: Duck, duck, and a goose believe it or not.

Cam: And some big dog about to pull their owner's arm off trying to smell every other dog's butt?
Grace: I feel like you're speaking from experience here.
Cam: Buddy likes butts and he cannot lie.
Grace: I see bowls of free treats everywhere and yet there are no vending machines for the owners. Not even coffee!
Cam: You could probably just snag a dog treat.
Grace: No, those are only for good dogs.

I hesitate for a moment and take the plunge.

Cam: Haven't you been a good girl?

There's a lull, and I only see three repeating dots flashing across her side of the conversation as she types, erases, and then reenters the text. The phone buzzes in my hand.

Grace: No, I haven't.

I exhale and let my fingers hover over the phone, looking up to see if Mr. Feldman has noticed anything, but he seems none the wiser. I'm just some first-time boss, but this guy means business. I'm sending vaguely sexual texts to my direct employee, and he's probably solving the next big architecture project—just as I should be. Eventually, I lock my phone back and set it on my lap. I don't need to keep annoying her. I need to focus.

My eyes glaze over and then the phone buzzes again.

Grace: I'm sure Hank would love the company if you get the time. At this rate, we'll be here all day.

The next text that follows is a street address.

28

GRACE

I'M STARTING to wonder if I'm in a vet's office or if I died in my car on the way here and I'm sitting in Purgatory. Hank and I have been transferred from one waiting room to another since we arrived this morning. By the time we're placed in one deeper in the vet's office, I'm fairly sure we've been here for half of my life.

Did you know people camp outside of a vet's office before it opens? I sure didn't. I pulled up five minutes before they unlocked the doors and you would have thought it was the night before Black Friday with the amount of people already waiting. I had to park across the street in what I hope is a legal place to put my car, but really, who knows. This place needs a bigger parking lot.

At the time, I thought, *Do these people think they're going to get a deal on the services?* But after this ridiculous waiting room hop-fest, I'm realizing those people had the right idea. You would think I hadn't owned a dog that's been to the vet regularly for eleven years to know that waiting rooms are serious business.

I've been passing the time by occasionally checking emails,

sketching, or shamelessly texting my boss like we're two friends that have known each other since elementary school.

Grace: Am I missing anything important today?
Cam: Meetings are running smoother but that's probably because I don't have some red head blurting out things every two seconds.
Grace: Boo.

Hank and I are finally waved into a private room to wait, yet again.

Grace: We're in the last room on the left. Am I the only one that finds that eerie?
Cam: You're both gonna die.
Grace: Knew it.
Cam: How is the old guy doing?

I look down to Hank, who's already splayed across the tiles. His eyes are closed. If I didn't know better, I'd say he was meditating.

Grace: Not miserable.
Cam: Stronger dog than I am. Vets freak even me out. Buddy and I are a wreck whenever we have to go.
Grace: Is Buddy's tail between his legs the whole time or is yours?
Cam: Even the cats bully me when I walk in.

The door to the waiting room creaks open and a tall curvy woman walks in. She has a clipboard in one hand, and her other placed in the pocket of her white coat. She's wearing lime green crocs, but for some reason she totally pulls them off. She smiles at me and it's like sunshine radiating from her pores. Without hesitation, Hank gets up and walks to her.

Animal whisperer, I think.

"Well now, how are we today?" she asks, bending down to take Hank's face in her hands, moving it back and forth, lifting his lips up to inspect his teeth.

"Good," I answer for him.

"Bit of some gum bleeding," she says, tutting. "Tsk, tsk, not good, huh?" She removes her gloved hand from his mouth and gives him a pat on the head. She goes on to tell me that he's got a tooth issue. Apparently, a lot of older dogs have it and a simple surgery will fix it. Simple, but not cheap. But I'd spend my entire life savings on this dog, so I sign some paperwork. There was a lucky appointment cancellation, so they can fit us on the schedule in a couple hours.

And back to the waiting room we go. Although, this time it's a nicer one in the back with comfy couches instead of hard, cafeteria-esque chairs. And there's a coffee machine. They must save the good stuff for the patients shelling out the big bucks.

I make a fancy cappuccino for myself and plop down into a chair, booting up the laptop to check emails and see any adjustments to designs before taking out my tablet to work.

I check my phone one last time. No more texts from Cameron, so I stash it away and do some warm-up sketches before jumping into my project. Sketching calms me; makes me feel like things aren't completely falling apart. Let's look at the bright side of things: My dog is fairly healthy, I'm settling into work with confidence, and I didn't kiss my boss. Could be worse.

I heard once that one hour of coloring is equivalent to one session with a therapist. Ever since I picked up art again, I can attest to the fact that it's true. I zone in and lose track of time. My phone rings and draws me out. My heart hopes it might be Cameron, but my brain is relieved to see it's not.

"Hey, Mom." I lean the phone between my shoulder and ear, filling in the remainder of the design with block colors.

"Oh, how is my poor boy?" My mother's southern drawl coos out from the phone.

"Hank is fine," I reassure her. "Just a tooth issue. We're going into surgery in a bit. They say it's a pretty low-risk procedure."

"Is he scared?" she asks.

I look over and see Hank lying on the floor, eyes closed, a small snore leaving with every deep exhale.

"Absolutely terrified." I can't remember the last thing that stressed him out. Even the vet's office is a breeze. Moving was the only slightly unnerving thing, but after one night, he found the part of the apartment where the air vents pointed and he was good to go.

"I found a recipe for little dog treats," she says. "I can see if there's one specifically for teeth cleaning." I hear her fingers clacking over a keyboard. "Alfalfa?"

"Isn't that for rabbits?"

"No, hang on a moment," she says, pausing.

I just picture her glasses lowering down to the bridge of her nose as she leans closer to the screen. I give her time to decipher, reaching down to pet Hank. His ear twitches at my touch.

"They're just selling hygiene chews," she huffs.

"That's the ingredient? Hygiene?"

"Very funny. Ah here we go!" Mom says, making me jump. "Now, do you brush Hank's teeth regularly?"

I look down at him and he lifts his head to look at me as if saying. "Don't even lie to yourself."

"Maybe once a week."

Hank barks in protest. *Smart ass.*

Mom sighs. "I'll buy some teeth cleaners for him. But swing by my house to pick them up. It's been a while since you've visited me."

My Mom. The queen of guilt. She isn't exactly wrong.

"Will do."

"Good," she says, satisfied. "So how's work going?"

My design stares back up at me, filled with colors, heart, and my purest form of relaxation.

"I finally feel a little bit like myself," I say, almost surprised at my own words.

It's odd to think I procrastinated on this career for so long. What was I waiting for? The depression from a relationship heading south to kick me into high gear? My resolve to overcome said relationship trauma?

"You were always meant for this. I couldn't stand that collections agency place," Mom says, almost like she's angry at the company itself. I'm not sure where her decisive temper comes from, but she could be mad at a brick wall for being lazy.

I sigh. "Geez, neither could I."

"And your boss?"

I pause—my heart stopping. I'd forgotten about Cameron for a bit, but the thought of him sinks into my chest and my limbs feel like they turn to jelly.

"What about him?" I try to sound nonchalant.

"I just want to make sure this job that you love isn't going to disappear. Your career means more than a man."

"You're right. Look, nothing is going on. We're just co-workers."

"No," she presses. "You're not co-workers. You're his employee. There is a distinct difference, Grace."

I know when she uses my name, she means business. But it's not like she's wrong. And it's not like I don't know that. I glance at my tablet again. I need this job. I want this job more than I've ever wanted anything before—even more than Cameron's muscular arms and mouthwatering abs.

"We're just working together." I pick up my tablet and put it in my lap again, sliding the pen out of its looped holder and start to work again.

"Clever girl."

Two hours pass, and I've made some progress on my project, but my hand is starting to cramp up and Hank's pacing the empty waiting room. He may as well have been crossing his legs and jumping side to side. Yikes, how long has it been since he went to the bathroom? I'm such a crappy dog owner.

"Want to go outside?" I ask, standing up and stretching. His tail wags and he walks over to me with a small whine.

I go toward the door, crack it open, and look out. "Hello?" Thankfully, a nurse is walking past the hallway looking down at her clipboard. Her eyes widen.

I just know these people totally forgot about us.

"Oh, right, right." She looks back down to her clipboard again, running her finger down the page then stopping halfway. "Grace and Hank? We're almost ready for you. The doctor is washing up right now."

"Wow, what stellar timing," I say, resisting the urge to roll my eyes. "But I think the ol' boy needs to pee."

"You can head out through this hall." She points. "Down to the first door to the left. Once he's finished, just knock on the door and I'll let you back in."

"Thanks." I turn around and pat my leg. Hank hurries over and squeezes past me in an effort to get to the door faster than I can. I take his leash out of my pocket—the only jeans I own with deep enough pockets! Darn you, fashion—and clip it to his collar before he can dart off.

We almost turn left at the door when I hear a very familiar, low voice.

"Grace Holmes. I think she's in the waiting room?"

"Which waiting room?"

"There's more than one waiting room?"

Hank pulls me toward the door, but I can't help stopping in the hall and calling out. "Cameron! Down here!"

A head pops around the corner and there he is, devil extraordinaire. Mr. Cameron Kaufman, with his bearded grin and his tousled hair. He turns back behind the wall. "Found her!"

"Can't believe you actually came," I laugh, barely concealing my anxious nerves at the sight of him.

He's wearing a raglan baseball tee with the sleeves a dark navy blue and, like most of his shirts, it's fitted to his torso. His skinny cut jeans rest on top of the dark brown, lace-up boots that are slightly worn and practically scream, "I am man!" I have to keep myself from drooling.

He's actually here. I sent him the address, but he stopped by?

"I needed a break from work stuff." We take the left toward the door and head outside. Hank reaches the heaven full of grass just waiting to be claimed as his bathroom. I drop his leash and let him roam.

"So," he starts, "you weren't avoiding work today?" The edge of his mouth exposes a grin and his dimples deepen enough to be seen through his beard.

Those damn dimples.

I bark out a laugh. "Last time I checked, I have a dog going into surgery."

"Surgery?" His thick eyebrows shoot up and he looks to Hank. His concern is enough to make a girl swoon.

"Teeth and gum issues," I say. "Simple procedure."

"Do you brush his teeth?" he asks.

"Why does everyone keep asking that?"

"Unbelievable." Cameron shakes his head in mock disappointment.

I squint at him. "Don't mess with me, guy. I've got enough stress on my plate."

"And what stress is that?"

He's testing his limits and I want to test mine. I want to grab his shirt, pull him close, and say "Hey buddy, *you're* killing me here." I want him. But that just isn't in the cards for me.

"The kind of stress put on by work and my dumb boss," I say.

He points a finger at me. "Watch it, Holmes. Are you ever not trying to push your luck?"

I'm always pushing my luck.

29

CAMERON

Once they take Hank back for his procedure, Grace and I are left in a comically large waiting room without a single other soul for a little over an hour.

I look over to Grace as she bends her slender neck just slightly to concentrate on her tablet. Her delicate hands move deftly across with screen, and I can just see the gears turning. I take a deep breath and look ahead at my laptop, clicking through email after email. A meeting invite, a sample from a designer on the team, and then a demand for a deadline that's next to impossible to meet.

The door to the room opens and in walks Hank, his tail wagging a bit slower than usual. Grace stands up and goes to him, crouching down and petting his head. The love she has for him practically radiates off her. It's even more of a turn-on to see her so caring. Abby could never express that kind of love even if she tried.

"He'll need these," the doctor says, handing Grace some pills. "And the back"—the doctor gestures to his own gums—"will need to have gauze every couple hours until the bleeding stops. Keep an eye on him and come back in a week. Katie will schedule your next visit up front."

I pack up my things while Grace makes an appointment at the front desk. By the time I meet her up there, she's ready to head out.

"If you need a couple days off—"

"Yeah, if I could work from home tomorrow at least, that would be great." She turns around, looking from side to side, and her face contorts into a mix of exhaustion and despair with a full dollop of irritation. "You've got to be kidding me," she snaps, letting out a long, raspy groan.

"What?"

Oh God, what did I do?

"My car."

Oh.

She throws her hands in the air. "It's gone. Towed. I knew I shouldn't have parked there."

I'm questioning my next sentence, but it comes out anyway. "Do you need a ride?"

Good job, idiot. Yes, let's definitely give the hot employee a ride home alone. Way to go.

Grace looks over to me, cringing a little. I'm sure she feels the same awkwardness I do. It was a dumb suggestion. "No, no, I can find a ride or something."

Yep, you're a genius for making this weird.

And yet I continue. "Well, you have one right here."

Stop it! What are you doing?

"No really, I..." She hesitates then shakes her head and laughs as if shaking off doubt. "Sure, yeah. And you don't mind?"

Do I mind? Not at all. I definitely don't mind having the woman I desperately want to sleep with but can't because it's absolutely forbidden sitting next to me in a close environment. No, I don't mind one bit.

"Not a problem." I smack a smile on my face and lead the way to my car.

You idiot.

As we ride down the road—her giving me instructions here and there—I wonder what the hell has happened to me. She's funny, feisty, and wears tops that almost always give a glimpse down her shirt, which I am *very* grateful for. But I went from hating her to being her friend? When did this happen? Oh right. I got drunk and she blackmailed me.

What a charming girl.

Except she is. That's the worst part. She's so incredibly adorable and sassy, and I just can't get enough of her presence. I feel like I've both met her a month ago and that I've known her forever. She's hilarious and caring, and I want to punch myself in the face for having these thoughts at all.

I zone out, but then see that we've definitely passed by a particular convenience store a second time. Plus, we're less than a mile from my own apartment complex, and I know I need to take Buddy for a walk before he destroys the entire place out of boredom. It's like being on a bus while it's parked for more than five minutes, but it's the stop right before your own. You think, *"I could have walked there by now."*

But when I look over at Grace, she's glancing out the cracked open window, her fiery hair billowing around her face, I'm actually not all that mad.

"Hey, Grace?" I ask. She jumps and looks over to me. "Not to be rude, but are we lost?"

Grace clears her throat and shifts in the passenger seat, adjusting her bag and reaching over to pat Hank whose head is resting on the center console. Damn it, she's uncomfortable. Though why wouldn't she be? I'm her boss and I'm driving her alone. This is a lawsuit waiting to happen.

"N-no," she stammers. "Not lost."

"Then why have I seen Dime-A-Dozen a couple times now?" If you thought dollar stores were cheap, you're dead wrong. It's one block from my apartment and I have visited there more times than I can count. The bread may be expired, but it still tastes just fine.

She exhales and then concedes, "Just take a right up here."

I slow down as we approach my complex—the one on the right.

"Here?" I ask, glancing over to her.

She nods, embarrassed.

Did she mean to take us back to my place? Am I misreading signals? I thought we were just co-workers, and yet here I am, being directed back to my own apartment with no words exchanged from the passenger next to me. Is she seriously that bold?

She starts laughing, but I'm pretty sure it's because she can't think of anything else to do. Hell, I can't think of a damn thing either. Are we going to sleep together? Is this is happening? Should it happen?

"You know I live here," I say. I don't want her to think I'm assuming anything. Maybe she meant to come here or maybe she was lost and too proud to say otherwise. "Why did you direct us... to where I live?"

She laughs again and I'm less turned on and more freaked out by each passing chuckle.

"I actually live here, too," she says.

Wait—what?

"You what?"

She plays with the strap on her bag, buckling and unbuckling it absentmindedly. "I, uh, it's funny, yeah, I live here." The words stumble out with confused and awkward laughter.

I'm not laughing back. "Why didn't you tell me you lived here?"

"I was afraid of what would happen." Her eyes glance up to me, glazed over and reflective. "I was more afraid of what we would do. No, what *I* would do if I knew we were so close. It'd be... easy." Whether she's doing it intentionally or not, her eyes dart from my face down to my pants, then back up.

Goddamn.

I run my hand through my hair, rustling it, trying to think of anything else to say without crossing more lines than we already have. I can't think of a damn thing.

"But this"—she gestures between the two of us—"can't happen."

"Right," I say, putting the car fully in park and turning it off.

The silence of the night surrounds us; the only thing I can hear are actual crickets.

But then—the entire moment shifts. Before I can process what's even happening, Grace grabs my collar and pulls me in. Our mouths touch and my body lights on fire. She tightens her hold on me. I run my palms up her neck, grip her hair in one fist, our mouths pressing harder, hungry for more. I open my lips and she welcomes me, inviting my tongue in to meet hers as they wrestle for dominance. My pants get tighter; I can feel the blood pumping down, begging for her—needing her.

She pushes against me, asserts herself, but I just push back. My strength is greater and her back hits the window. I wrap my other hand around her, reaching for her neckline. I stroke the back of her neck, my desire for her soft skin against mine, overwhelming me. I reach for her seatbelt buckle, fumbling to undo it, but she pushes against my chest, pulling away.

No, God no, please don't stop.

"That was stupid," she says, her voice strained and out of her breath. My hand is still tangled in her hair, but I slowly remove it. "That was so dumb. I am so sorry."

"Don't feel dumb," I say. "I wanted it, too."

We exchange small smiles, and it just feels right. This whole situation almost makes me forget how absolutely wrong it is—and how many issues this could cause for both of us. But she's so beautiful and exciting and I want to grab her face and keep kissing the shit out of her. She averts her gaze, adorable when she's embarrassed—mostly because I never see this woman get embarrassed. She's vulnerable. It's exciting to know she's letting her guard down with me.

"We can't do that again." She shakes her head, placing her cheek in one of her hands and looking back at me with those blue eyes. I'm absolutely lost. "But God, do I want to."

I let out a mix of a laugh and a breath of exasperation. "You're killing me, Holmes."

"It's just... you know... you're *you*," she says. She's drawing a line in the sand and I don't like it. "You're my boss. And I'm your employee."

I can't help but laugh again. "We were never really that, were we?"

Her face falls. "We need to be, Cameron."

I understand. I do. I know I let this get too far and she's right: It's best to stop this right here and now.

We're quiet; it's almost too quiet. We've never had an issue with awkward silences—even from the first moment I sat down next to her in the front lobby. All that red hair in a short bun, her skirt even shorter. I should have known I was a goner then.

"I'm going to work from home for a couple days to be with Hank." She unbuckles her seatbelt—the seatbelt that seconds ago was my responsibility to take control of—and starts gathering her bags on the passenger floor.

"Do what you gotta do."

My hands grip the wheel, knuckles whitening. She exits the car, opening the back door again to call for Hank. He steps out gingerly, then heads over to the right side of the complex. She climbs the stairs to the second floor and unlocks the door to her place.

For a second, I wonder what different decisions could have led to me going in there with her. But I know that nothing would be different than it is now.

Because I'm just her boss. And I'd do anything she wanted.

30

GRACE

CAMERON KAUFMAN and I don't speak for a month.

We still have team meetings, and I say my piece. I'm just as involved as ever at the company—if not more—but it's only business talk. No conversations regarding giraffe socks or food stealing adventures; just design.

Oddly enough, Saria has become my go-to work friend. We have lunches together, where she whines about her latest boy toy, which, it seems is about three at a time. (Did you know having a backup for your backup boyfriend is recommended nowadays?) I stay silent and soak in the nineteen-year-old's advice. Initially, I tried to start in a two-sided engagement, but I quickly realized she didn't need that to thrive in a friendship. The conversation flows much better when we only discuss her life.

Needless to say, it's been a bit lonely lately.

This is not to say I don't still have Ramona (who insists on calling every night), or my mom (who is adamant about Hank and I coming over for dinner now that she's getting the hang of avocados), but work life just isn't what it used to be.

For my first week back following Hank's surgery, I would

stay until exactly five o'clock, then head home and tend to Hank. We go on walks after I survey the street outside my window and ensure there's no hunky, shirtless, floppy-haired man and his golden retriever.

But one week of this, and Hank's bored to death of staying indoors most of the day. Once an eleven-year old normally behaved dog starts chewing throw pillows, you know you've made a mistake somewhere down the line.

Cameron stays late, but holes up in his office with the door closed. There's been one day Cameron left before me and we sort of interacted. His office light turned off and the door opened to the taps of Buddy's nails on the concrete floor. He dashed down the aisle toward Hank, who greeted him with a gruff, sleepy bark without even lifting his head from the bed. Cameron didn't follow his lead.

We made eye contact and he gave me a half smirk with a small wave. Before I could even wave back though, he whistled and Buddy came running. They left, only the tiniest spots of drool left behind from his over-eager dog just ready to play.

Now it's Beer Friday, and I'm here late again. I avoid the warehouse on Fridays so I don't have to look at Cameron. He always seems like he's having the best time. I went to the first Beer Friday we stopped talking, and it killed me to see him and Ian at the bar, Cameron's sleeves rolled up, one elbow angled behind him on the counter. He looked so at ease and even a little happy.

Not that I don't want him to be happy. I wish only the best for him. I just wish it could be me making him laugh, though.

The noise dies down eventually, but I only notice how late it is when I look at my watch and realize that the volunteers for Beer Friday must have packed up hours ago.

Crap.

I promised Ramona I would come over for dinner tonight and we would watch any movie she wanted. In return, she promised Cajun chicken with enough spice to burn my tongue for days. Bring on the challenge.

I pack up my things before calling Ramona. She answers in one ring.

"Okay, so how about we watch *Little Mermaid*?" Blasting into conversation without even a hello.

"Uh, hi, and why in the world would we watch *Little Mermaid*?" I ask, opening the passenger-side door to my car to letting Hank hop in.

"I don't know. She's red-headed like you? A good heroine ready to kick ass?"

"I don't think she's kicking anything."

"She gets feet eventually."

Wes's echoing voice comes over the phone. "And a vagina!"

"Geez, am I ever not on speakerphone?" I ask, closing the door to my car and starting it. After a moment, it transfers to the Bluetooth car speaker and Ramona's groan comes in surround sound.

"I can't contain the beast, Grace," she says. "It's either speaker phone or repeating the conversation later."

I laugh and Hank barks.

"Oh oh ho! Who's on speakerphone now?" Wes calls, and Hank barks once more.

I turn around after putting my car in reverse but stop before I can back out of the spot.

There's Cameron, waltzing out of the building, his keyring swinging over his index finger as usual, trusty golden steed following after him.

"*Little Mermaid* sounds fine." I'm barely focused on the conversation anymore. "I'll see you guys in thirty."

"Sure thing. Come ready to get your mouth on fire!" Ramona and Wes yell out in unison. They're too cute for their own good.

I stare at Cameron as he walks to his car. Sure, it's creepy. So sue me.

I hesitate for a moment, wondering if I should get out of my car and talk to him. We could say anything. We could talk about the project, lunch, hell, even his socks, I don't care. But I don't move.

I see him reach up and run his heavy hands through his hair. Why does he even bother? It's just going to fall back over in ten more minutes and then he'll have to fix it again. In fact, he's probably just making it worse by running through it over and over.

There. Now I have a reason to hate him.

He starts his car and drives through the parking lot, stopping at the entrance, looking both ways and turning out on the main road.

I wonder if he's going on a blind date. I'm willing to bet Cameron has forgotten all about what happened between us. It probably ended for him the second I left his car that night. I really give myself too much credit to think there was something more.

I buckle my seatbelt and look over to Hank, who has his nose smashed up against the glass. I roll my eyes and lower the window. He sniffs the fresh air. I wonder if I could even remotely be that happy.

I ARRIVE at Ramona's house and Wes greets me and Hank at the front door with a large plate of onion rings, stacked and still steaming.

"Is this how you greet everyone that walks in?" I ask, grabbing a ring and shoving it into my mouth.

Rookie mistake.

"Oh wait—" Wes doesn't finish before I spit it back on the

plate. My tongue burns and I'm breathing with my mouth wide open in hopes of letting cool air waft inside to simmer the blazing oil-dunked fire that just destroyed my mouth and taste buds. So much for fun food night.

"Yeah, they're hot."

"Ya think?" I shoot at him.

Wes moves to the side to let me in, closing the door behind me and yelling out, "Ray, she's still an idiot!"

Okay, so I *may* have burned my mouth within the first five seconds of being here, but I'm still dead set on this being a good night. For the entire car ride, I've been building up this idea of *The Little Mermaid* in my head. Ariel is a no-nonsense, see-the-world type of girl that's taking what's hers. I'm going to find my legs, too. I'm going to best this ocean of emotions. I'm going to—*Cameron?*

On the couch, ankle crossed over his knee in classic Cameron Kaufman-style, is the one and only bearded man I thought I wouldn't have to see for two days—complete with those damn corgi socks.

"Let's not all act surprised!" I hear Ramona yell back to her husband. "Give Grace food and she'll eat it!" It's hard to gauge Wes's reaction when I can't tear my eyes away from Cameron.

Good lord, he's the only man I know that can pull off a salmon pink polo and still look like a whole hunk of a man. His head is cocked to the side and he's laughing good-naturedly at Ramona's comment. His dimples are deep, and he has a hearty smile that's just ready to burst with another bark of laughter. But then he sees me—the person they're referring to.

His smile doesn't go away, so I guess I can take that as a win. But the dimples disappear, which is the real tragedy here.

"What." That's all I can get out once I find my voice. Hank trots over to him, licking his hands as Cameron absentmindedly pets his head. It's like we're both trying to remain calm but, seriously... *Am I in a flipping nightmare right now?*

The familiar tapping sound of Buddy's nails come skidding around the corner and there's that excited face I know so well. His tongue lolls out and he's already sniffing Wes's crotch. He laughs and pushes him away.

"I hope you don't mind." Wes's voice brings me back, making me jump a little. "We invited Ian over too, and he brought a friend who apparently also doesn't have a life on a Friday night. Sorry, dude." Wes waves his hand to Cameron, who forces a laugh out and pats the couch arm to direct Buddy over.

Wes stares at me. "Eek, you want some water?" I'm sure he's wondering just what type of number that onion ring did to me, not realizing the new guy on the couch is the real reason I've lost my marbles.

"What?" I repeat, darting my eyes over to Wes. He squints at me.

"Honey, you need to change that recipe!" he calls, walking toward the kitchen, the plate of rings stretched out in front of him as if afraid they may jump off and scald him, too. "Pretty sure those rings killed Grace!"

Well, at least something here has.

I hear the *clip-clop* of high heels and around the corner comes Ramona, with a red apron that says *Fri-YAY!* and is covered in flour. Her thick black hair is piled in a bun that probably tried its best to hold shape at the top of her head, but now it looks like a deflated beehive, curly strands sticking out every which way.

"You'll get over it," she says, pulling me into an embrace. "I'm trying to perfect the recipe! Your mom asked for my onion ring recipe and I lied and said I had one. I just want her to like me—is that too much to ask?"

I look over her shoulder to see Cameron staring back at me, his hand clutching a beer to the point of nearly crushing the can.

She pulls out of the hug and places her hands on my shoulders to keep me situated in front of her. After looking me up and down and letting out a heavy sigh, I give a half-hearted smile back.

"You really got to stop staying so late," she huffs. "It's a Friday! Relax!"

Well, yes, I would relax but there, right there, is the one man who can make me feel the least relaxed.

This Friday sucks.

31

CAMERON

"Come to my sister's house!" Ian told me. "She's making Cajun chicken! It'll be great!"

The only advantage of no longer hanging out with Grace, as if there really are any, is that after I'm exhausted from the day-to-day, I've been jumping into architecture again. I don't know what I want to accomplish with it—hell, I'm not even sure where to put the sketches. My apartment wall is starting to look like the ravings of a madman. There may as well be red string and a massive cup of cold coffee on the desk. At least one half of that is true.

But it's relaxing to focus on a dream that isn't designed around someone else's wants. Plus, my brain just keeps buzzing with ideas. A house with two bedrooms. Maybe three for an office. Or four for a kid or whatever. It's not like I'm thinking about a kid or anything, but I guess for some reason the blueprints just feel a bit more complete with a nursery.

So, while I could have been completing another project, I'm living Ian's lie about tonight being decent.

I'm aware that Grace is Ian's sister's best friend. They've apparently been almost inseparable since elementary school.

Ian was part of the reason she got an interview. But the last thing I expected was to see her stumbling into his sister's house, tongue hanging out of her mouth and a look of pure anguish over her face. Though the look of surprise that followed when she spotted me was worse.

"What."

Well at least she gets a word out. All I can think to do is leave the room in silence.

Fantastic manners, Cam ol' boy. Good job making her instantly feel like a giant piece of shit.

I somehow find my way into the kitchen without even realizing it, and Ian's sister Ramona follows behind me, arm-in-arm with the woman who's making my appetite for Cajun chicken disappear.

"Have you met Grace?" Ramona asks.

"Yeah," I say, refusing to make eye contact with Grace. "We know each other."

She unhooks her arm and raises an eyebrow. "Odd. How do you guys know each other?" She goes back to stirring the Cajun mix in a bowl without waiting for an answer. Grace takes a deep breath and hops herself up on the countertop. It's unfortunate she's not wearing a skirt, but I try to wipe that thought away as soon as it comes.

"Cameron is her boss," Ian says as he pops a cube of cheese in his mouth. He'd been lingering near the cheese tray since we got here, and I'm fairly sure that he's single-handedly wiped out the cheddar and pepper jack.

Ramona stops mid-whisk and looks over to me. It's like she is having some epiphany as if my job is some piece of information she's been looking for her entire life.

"Oh really?" she asks, shooting a quick look over to Grace before going back to the mix, which I'm pretty sure she's tossing around more feverishly than the recipe calls for. "Sorry for bringing work to the party." She seems more irritated than apologetic.

I shouldn't be surprised that Ian's sister is just as turbulent in personality as he is.

"Cam doesn't deign to be among the commoners anymore." Ian's mouth is full, but he pops another cube in with a wide smirk. "I'm sure this is a lovely reunion."

Sure. Absolutely lovely.

I laugh to try and ease the tension. For a second, I look over to Grace, but she watches Ramona sprinkle the mix onto the prepped chicken. I wish I could see her blue eyes for even a moment.

"More like I'm trying to get things done," I say.

"Nia says she's gotten three complaints about you not being present anymore," Ian laughs, transferring a cube from one hand to the other before tossing it up in the air and catching it in his mouth.

"Ian James, I swear if you eat one more cheese cube, I'm going to throw it all in your face." Ramona tosses a small pinch of Cajun mix at him.

Her husband, Wes, comes around the corner and grabs a handful of cheese. He looks to Ian. "I'm hoarding my share. I wouldn't test her."

Grace lets out her first laugh of the night and it's like Christmas bells. I'd missed that.

Dinner is served an hour later, and the entire house smells like spices. It's thankfully drowning out Grace's flowery scent, which has been driving me insane since she came in. This, plus the fact that Ramona's food actually smells quite good, has given me my appetite back.

We sit at the oval table in their dining room. Ian is beside me on one side with Ramona across from Ian and Wes at the head of the table, leaving only the seat across from me for

Grace to sit at. She's doing everything in her power to avoid my gaze and I'm doing everything in my power to meet hers.

I settle into my seat and take my first bite. I expect something deliciously spicy and juicy, but instead I'm greeted with something sort of spicy and very, very dry.

"Just like Mimi made it, but a tad bit worse," Ian says, flashing a grin at Ramona who already looks like she's ready to rip his head off.

While Ian is generally jovial and fun-loving, Ramona seems like she inherited all the rage to make up for Ian's lack thereof.

"I can't exactly taste the food due to the insane amount of pain from those onion rings," Grace muses, "but I bet it's really good." She's trying her best to be nice to her best friend. I've never seen Grace in an environment where she isn't sending sarcastic bites in someone's direction.

"Damn, yes! I couldn't put my finger on why it was a bit off, but your Mimi's chicken is good," Wes says dreamily, pushing his food around.

Ramona's eyes bore into him and I swear she could scare the tattoos right off his arms. "Mind repeating that?" she spits.

We all get quiet until Grace lets out a bark of a laugh. "Ramona, it's wonderful." She says it through a muffled voice. She's storing the chicken in her mouth like a hamster with sunflower seeds.

"Yes, please, finish your food first," Ian goads with a smirk.

"Hey, wait, weren't you the one struggling with her spaghetti last week?" Wes leans forward on the table, shoulders hunched and pointing his accusing fork directly at Grace, who copies his movement in defiance.

"Stop putting me in the doghouse, Wesley." Grace's words are muffled through the chicken in her mouth.

"You know what would never happen at Mimi's?" Ian says matter-of-factly. "Fighting." His posture is filled with slimy poise and an eat-shit grin spreads across his face. I can practically see the steam leaving Ramona's ears.

"Well, I think it's great." I say, taking a swig of my water to wash down the chicken. It goes down with a fight, but I'm sure not saying that.

"Suck up," Grace mumbles, but when I look to her, she's finally looking back at me and there's the smallest hint of a smile tugging at the side of her lips. It's like my muscles tense up, then a wave of relaxation begins to pool across my body. I desperately need her to smile again.

"Spaghetti," I shoot back.

"No, no, no, you are not in this argument!" Grace laughs. Her eyes crinkle while her cheeks flush a very soft pink.

"He's learning," Wes says, moving his eyes over to Ramona, who discreetly passes a wink back to him.

I wonder how long they've been married. I don't have any married friends and it's odd to see people in such a happy state in their relationship.

"I can ask you to leave at any time, new guy," Ramona sneers.

"He's shaking in his boots," Ian says.

I tap my shoes together and wiggle my shoulders in response, causing Grace to laugh.

"The most I can do is wish you luck." Grace grins.

God she's stunning. I want her smile, her laugh, everything.

"You know, when we were in middle school, Grace was the girl you had to watch out for—not me." Ramona says.

I look between Ramona and Grace. I can't help but let out a chuckle. It comes out of me without willing it, like I'm more excited to hear about Grace's past than even I know.

"Oh really?" I ask. I can only imagine younger Grace with a much more feisty, preteen sense of purpose.

"Absolutely not!" Grace drops her fork and slams her hand on the table. "I was super kind!"

"You would ride your bike down the road like some rebel without a cause," Ramona said matter-of-factly. "Fire on wheels!"

"Were you a bully?" I jest.

"No!" she says and there's a hint of adolescent resistance in her tone.

"...Were you?" I repeat with mock trepidation.

"Yes, she was," Ramona presses on. "She totally called people out on their bullshit."

"That did not go away," Wes interjects. "The first time I met her in college she said that my tattoos were a clear indication that I was not good enough for Ray."

"Hah, well yeah. 'Cause you weren't," Ian says. "We pretty much tag-teamed giving you hell. High five, Grace!"

They air five and I'm suddenly a little jealous. All these people have memories that I'll never get with her. We stopped before we could even begin.

"And last time I checked, your intentions weren't very chaste," Grace says. "So, we were right!"

"What happened to your bad boy image, Wes?" Ian asks. "You're a total push-over now."

Ramona laughs. "Yeah, what happened to my rebel punk hunk?"

"Excuse you, we are married. I don't deserve this type of shit talk from any of you three anymore." Wes crosses his arms and looks between the three of them in silence.

"Well, I'm new, so can I shit talk?" I mumble.

Everyone busts out laughing.

Dinner talk ranges from stories about how Ian was uncharacteristically more responsible in law school, how Wes's contrasting rebellious days resulted in sleeves of tattoos and a motorbike, and how Grace was always a little firecracker.

I soak in the talk, letting every bit of their nostalgia paint a more vivid picture of Grace in my mind. None of it is surprising, but that's the charm. And the more she talks, the more I respond, and soon we're riffing off each other's sentences just like we did before. I'm dying to hear her take another stab at me just so I can throw it back.

When we clean up after dinner, I take over washing dishes. As a guest, it's the least I can do. Grace clears the table of plates and brings them to me.

"You're missing spots." She passes a grin my way every time she drops something off and a part of me wonders if she's taking extra trips just to come back and tease me again on my washing technique.

We sit down for the movie—why *The Little Mermaid?*—with Ramona and Wes cuddling in a recliner, Ian stretched out to fill half the couch with a glass of wine in hand, and somehow Grace and I end up on the other side with only a couple inches between us. A singing mermaid is the least of my concerns as I try to maintain a decent distance between Grace and I, but it's difficult when we're constantly exchanging secret commentary for the movie. Although, it's more like Grace is leaning in and whispering to me.

"Why doesn't she just flop around when she hits the surface?" Grace whispers. "Isn't she part fish?"

"Do you think the prince guy would really want a flopping fish?" I ask.

"Hey, I don't know what he's into."

My head is dunked into a sea of possibilities about what Grace's preferences are. I want to discover them all. I want to see her lying on my bed, hands above her head, nipples exposed, begging me to be inside her. I cross my ankle over my knee and place my arms into my lap. I can feel my heart pounding and I know exactly where all that blood is pumping to. With every whisper she makes, my hair stands on end and I'm lulled into a rosy haze surrounded by her red hair and flowery perfume.

"I wonder what a shock it would be if she saw a penis for the first time," she says, causing my head to swim once more. "Do mermen have penises like human men?"

"Wouldn't you want to know?" I say, nudging her. My cheeks are starting to hurt from smiling so much.

I try to stay quiet, but every time she leans over to talk to me, I only lean back in as we scoot closer and closer together on the couch. I don't know what she wants from me. We agreed to not pursue anything, yet her thigh is caressing mine, she's talking about mermen genitalia, and I'm trying to come up with a million reasons as to why we aren't sleeping together already. The only one coming to my mind is the obvious: Because we simply can't.

The movie ends with applause from the room, but mostly from Ian who has downed five too many glasses of red wine and is whistling and yelling, "Get your man, mermaid!"

Wes, whose hands are no-so-discreetly creeping along the hem of his wife's shirt, asks, "Ian, are you staying the night?"

"Can Ariel talk?" Ian slurs, winking to him. I've been around Ian for years and he never drinks, so it's unsurprising he's as smashed as he is. Wes kisses Ramona's neck with regret before directing her out of his lap. "I'll prep the guest bed," he says.

Ian's oblivious to being a total cock block for his brother-in-law. Although, knowing Ian, he probably *is* more than aware of it.

"Do either of you need to stay, too?" Wes asks us, and both Grace and I shake our heads simultaneously. She seems almost eager, and it makes my chest beat in anticipation. I want to talk to her without the company of her friends. I don't know what to say, and my best bet is that we'll simply say goodnight and part ways. But why do I feel like my blood pressure has been escalating this entire night for something? Why has she been flirting for the past three hours? Has it been flirting? Do I just want it to be?

I gather my wallet and keys, leashing Buddy with a pat on the head, and Grace grabs Hank's leash, clipping it on his collar. We wave and close the door behind us. The humid night air washes over me and it's suddenly dead quiet.

I walk her to her car, even though it's only a few feet ahead in the driveway but it feels like the gentlemanly thing to do.

"I parked on the road," I explain, and she nods, a smile beaming on her face though I really didn't say anything funny. It's absolutely contagious so I can't help but grin back.

We stare at each other for probably a moment too long, causing her to laugh.

"What?" I ask, laughing back.

"Do you think she ever regretted not keeping her mermaid tail?" she asks.

"I don't know. I think she honestly lived with no regrets."

"I live with no regrets," she says, sparking a second of something else in the air. It's like we're opposite ends of a magnet and I'm doing everything in my power to resist the pull.

"Me too," I reply.

Her chest rises and falls quickly, betraying her attempt at concealing her nerves. I can feel them, mixed in with whatever otherworldly power that's drawing her closer to me.

"So, you're a mermaid?" I ask and the sentence runs through my head again and again in the span of one second because I can feel the mood break slightly.

"Wouldn't that make you one, too?"

"I like to think I'm a manly mermaid—merman."

"Whatever," she says, rolling her eyes.

We stand there just looking at each other. I've missed those blues, the freckles scattered across her nose, her cheeks, her ears, the fullness of her lips tinted with a slightly deeper shade of red lipstick.

I move forward one step, my head tilted down and slightly turned to the side. I present the opportunity, if only she would take it. We both agreed this wasn't possible, but I feel something more—some sign that maybe we can forget work, responsibility, and give in to what we've been resisting for months. But I don't want to be the one to make the call. I can't be.

Her eyes move between mine and she pulls her lower lip into her mouth, biting it. It's testing my limits.

I fail.

My hands move to her neck, running my fingers across her jaw and then crushing them into her bright red hair. I pull her toward me with everything I have, every bit of energy that's consumed me and begged to be released.

Finally, we both stop swimming against the current. She rises onto her toes and our lips smash together. It's like flames licking across my chest, fury in the soul of me that hates we waited this long, and chaos in my head urging me to possess her more.

Her lips part just a bit; I can feel her smiling against me. Her enjoyment drives me wild. I take the opportunity to slip my tongue in her mouth which she welcomes, sliding across mine slowly as if teasing the skill of what else she can do with it. I inhale sharply, pushing my hands through her hair and pulling the back of her neck to deepen it—to let me explore her further.

I take a step closer, pressing her back against the car, letting her arch into me. I can feel her chest heave against mine and her nipples harden, which only makes my hardness press against my zipper, aching. I let my hand roam her back, finding their way up to caress just below her the curve of her chest, the feel of her thin shirt being the only barrier between me and the pleasure I want—what I need—to provide her.

She pulls away and I'm left with no soft skin in my grasp,

craving more of her taste. My stomach drops and I'm waiting for it—the expression that says "this isn't right" or any clear resistance against this moment. But all I see is her smile and that devil of an eyebrow raised as if challenging me.

I growl and take a step toward her once more, but her hand goes to my chest, stopping me.

"I should take Hank home," she says.

A feel a head bump my thigh and am brought back to this moment: The driveway, her yellow car, the two dogs demanding more attention. I reach down to pat Buddy's head. but my eyes refuse to part from hers.

Only one side of her smile gives in, and its more curiosity.

Fuck me, it's sexy.

"So, I guess this is it," she says.

It feels like she's toying with me, but I like it. You don't have a kiss like that and not expect to pick up later. What is her game?

I pull my keys from my pocket, giving them a quick swing around my finger before clutching them again. I'll play along.

"Fine, I'll see you when I see you, Holmes." I take a couple steps backward and she's already got her keys out, dangling over her shoulder as if teasing my resolve. But I turn on my heel and start walking back to my car. I'm trying my best to remain cool, but my hard cock is tugging at my pants. I don't know what just happened, but I can't stop smiling. Are we finished here? Is this all for tonight? Or is there more?

I hear Grace's start and car back out of the driveway. She stops when she reaches the end where I'm walking onto the street, and she rolls down her window.

"Can I help you miss?" I ask, stopping to a slow stroll.

"I just want clarification here: You are coming back to my place, correct?"

Fuck yes.

I throw my hands into my pockets and lean back a little,

letting her see the curve in my pants. I want her to see how hard I am—just how bad I want her.

"Yes ma'am."

"And you're going to fuck me until I can't stand anymore?"

I grin, barely able to contain myself. *What a fucking fox.*

"I'm going to fuck you until you want me to stop."

Her eyebrow rises once more and her bottom lips barely slides in, biting it—teasing me with just a look.

"Good luck getting me to say that."

With a smirk, I lean down to her open window and whisper, "I'll get you to say a lot of things."

32

GRACE

THE DRIVE HOME IS MADDENING. My feet can't stop shaking against the pedals and I'm giving myself a crazy pep-talk all while pretending this conversation is to Hank.

"This is a good idea, right?" I ask him. He looks up at me with his head turned to the side, but I just laugh. "I mean, you've seen him, right Hank? I know you don't swing that way, or I don't know, maybe you do, but good God, he's gorgeous, right?"

I picture him. His bare chest. The rows of hard abs that adorn his body, the strong shoulders that will soon be ravaged by my hands and my mouth. I want to kiss him. I want to taste every inch of him.

Dinner was everything I needed. I wasn't sure how the night would turn out, but just one look into his eyes and I knew I was going to give in. For the past few weeks, I've wanted to talk to him, be around him, breathe in his manly scent, and have his hands wind their way through my hair just one more time. And now my mind is caught on the same thing: His lips on mine, and that bulge in his pants buried deep inside me.

The thought makes me take deep breaths and I've gotten so

lost in my head that I didn't realize I'd made it back to the complex. I pull into a parking spot and Cameron is already out of his car, leaning against the trunk with his arms crossed and his dog pacing beside him. I can see his biceps pressing against his sleeves and his pants fitting snugly on his hips. A grin lights up his face, and I know it's for me. He's all for me.

I open my door, escorting Hank on a leash, and Cameron's lips are already upturned in a sexy smile. I scan every part of him—his strong shoulders, his prominent wrists guiding veins along his forearms, and his large hands, waiting to grip me once more. He's looking me up and down, scanning me from my legs, my skirt, pausing at my breasts, and continuing up to my eyes where he arches one eyebrow.

"Fancy seeing you here."

I can't help but return the look, hoping I exude even half the confidence that he does. "What a coincidence."

He's focused on me for a moment more before looking down to Hank. "Do you think Hank would want a slumber party with Buddy?" he asks. "I can put on *Air Bud*."

"Yes, good idea."

He takes a step forward and I clutch Hank's leash a bit tighter. The nerves are shooting through me, and my face grows hot. His lips hover above mine and I can feel his minty breath when his lips part. I rise to my toes to kiss him, but he pulls away with a chuckle.

I click my tongue, guiding Hank over to Cameron's apartment. I'm walking a few paces ahead of him, leading the way and swinging my hips more than I usually might, hoping my ass is right in his line of vision as we walk up the stairs. Two can play at this game.

If only I can reach his apartment, drop off Hank, and make it back to my place. Every minute that passes is another minute he's not running every bit of his hands over me. It's another minute I'm not holding his cock in my grasp.

Why is this so far away? It's actually a tiny lot and the apartment buildings are pretty close together, but it feels like I'm walking three miles just to reach his front door.

Finally, it's in front of us. He catches up to me and pulls the keys out of his pocket. I can see a clever smirk tugging at his lips, and I know he's purposefully teasing me as he takes his sweet time fingering through the key fob looking for the correct one. My hands run along his stomach from behind, feeling the peaks of his abs. His lets out a low groan and I relish the sound.

He finds the key and inserts it into the door, letting me walk in first. Behind me, Cameron grabs my ass. It's something so simple and so shocking, and I'm dying. He rubs across one of my cheeks and gives it a hard slap, making me jump.

Goddamn it.

As promised, he loads in the DVD of *Air Bud* (who actually owns that?), reaches into a drawer, draws out a couple condoms, and pockets them. I expect us to begin pawing at each other once the door closes behind him, but he locks it and we walk in silence to my apartment. He's testing my patience, making me wait every single second he can, prolonging the anticipation.

I'm less graceful with my keys, fumbling for the correct one and trying my best to jam it in the lock. It's even worse when I feel Cameron's breath warm my neck. His rough hands ride under my shirt and settle on my hips as he pulls me closer to him. I can feel his hardness against my ass.

His mouth closes over the lobe of my ear as he whispers, "You want me to fuck you, Grace?"

The words send shivers down my spine. I know I'm wet. I know how bad I want him.

"I think you want it more than me," I lie.

"I'll make you eat those words."

"Or maybe something else?"

"Get inside," he demands.

We walk in and the second I close the door behind me, his hands on my shoulders. He pushes me against it, lips devouring mine. I eagerly push back, forcing my way into his mouth, letting our tongues meet once more. Our bodies cannot be contained. I'm burning from the inside out.

I clutch the collar of his shirt and tug him closer, if that's even possible. Our bodies are slowly molding into one as he presses himself against me, moving his hips to let me feel just how hard he is for me. I feel for the edge of his shirt and pull it over his head in one movement. I let myself rub over his abs, taking in the feel of it all, soaking in the smell of him— bonfire, cedar, sweat. He moves my arms above my head, holding them in place with one hand while his other finds its way behind my back and unhooks my bra with one snap of his fingers. There's no fumbling fingers or breathy apology. It's like he's meant to be here and now and his lust for me flows through every calculated motion. The bra didn't have a chance.

I can't move my hands, and squirm under his dominant touch. I arch my back, willing my body to move and touch his. I make sure my chest is pressed against him. He lets out a low breath, lifting my shirt and moving my now loose bra out of the way.

He takes my breast into his mouth and flicks his tongue back and forth against my nipple. The sensation runs down my chest into my thighs. I want to clench my legs closer together as I've gotten used to doing, but then I remember I don't need to. This is happening and he wants me. I don't need to hide anymore. He rubs his bulge against my hips, but there are clothes between us, and that simply isn't good enough.

"Please let me touch you," I whine.

He stops licking me and I miss the warmth of his mouth, but his breath against me makes up for it. Shivers run over my bare skin.

"I want you to beg." His words rumble in his throat, a carnal sound.

I buck my hands against his hold, but he doesn't release them.

"Make me," I challenge.

He takes me into his mouth once again, licking, biting, sucking. He's devouring every bit of me that he can. A moan escapes before I can halt it.

"Moan for me again. Beg for me," he rasps.

I whimper under his touch as he circles my nipple with his tongue before whipping it across once more. My knees buckle.

"Please," I moan.

"More." He swipes his tongue against me; my hips buck forward in response.

"Please let me suck your cock."

At that, he moves his hand from my wrists, bringing it down to lift my skirt and explore me underneath. He lets his hand run along my thighs, trace the edge of my underwear, then slowly rubs against the outside of the thin cloth to find my sensitive spot.

I let out a moan and I hear him chuckle, as if winning the fight for initial pleasure. I will not have that type of confidence from him overpower me.

I force myself to release from his hold and lower to my knees, wanting more of his touch, but I'm too excited about my frantic hands unbuckling his belt and pulling his pants down. I kiss his underwear line, slowly tugging them off until his length is released in front of me.

I can't help but grin as I look up at him and meet his eyes. It should be impossible that he's as good looking, funny, and charming as he is. It's almost unfair he's well-endowed as well. "I'm a lucky girl."

A smile tugs at the side of his mouth. I can see a lone dimple deepening through his beard, and I know that before this night is over, I will have that beard against my thighs. He wants me to beg, I'm not afraid to do exactly that.

I take only the tip of him inside my mouth, running my hand along his length, teasing him with small kisses along the side. He growls and runs his hand through my hair, gripping it into a ponytail and trying to ease the rest of himself into me. I resist. I need him to want this.

"Baby," he groans as I pull him out of my mouth and kiss his base, licking my way back to the top, purposefully drawing out the motion. I stop at the head and look up at him before I take him into my mouth completely, bobbing back and forth, letting my tongue flick against him, and pumping my hand. He lets out a struggled mix of an exhale and a moan. He's mine.

I continue for a minute or so before his patience wears thin and he pulls me up by my arms, slipping his cock out of my mouth before gripping my thighs and picking me up to let my legs wrap around him. He steps out of his pants and carries me to my bedroom. I kiss every part of his skin I can find: His neck, his collar, his shoulder. I bite it for good measure.

He throws me down on my bed, hovering over me. There's a moment where all I can see is his eyes as they dart between mine. He runs his hands from my neck down to my stomach, following them with a raised eyebrow, taking in my body. I suck in. I try to make my stomach flatter, my boobs perkier, and my pussy tighter. His hand glides over my underwear and he lowers himself to kiss the fabric.

"God, you're sexy," he breathes.

I exhale and all my insecurities feel so distant and irrelevant. He wants me. All of me. For who I am.

Cameron slides my panties down past my ankles and off my feet. His hand drifts up my legs. Thank God I shaved this morning. His palm rests on my knee and spreads my legs apart as he kisses the inside of my thighs slowly, taking every bit of care in building my anticipation. *God, is he ever.*

His scratchy beard reaches my lips and he kisses them, letting just the flat of his tongue rub against me. It's like fire igniting every single nerve. He needs to move lower and before my hand can reach his head to direct him, he just fucking knows. My body is his for the taking, and he navigates me with his tongue like he's known me forever. His fingers curl into me, pushing in and out as he continues to lap me up. The sensation spreads to my hips, my arms, my fingers, my now shaking legs. I'm getting close, but my mouth can't form words—just moans. My eyes close tight and I bite my lip to stop emitting more embarrassing noises.

"Look at me," he demands, and I do as he commands. His eyes meet mine, the edges of his beard soaked from my wetness, but a grin spread across his face. "You're delicious."

I can feel my face growing hot.

"Really," he insists with another flick of his tongue. My toes involuntarily curl. "I can't get enough, but I need to be in you now."

My hands clutch the sheets, balling the fabric in my fists as if they will keep me grounded. I don't know if the sheets can handle the weight of this responsibility, or if my nerves are even capable of being controlled at this point. All I know is that I need his mouth against me again. I even lift my ass from the bed to coax him back, but he pushes my pelvis back down. His circles his thumb across my clit for a moment before standing up and walking toward the doorway.

"No," I moan, begging for him to return. My chest hurts at his sudden absence as if it can't survive without the heat of his body near mine.

Cameron turns around at my call and passes his eyes over me. I'm on display for him, legs apart, feeling both vulnerable and empowered by it all.

"Touch yourself," he demands.

I oblige without thinking, but go slower so I don't put

myself over the edge without him here. I want him to have the honors. I need him to own me. He could ask me to jump off the top of the office building and I'd probably do exactly that.

He comes back moments later with a condom in hand, ripping the package open with his teeth. The immediacy and carnage in the motion sends my mind whirling. I'm lightheaded and very thankful I'm laying down. I watch, hungry, aching, as he rolls it down his length.

I move my fingers in slow circles against myself as he walks up to the edge of the bed, separating my legs further to position himself in front of me. The head teases my thighs while his other hand is running up my stomach to my nipple. He pinches it between his fingers, rolling it through them. He could continue doing that and it would be enough, but when his tip rubs against my opening, I know I will be happily mistaken.

"Tell me you want it," he urges. His voice is gruff.

"I need it."

At that, he groans and pushing himself into me. My stomach curls in on itself and I feel blinded, but full and content. We fit like we're made for one another and every ridge of him sets my insides aflame.

He pulls out slowly and I already miss being filled by him. He eases his way inside again, pumping in then pulling back out. I watch his eyes close and his head fall back, a groan escaping his lips. His dark brown hair is flipped to the side, unruly and swaying with each dip of his head. I move myself closer to the edge of the bed, desperate for him to be deeper inside of me.

"Cameron, fuck me now."

His eyes open and he looks down to me. He pinches my nipple harder and, with one movement, sends all of himself into me. I groan his name, finding no other words to express how perfectly he fills me up. He moves against me with force, grabbing my legs and placing my ankles on his shoulders. He grips my hips, possessive, as he pushes deeper and deeper with every forward thrust. The sound of our skin together wills me further into submission. I let him guide me, consume me, and I take every thrust against me like it's the last.

I keep rubbing circles with my fingers against my clit. A building sensation starts in my pelvis and low in my stomach.

I don't want this to end. I've wanted him for so long, and now I have him.

He increases the pace, tightening his grip on my hips, calling my name with expletives. It's animalistic, a sound demanding more of me. He's insatiable, and I want him to be the one to ultimately satisfy him.

I move my hands away, moments from imminent release, and instead grip the sheets beside me. I use them as leverage to push myself against him in the same rhythm. He groans and grinds harder, a dance of desire and want.

My stomach clenches, the yearn to let go oncoming. I don't want this to end yet, but he knows this is it for me.

"Come for me," he says, moving faster, clutching my hips harder.

The sound of his voice sends the pleasure radiating through me; pure elation carrying up to my stomach as I come hard. My head is numb as he pushes in and out, huffing out deep, grumbling breaths.

"Baby—" he growls, but before he can finish, he's leans over and bites my nipple. With a sound like relief, he releases inside me and collapses on my chest.

He lays there panting for a moment, then kisses every inch of my chest, my collar bone, my neck, and ends at my lips with soft, light kisses. Our mouths are perfect for each other as they move in unison. He pulls away, planting one small kiss after another on my chest before looking back into my eyes, the mix of brown and green tantalizing as a smile tugs at his lips.

"I need more of that," he says.

I laugh a little, reaching up to run my hands through his hair, mussing up the top as he generally would. But it's not him this time; it's me. This is me playing with his thick hair, me with my fingers running along his beard, caressing his jawline. I'm the one placing my forehead against his.

"Do you want me to call you 'boss' next time?" I whisper.

"Mmm," he groans, placing his head in the crook of my neck. "You're an absolute fox, do you know that?"

"It's the red hair, isn't it?"

"It's absolutely everything, Holmes."

33

GRACE

"Twirl for me again."

"Don't be such a pig," I say.

"Please," Cameron begs, bending a little at the waist in prayer. How am I supposed to say no to that? I spin in a circle with my hands raised above my head, my shirt lifting to expose my backside and cheeky underwear.

"That should last for at least tomorrow," he says, pulling me toward him and kissing me deeply. I melt like butter in his arms.

Cameron is at my door with it opened, standing in the threshold. A part of me wonders if neighbors can see us, but the other part is a willing prisoner in his grasp.

As of tonight, we've had sex a total of eight times over this weekend with other delights sprinkled in. Most notably, there was a time when his head was between my legs as we attempted to watch some movie I don't even remember. He spent the night both Friday and Saturday, and we agreed to go our separate ways on Sunday.

Tomorrow is work, and our joy ride will lessen significantly.

A smirk stays nestled behind his beard, and his eyes practically bore into mine. Just his gaze turns my legs to jelly. I have the sudden image of him taking me again—maybe on a piano *Pretty Woman* style—but it's getting late and, hey, we're responsible adults that don't even own a piano.

I've occasionally thought about the concept of responsibility tonight—how what we're doing is pretty dumb, how I almost feel like I've doomed my career to hell. But when I rolled over this morning to see him sleeping beside me, his arm laid over my waist, I couldn't help but think that it may have been worth it.

Is it possible to have both? Can we hide this mess we've gotten in and still maintain professionalism?

I want Cameron. I like him. I know for a fact that I've started to fall for him like a damn fool. But I also want my future. And who knows if Cameron will be in it? Design will be, of that I'm certain. I hold out my pinky.

"Oh boy, this again," he says with an eye roll and a smile.

"Pinky promise this doesn't affect our working relationship." I say, quirking an eyebrow.

"Darling, I think we're a bit past that," he laughs.

"I'm serious, *darling*," I insist. He edges toward me, placing a hand on my hip. I melt in his touch but try to maintain my resolve. "I don't want favoritism or more opportunities with clients or whatever. I want to succeed on my own merit."

He grins, exposing both dimples.

"Okay," he agrees, tilting his head to the ground and running his hand along the edge of my t-shirt. "Boss Cameron and Employee Grace. Got it."

"Well," I laugh. "Boss Cameron is my bitch, so maybe not that."

His eyebrows raise almost up to his hairline, and his other hand trails along my spine. It's like a volcano erupting across every single bone, deepening as the sensation travels into my thighs.

"Last time I checked, it was the other way around," he whispers, his voice low and gruff, demanding more.

I *want* more.

No, we have work tomorrow. He's had a hold on me all weekend, and we have responsibilities. Right. Like adults. Sure. Oh hell, I don't even believe myself.

I back up, extending my pinky out. "What we do here stays here. Outside of work. Just in this complex."

His eyes scan across my entire body, pausing at my exposed panties and again at the low-cut V-neck that's close to exposing my braless chest.

He smiles. "Deal."

We tie our fingers in agreement and part ways, but not before he plants one more kiss on me. I close the door behind him and exhale. It feels like it's an exhale I've been holding in all weekend, and I'm so exhausted that a bubble bath sounds incredibly necessary. Anything to relax. I can only imagine how irresistible Cameron will be on Monday when I can't reach out and touch him, mess up his hair, and feel the strength of his arms around me.

I bet he'll be wearing a suit. That d-bag.

I turn on the faucet in my bathroom, pouring some Epsom salt bubble mix into the water—because boy am I going to be sore—and walk back into my bedroom to exchange my Cameron-scented clothes for something that won't drive me crazy through the night.

I knew it would be like this once we were both aware of our shared apartment complex. It's too easy to think that I could simply walk over there at any moment and demand more of him. He would probably oblige with no objections, too.

No. I'm filling up a bath. I'm gathering myself for the week ahead. I need to concentrate. Until five o'clock, he is Boss Cameron—and not the Boss Cameron that orders me around in a fun way, either.

On my dresser, my phone lights up with a new text. Oops, I hadn't thought to check that all weekend. My stomach flips when I see "Cameron Sex God" pop up as the sender. Hah, he must have changed his contact when I was in the bathroom at some point. I never bothered to set up a lock on my phone. I always figured I had nothing to hide... But now I *do* have a dirty little secret, I guess.

Cameron Sex God: I can see your light on. Aren't you supposed to be in bed?
Grace: Why are you looking in my window, weirdo? Aren't you supposed to be in bed, too?
Cameron Sex God: I'm taking Buddy for a walk. I figured I'd see if the hot redhead across the street accidentally left her blinds open while she was changing. Sadly not.
Grace: You're distracting me from pretending Cameron Sex God doesn't exist.
Cameron Sex God: Haha, I think the new title is fitting. Much less stuffy than, "Boss Cameron." Plus, I thought we agreed that Boss Cameron was what you called me when you were incredibly happy?
Grace: Define happiness.
Cameron Sex God: Begging for more orgasms?
Grace: Goodnight, Cameron.
Cameron Sex God: See you tomorrow, Holmes.

Although it admittedly kills me to do so, I change his name back to Cameron Kaufman on my phone. God forbid the nickname were to pop up at work.

I look at my full page of texts and noticed that Ramona has texted me upward of ten times, stopping the barrage once to call and leave a voicemail. I skim the first few texts and they all say about the same thing: *Cameron is your boss?!*

Oh, right. Ramona connected the dots between Cameron

and "hot boss" right when Ian opened his damn mouth at Cajun chicken night. Thankfully, she didn't say anything while we were there, but I should have expected calls or texts on the matter. It'd be cruel not to text her back, but I'm not even sure I want to reveal this weekend. I almost want it to just be between us—just Cameron and me. Our secret.

I end up dialing her up anyway, pressing the phone against my ear. She answers within a few rings already screaming.

"No wonder you had trouble focusing at work!" she yells. "My God, Grace, I'm pretty sure he could be a model!"

"Yep, I'm still in the room." Wes's voice comes through the line, and he's much less excited than Ramona.

"You know you don't have to yell on the phone, right?" I say, which she ignores.

"I saw the way you guys were talking during the movie."

"I knew you were distracted..." Wes mumbles.

"Something totally happened afterward, didn't it?" Ramona squeals. "You went home with him!"

"No, I didn't," I lie. "The best thing that came from that night was that now things aren't as awkward."

Wow, I am a master of lies. "Aren't as awkward?" Try more awkward than ever. But at least it will be a good awkward. Is that a thing?

"Well, work will be easier," Wes says, but Ramona's already letting out her sorority-fueled scream. I'm fairly sure that's the first thing they taught her there.

"Girl! There. Is. A. Connection!" Her hand hits the counter with each syllable. She doesn't know the half of it.

I want to tell her. I want to scream from the top of this complex that Cameron was right: He *is* an absolute sex god. But he would get too much satisfaction from that, and I couldn't handle his smug grin—or the police report when I get arrested for climbing to the top of an apartment complex and yelling at two in the morning.

"You're doing the right thing," Wes says, interjecting into his wife's hysteria. "I do like the guy, but the same issue remains. It's work. Don't dip your pen in company ink. Or... I guess it's his pen?"

"We use tablets."

"You get my point."

"Can I keep inviting him over?" Ramona asks, giddy with excitement. "He's Ian's best friend, you're my best friend... it's a connection from heaven."

"Ray, honey, are you even hearing yourself?" Wes asks.

"Office romance can be hot!" she says, and I can hear small kisses being exchanged between the two.

Oh God, I really hope I didn't just accidentally spark some new kink in their relationship. The last thing I need is that mental image.

"Okay, well, I was just returning your call and thousand texts," I say, eyeing my now nearly-full bath.

"Is that a bath?" Ramona asks. "Is he over? Are you guys going to have hot bathroom sex?"

"And I'm hanging up now." I press the button as she is mid-scream saying something about bubbles.

I settle into the water, letting the heat overtake me. I make a mental note about Ramona's bath suggestion, and then let myself drift off, reliving every moment from this weekend and praying for Friday to come once again.

34

GRACE

As I walk in the office today, I keep having the same repeated thought:

I had Cameron Kaufman inside me. I had Cameron Kaufman inside me.

When I make eye contact with Saria, she gives a bored "hello" and I just wave back because I'm scared of what may leave my mouth if I try to greet her with words. Probably something along the lines of:

This hand was on Cameron Kaufman's cock. This hand was on Cameron Kaufman's cock.

But when I get to my desk, I notice possibly the worst thing I could have imagined: An email announcing a workplace harassment seminar for the entire company later this week. My morning went from a mug full of warm coffee to sludge in a cup. I realize I'm staring at my laptop accomplishing zero work, so I pull out my sketchbook with my pen in hand just to look busy, yet no motions flow on paper.

My mind races. Who could have possibly discovered Cameron and I before we'd even had time to process this ourselves? Did HR sit outside of my apartment with binoculars and a ghillie suit, whispering, "Gotcha!" in classic spy fashion?

No—there's no way anyone could know our secret. We stayed in our little apartment complex for the entire weekend. We barely moved between each other's places unless we were out walking the dogs. Hell, we barely moved away from each other's thighs. But maybe someone else lives in our complex, too. Cameron had no idea that I lived there, so why should I expect to know all of our other neighbors?

Before I know it, I'm up from my desk and power walking to Cameron's office, arms pumping beside me as if propelling me forward. I look like some mad woman in an 80s aerobic video. I may as well have five-pound weights in each hand. Yet when I arrive to Cameron's office, Ian's already inside running his hands through his hair.

"She's doing this on purpose, man!" Ian practically yells.

Cameron has his hands out, lowering them repeatedly to signal silence from the madman pacing his office.

Me. He's talking about me. Ian thinks I'm trying to get Cameron fired or get ahead in the company. That's the only explanation. Cameron told him what happened and, even though I've known Ian for years, he's already assuming that I'm plotting some elaborate plan for my boss's demise.

I'll let him have a piece of my mind.

Cameron sees me at the door and waves me in with a small smile on his face.

How is he so calm?

"Keep it down, Ian," Cameron says, turning his attention back to the tall, angry giant pacing back and forth.

"Grace, I need your opinion," Ian snaps.

"Is this about me?" I ask. If he has anything to say, he can say it to my face.

"What?" he asks, his face scrunching up as if offended I would even make this about me. "No. And shut the door."

Cameron exhales. "Sometimes I don't even think this is my office."

Ian misses the humor in it. Or probably doesn't care.

I follow Ian's demands and shut the door. I try to get out of the way as he storms from one end of the office to the other, his long legs completing the distance in only three steps.

"I'm getting a write-up and a harassment prevention seminar!" he bellows. "All I did was say she looked nice on Friday. That's it!"

"Who?" I ask.

Without skipping a beat—almost to the point of interrupting my one-word question—Ian snaps back: "Nia!"

I look over to Cameron as he rises from his chair. He looks so calm—there's not a hint of worry on his features. He's wearing a dark gray button-up with the sleeves rolled up and fitted black jeans, the picture of elegance with his hair perfectly tousled and thrown to the side. Even his beard looks as if it's recently been trimmed.

That beard has been between my thighs.

He takes a seat next to me with just enough distance that I could make one slight movement and we may touch, but also sitting apart so it wouldn't seem like we're trying to do so.

"I think we're all getting this seminar. I'm sure this was a scheduled compliance thing or whatever," Cameron says, attempting to be the voice of reason, but Ian continues to pace.

I'm too busy measuring every centimeter that we're apart.

"She finally wrote me up. And now this?" Ian scoffs. "Doubt it. She's just trying to use her little HR magic to make it seem like she's not singling me out."

Cameron leans forward, resting his elbows on his knees. The movement makes his legs spread outward, shins just barely touching the edge of my knees. It's like nothing else exists in this room apart from this touch. Does Ian seriously not know that the world's axis is now spinning around Cameron and I? How can nobody else feel this shift?

"Is this an annual thing?" I ask in some effort to contribute to the conversation, and Cameron nods.

Our eyes meet and my chest thumps faster. I turn my head to look away as he gives me the most devilish of smiles.

"It's normally in the fall," Cameron says, "Looks like she's moving it up this year."

"And for whom?" Ian shouts.

"Ian, stop it." Cameron raises his voice.

I quiver. Its demanding nature reminds me of this weekend and how he spent quite a bit of it ordering me to do whatever he liked. Is it getting hot in here, or is that just me?

"I'm not an idiot, Cameron," Ian continues. "I would never actually date an office employee. It's a fucking stupid thing to do."

My heart stops, and I can't help but glance over to Cameron to find that he's already looking at me. *Shit.* We avert our eyes and I'm going to straight up pretend that didn't happen.

"Grace, you're smart," Ian says, breaking my thoughts.

"Sure," I choke out. *No, not really.*

"Would you date a co-worker?"

Ian knows. Ian—lawyer shark extraordinaire—totally knows what we did. He can smell it on me like blood in the water.

"No," I say as convincingly as I can.

Ian huffs, too distracted by his own issue to notice my apprehension. "Exactly. Because only idiots would do that. We don't need a fucking seminar or training or whatever the hell this is!"

He stands there, breathing hard, and I avoid eye contact with Cameron. I'm too ashamed to admit that I might be exactly that type of fucking idiot.

35

CAMERON

I shift in the folding chair at the back of the warehouse where we normally hold Beer Friday. Except it is not Friday, there is no beer, and this is definitely *not* fun.

Nia could not have found better timing in scheduling our annual workplace harassment seminar the following day after I do the very thing they're training us to avoid. Employees are scheduled for Thursday, but managers get the lucky task of completing their portion on Monday afternoon. Whoopee.

"Nice to see all your happy faces!" Nia's voice is entirely too peppy for this subject matter, but at least she can express some form of sarcasm because I know as well as she does that there are zero happy faces in this audience. "I hope you have your afternoon coffee!"

I can honestly never tell if HR is actually excited about these subjects, or if her smile is just there for show and all a part of the human resources face that she needs to put on.

"Who's ready for one hour of fun manager trainings?"

No thanks.

Ian's sitting on the spare stool next to me with his arms crossed. To a common bystander, he does look like the "good lawyer," as today he's dressed in a clean-cut suit with an expression of concentration as Nia spouts off more information regarding the seminar. But I can tell he's dying inside by the way he's tapping his foot on the final rung of the stool's leg. He was late enough to the seminar that he could have been holding a private protest, too.

"We have our in-house lawyer, Ian, here to help with any questions you may have at the end," she says, pointing him out.

I turn to look at him and he does not break his stoic eye contact with Nia. That's probably the most I've ever see her smile. It almost has an edge of a smirk to it, if I didn't know any better. She's totally loving how irritated he is.

"We also have gift cards for the first five people that jump in with some good questions." She waves some local convenience store cards above her head.

There's a whoop from the other side of the warehouse. Some of us may hold the title of "manager," but at the end of the day, we're just kids that became adults and were mistakenly given responsibility. This is never more apparent than during seminars geared specifically toward the management.

Ian scoffs and leans down to speak in my ear, "My write-up punishment included extending my office hours during this week to answer questions."

"Shouldn't you be doing that anyway?" I whisper back.

He shoots me a glare that clearly states, "whose side are you on?" I cringe and turn away from him. Might be best to not to wave that particular flag at this bull for the time being.

Nia clears her throat. "This seminar should serve as a reminder of the need to maintain cognizant of employee boundaries."

Employee boundaries? I think I may have crossed those when I was balls deep in my employee this weekend. A side smile works its way up my face, and I have to force it back down.

Nia goes on to start the presentation. It's the same thirty-minute video we watch every single year as a company, except there's an additional twenty-minute segment at the end where they review your responsibilities as a supervisor and "doing your due diligence." You know—that one thing I didn't practice this weekend.

The man on the screen asks the audience why it's no longer acceptable to tell a co-worker they're good looking and what direction the world is going in if even that's offensive. He seems genuinely confused and exhausted at how much trouble he's gotten himself into with this fictional company as the video continues on to explain why his actions were wrong.

I feel ya, buddy.

I'm too busy reliving my own wrong doing over and over. Grace's legs spread for me, my hands across her body, her mouth against mine...

I reach into my pocket to pull out my phone. I keep it flush with my thigh so that hopefully nobody can see, but my expression gives away my disappointment. No texts from Grace at all. I'm not sure what I expected. Some dirty picture? No... but I can't say I'd be disappointed if I got one. It's just that we haven't spoken one-on-one since last night and, by the time this meeting started, she was already so nose-deep in work that I felt making up an excuse to talk to her would just be obvious and unwelcome.

"That is the final straw," the woman in the video says, monotone, pointing her finger in the chest of a man in a suit. "I am filing a complaint. I mean business."

I look up when Ian exhales, but he's not looking at me or my phone. His arms are still crossed in defiance. I understand his frustration with it all, and I did admittedly have a small panic attack when I had noticed the annual harassment compliance had been moved from October to June, but how important do I think I am to assume this whole seminar is about Grace and me?

It took some moments of composure, but by the time Ian stormed into my office also assuming it was because of *him*, I realized our secret was safe.

I move to the text message window and quickly type out something. It's not anything special or intelligent, but I need an excuse to talk to her. It's already been too long.

Cameron: Hi.

Masterpiece right there. I place my phone in my lap and flip it over, inhaling deeply.

I can't remember the last time I was this nervous for a response. It was definitely before Abby. I'm not sure I've *ever* been excited by the prospect of receiving a text back.

My phone buzzes and I fumble for the unlock. There, in the sender line, in big bold, beautiful letters is the name I so desperately want: Grace Holmes.

I swipe the text open, hoping to see anything that suggests another late-night session or simply asking if I'll be at the apartment.

Grace: What an opener. Real pickup artist.

I stifle a laugh, look to make sure Ian isn't watching (nope, still brooding) and text her back.

Cameron: Seems to work out okay for me so far.
Grace: You and that well-endowed charmer of yours.
Cameron: I'll have you know I am currently sitting in the
harassment seminar for managers and I feel personally
harassed right now.

She doesn't text back right away. I see a couple dots cycle in bouncing motions then disappear, reappear again, then nothing. She must have gotten busy. It's still a work day, and I'm willing to bet she's overanalyzing her designs as usual. I wouldn't know—I haven't done a lick of paperwork this morning. I've been too distracted by Grace and the memory of her body.

I glance back up to the screen. At some point the video changed to a scene of a guy leaning forward to kiss a woman, but she backs up just before they make contact. Then I see my phone light up in my hand. I peek down.

Grace: Getting any ideas?

A wide grin spreads across my face and I shift the phone against my leg once more, partially moving it closer to my center in an attempt to cover myself. She has this pull on me. And by me, I mean my dick. It's like a magnet constantly searching to find its mate.

I inhale sharply before flipping it over and typing fast, peering out of the corner of my eye to see if Ian has noticed just yet. Thankfully, no.

Cameron: Why? Do you want to drop by the boss's office later? I bet there's an assignment he can give you.
Grace: I'll expect a calendar event for 4:00 p.m.
Cameron: I believe you should.

"Do you want us to get yelled at?" Ian hisses to me, flipping my phone out of my hand from underneath. It clatters to the floor, and I raise my hand in apology to the various people glaring my way.

Nosy fuckers.

Ian raises his eyebrows in disapproval and I'm wondering

just when he became so concerned with good behavior. Probably the second Nia wrote him up. I bet it's eating him up inside.

My phone buzzes again and I peer down to read the message before pocketing it with a smile as Ian punches my arm in irritation.

Grace: To wear underwear or not to wear underwear. That is the question.

She's a siren; a succubus just waiting to swallow me whole. My own fiery goddess.

And I'm the fool surrendering to her willingly.

36

GRACE

"Is it weird that harassment prevention videos are an aphrodisiac?" Cameron asks.

I shut the door to his office and lean against the handle, smiling as he stands opposite me, sitting on his desk. He runs his fingers through his hair, and it chills me to the bone. His large hands are much too far away from me. Like a candle to a flame, I'm already walking toward him, settling myself between his open legs.

"I think it makes you a sociopath," I whisper, reaching my hand up to stroke his jawline and ghost my fingers over his trimmed beard. His hands go to my waist and he pulls me closer, gripping my sides tighter as his hands run along the stitching of my dress. If I could read minds, I'd be willing to bet he wants to rip it off of me.

"Good. Now I have a medical excuse to ravage you."

I can't help but let out a quick exhale, shaky and longing for more. He leans down to kiss my neck, inhaling and nibbling every piece of skin he touches while his hands trail down my dress to the slit on the side, parting it to stroke the outside of my underwear.

"Damn," he breathes. "I was hoping you'd gone with the other option."

"Maybe I wanted you to work for it."

He lets out a low groan, gripping my waist tighter and applying more pressure to the circles he's now forming against my sensitive spot. It's a part of me so excited to remove the layer of fabric that separates me from his deft fingers that I know can destroy me in only a few minutes.

His heavy breaths carry up my neck and to my ear. "Do you want me to take you on this desk?" he growls, moving his hand on my waist and caressing the underside of my breast, teasing how close he is to me. "Can you picture my hands pinching your nipples? My fingers deep inside you?"

Surely he can feel the wetness against his fingers. I will myself to not moan at the sound of the anticipation in his voice.

My gaze shifts to the windows. The blinds are as closed as they can be, pulled taut against each other. Nobody can see us, but my heart races. I can't tell if I'm nervous to be caught or thrilled that it's a possibility. It's the risk that someone could walk in and see Cameron's body pressed against mine as he possesses me body and soul that makes my heart pound. The feminist in me likes to think I would be on top, but I'm craving to be bent over the table, submitting to his will.

"Do you want to be mine, Holmes?" he croons, his voice vibrating between us. "I can feel you tensing up. You're close and we haven't even started."

He's not wrong. The area between my legs is practically shivering and his touch feels more and more pleasurable with each circle of his finger across my clit. I hadn't even noticed I was being pushed further to the edge as he spoke, but my breath is stilted and I'm trying my hardest to not make a noise.

I never imagined my job would lead to this type of opportunity. I'd hoped for advancement and learning the art of design.

I didn't dream that I would be in my boss's office as he teases me close to climax.

My boss.

I back away, causing his hand to slip out from under my dress and his grip on me to release. "I—I should lock the door," I stammer, pointing over my shoulder and giving an uncomfortable laugh.

He raises an eyebrow, and maybe in that moment I felt myself release all the tension that had building, but it's ramped back up when he leans forward to clutch my hips once more. Without any resistance, I step back between his legs. He hops off the table, whipping me around and bending me over, running his hand along the length of my back and pressing his strained zipper against my ass.

I spread my arm across his desk and knock over a couple items.

"Have you always wanted to do that, Holmes?" he asks with a laugh.

"No, I've always wanted to be fucked over the desk."

He groans unrestrained, and I laugh. He reaches across to cover my mouth with his hand and I moan against it. He's grinding against me and I hear his belt buckle coming undone. It's the sound of pure anticipation and want.

But then, just as quickly as I dive into his touch, a knock on the door sounds. I sit up and Cameron fumbles with his buckle. I straighten my dress and scramble to the couch.

The door handle turns, and then opens, revealing Mr. Feldman, clipboard in hand.

"Oh," he says and my heart sinks.

What must he think? Do I look as guilty as I feel? My heart is racing a million miles an hour, I'm clearly out of breath, and, God, am I sweating?

"I didn't know you had a meeting," he says. "I'm leaving for the day."

I open my mouth to speak but Cameron jumps in. "It was on our calendars. Four o'clock. We were planning to speak with you on this tomorrow. Hopefully flesh out some things."

He's smooth and more vocal than I am right now. I can't even form a sentence and I'm thankful he has his wits about him enough to cover for the both of us.

"Right, well, then let's do that," Mr. Feldman agrees, reaching into his pocket to pull out his phone. "I'll be in town until three tomorrow so let's try for noon, shall we? My treat for lunch. We'll order in."

I want to have more of this man's kindness spread across the room. I'm soaking it in like an antidote to the illness Cameron has bestowed upon me, paranoia and fear radiating from me like an aura. I'm terrified. The past minute could have ended badly, and I'm stunned that fate felt gracious enough to allow the moment to have passed with zero casualties.

I mimic his movements, pulling out my phone and seeing that Cameron was indeed smart enough to add the four o'clock event titled "Brainstorming" to both our calendars. I'll have to thank him later for his stroke of genius.

An invite comes in from Mr. Feldman, and I nod to him in acknowledgement. He takes his leave and we're left, just the two of us, phones ignored in our hands, eyes scanning every inch of each other's skin. I still need to feel his breath against me, whispering dirty words into my ear, but I think I just felt my career flash before my eyes. Heart in my stomach, I hope he feels it, too.

My pinky is extended when I walk back over to him and he's gripping the edge of his desk already laughing.

"You've got to quit with the pinky swears," he groans, rolling his head on his neck.

I keep my finger out. "Promise no more office hookups," I whisper, now that the door is wide open.

He inhales and exhales heavily as if being reprimanded by

a teacher. He's been caught doing something—cheating on a test, sneaking out of class, groping the girlfriend in the back of the theater—and he has zero remorse.

Reluctantly, he links his pinky with mine and smiles. I've signed a deal with the devil, and as long as he plays the game fairly, I'm quite okay with it.

Though, do I really expect fairness from a demon?

37

CAMERON

I TRY to cut out at exactly five o'clock to make my way home and clean the place. Grace sent me a text earlier saying she was going to leave a bit later so as not to raise suspicion. Smart girl.

All day I've been antsy, consumed by the need to touch her soft, freckled skin, to smell her flowery scent, to taste every inch of her. And now it's a little past six thirty, and my patience is wearing thin. I've done everything I can. I cleaned every surface of empty counterspace, took Buddy for a walk, and even attempted some architecture sketches. But nothing can distract me from my need for one thing: Grace fucking Holmes.

I hear a knock at the door and there she is: At my doorstep, purse slung over her shoulder, full lips slightly parted.

As soon as she steps inside, she's in my arms and our mouths are pressed against each other as if our lives will end should we part. She fumbles for my belt buckle, but I'd prepared in advance and changed to gym shorts the second I got home. She groans in relief once she realizes and rips my pants down with ease, releasing my cock, fully erect as if it's been waiting for her.

I run my hands through her thick hair, and she returns the

gesture, one hand scouring my scalp, the other grabbing my exposed length and pumping up and down with fervor.

"Where have you been?" I ask, pulling her head back to speak, trying to compose myself as she strokes me. I want to look in her eyes, but by instinct they close. The pleasure of her touch washes over me and I'm already lightheaded.

"Not driving fast enough, apparently." She grips my hair to pull me back to her, and our mouths smash together once more.

I back into my bedroom, kicking the door open wider. There are small whines coming from the kitchen, where I'd preemptively propped up a baby gate to section Buddy off from us. I couldn't risk him doing something unruly once we were naked. Sorry, pal.

I try to turn her to the bed, but she twists around fast and pushes me down so that I blink in surprise. It happens so fast: She reaches up the skirt of her dress and tugs down her underwear until they slide to her ankles and she steps out of them. I compulsively want to pull her down on me, but she's already making her way to the side table where she pulls out a condom. Seems she's gotten very accustomed to knowing exactly where they are.

She unpackages it and slides the condom over me before climbing on top. I grip her ass as she lowers down without waiting another second. She's so insatiable. Her pussy surrounds every inch of me. Wet and hungry, licking her lips and bending down to place one final kiss on my lips, she rises back up and down again.

Her hips move front to back, riding me like an animal, and she places her hands on my sides to keep herself steady. I continue to massage her ass, guiding her. It's the perfect size for my palms—round and moldable—but even my guidance seems fruitless as she continues to take control. She looks down at me with a vixen smile, and in this moment, and I can't imagine redoing any decisions that would have led me to this point. Work policies? Fuck that shit.

Grace grinds faster, head falling back as she moans my name. She even throws in a "Mr. Kaufman," which really sends me flying. I pump into her harder. Her cries of pleasure are almost distant and muffled. It's hard to concentrate on anything but the feeling of her around me.

I feel a rising sensation in my balls, and I groan. My gut clenches and I can feel myself releasing, filling the condom with everything I have. Grace is still going, sliding down to take all of me inside her, then rising back up over and over.

I reach back to slap her ass. She moans and I hit it once more, shuddering as she falls to my chest. Grace sucks in sharply as she comes, gripping my hair and tugging as the orgasm rolls through her.

We lay there for a moment, me still inside her as her body covers mine, until she sits up, both her hands on either side of my head.

"How was your day, honey?"

"Maddening," I say, sitting up to place a hard kiss on her lips. She licks mine once we part and another low whine escapes me. "You're going to be the death of me, woman."

38

GRACE

"When was the last time you were upset? Like, really, really upset?"

"I don't get upset," he deadpans.

"Heartless bastard."

We're lying in my bed with both dogs surrounding us, and Cameron is stroking my splayed-out hair on the pillows. We've been in this position for what feels like every night for the past few weeks. Cameron kept his promise and continued to keep work separate from our play time. Although, admittedly, he did slip up. There was that one time in the copier room…

We've been talking about everything under the sun as I try to capture every moment I can. I want to know about his childhood, what sports he played, when he first masturbated—okay, so maybe not that—or maybe just a little, but I want to know everything. I need to know how he ticks.

"Well other than Abby," he starts, making my heart sink. He rubs my templates and it instantly calms me. "I guess when my parents split."

"I didn't know you were a divorce baby," I say.

He chuckles. "That makes it sound almost sweet."

"Hah! No, no, just," I sigh. "You seem partially well-adjusted."

"Thanks?"

"You're welcome." I curl closer to him and he grips my shoulder in a side-hug, loosening his grip after a moment or two.

"Wait—let me guess your life," he says. "Dog by the fireplace? Cookies in the oven? Parents holding hands and reading a book as you color with crayons on the floor?"

I smile because, yeah, kind of. It's picturesque and everything I've always wanted. It's a life that's possible and one that I lived—in close proximity to the unconditional love my parents shared.

"Sweet potato fries in the oven, but close."

"Of course."

"Well you don't have to be bitter about it," I say, tugging his hair as he tugs mine back.

"I don't believe that type of happiness exists," he says giving a slight shrug as I balk at him.

"Come on, seriously? Of course it does."

"Nah, nothing lasts," he says, blowing out a raspberry in my direction. "Are your parents still together?"

My chest sinks and I give a weak smile. I never like discussing this. It's wonderful and tragic. We could practically be a Shakespeare tragedy. "My dad died a few years ago."

His eyes widen. "Oh." He looks away from me and repeats himself. "Oh."

"That's it?" I tease, trying to breathe normally and snuggle my nose against his shoulder to lighten the mood. "No condolences?"

Cameron's head turns to me as he goes back to stroking my head. "I'm sorry. How?"

"Side street. Mugging. The usual suspects."

"Don't let that lessen it."

"I don't," I say. "It hurt for a while. My mom was barely holding it together. I think Joe gave her hope."

Cameron's eyes give him away. His attempt at concealing a cringe at the mention of my ex fails, but I continue.

"It was supposed to be my chance at a love she lost. But a lot of good that did."

"And Joe?" Cameron asks, opening it to anything I want to share. But what is there to say? He was nothing like my father, and yet I wanted everything from him? I expected too much?

"I found a dating app on his phone. He didn't want marriage. We always fought. Once again, the usual suspects."

Cameron glares, shutting his eyes for a second and turning away from me once more to look up at the ceiling. "I'm sorry, Holmes."

"Now there's the sorrow I wanted," I giggle.

He turns to me with a smirk and tickles under my chin. I embrace the butterflies swooping through my chest and let them overtake me. When I close my eyes, I wonder if the stars I see are just my imagination or the hope pounding through.

I hear a whine from one of the dogs at the end of the bed, followed by a bark.

"Hank probably thinks I'm hurting you," Cameron chuckles. I open my eyes again when I feel him bend down to scratch Hank behind the ear. The old boy lets out a low huff in response, but drifts back off to sleep once he sees me smiling like a fool.

"You're so good with Hank."

"When you have a dog like Buddy, it's easy to love the calm ones."

"Why Buddy?" I ask.

"What do you mean?"

"The name. It seems so cliché for a dog name."

"How dare you," he gasps in mock offense. "Buddy was my first friend after my quarter-life crisis. Sure, that crisis included a lot of nineties movies, but Buddy is proudly named after a basketball champion." At his name, Buddy's head jerks up, instantly awake. Cameron pats him on the head and he falls back asleep just as easily as Hank did.

"Oh, tell me you're joking. *Air Bud*, seriously?"

"You know, you're a lot more of an asshole once you get to know you," he says. "You're more of an animal. Well, in one sense of the word, but, hey!" He laughs as I punch him in the arm. He lifts his free hand that isn't over the pillows and allows my fist to beat into his hand.

"And I'm still correct one hundred percent of the time, right?"

"Pssht, thirty," he says, rolling his eyes.

"One hundred."

"Sixty."

"One hundred."

He pauses then laughs. "You're not letting up this time, are you?"

"I think I'm destined to get your job," I say, not stopping myself before wiggling my eyebrows up and down.

He snorts. "Not if we're caught first."

The sentence punches me in the gut, but I try not to let it show. I keep forcing myself to forget the position we're in. I want to just enjoy these moments we have. I look down and see Hank's head on Cameron's legs while Buddy rests over the both of us, chest in the air and back feet kicking in his sleep.

I like this, but I also like—no, love—my career. The little spot I've holed my way into in this company has been a product my pushiness and my continued motto of "fake it 'til you make it" where even if an idea is lackluster, I want to be the first to yell it out in hopes it may stick.

Having all of that work taken away is the last thing I want.

My eyes trail to him and he stares off into space as well, his jawline tightening and his eyes steady, focused on whatever he's nursing in his mind. I feel a wave wash over my chest and it's like something is off, but I can't put my finger on what.

"Do you like your job?" I ask, and he turns back to me. His mouth contorts a bit as he thinks then he shrugs once more in ambivalence.

"I guess not," he says, no signs of remorse.

"Do you not want something more?" I ask. "What about architecture?"

"Let's talk about something else. Big life decisions aren't really my thing."

Big life decisions are my thing through and through. I thrive on the idea that if something isn't enough, I refuse to be okay with it. I enjoy the excitement when you know the choices made were the correct ones. I like the rollercoaster rides that come with something new.

"Don't you want a future?" I ask.

"Who really knows what that even is?" he asks, staring at me.

I wonder if I'm prepared for this rollercoaster. I wonder if he is.

39

GRACE

You would think with work and Cameron Kaufman being so intertwined, it would come naturally to balance the two but of course, it's impossible for me to have anything truly easy. My life is split between long evenings in Cameron's bed, and even longer nights completing work with only the light of my tablet to guide me into the following day.

Cameron and I went back to staying late at the office, leaving for a quickie at the apartment, then bringing back our dogs. We could have stayed at the complex, but there was work to be done, and the office has the network with all the files we needed. If we stay at our apartments, then I'd get zero work done. However, I *would* have a nice handprint on my ass which, you know, it's kind of a toss-up as to which I'd prefer. Instead, we're confined to late nights where we play fetch with the dogs and steal occasional kisses in the break room. He may or may not have made me orgasm under my desk once or twice, but how am I supposed to say no when a man buries himself under your dress while you work?

Not me, that's who.

But, as far as we know, everyone is none-the-wiser by the time we wrap up our project with Mr. Feldman on a Friday a month later.

We've gathered in a circle in the back of the warehouse, all of our drinks raised to the ceiling as we toast to the end of a project.

Cameron and Ian go to get refills. It's weird how much of a balancing game this has become. It's little things, like how I get a sense of relief when someone else asks to refill my drink before Cameron can. Even though it's common courtesy from anyone to ask fellow company if they need a favor while the person is up, it feels more obvious if Cameron tries to do it for me. So, I agreed when Ian offered to refill my drink first.

I stand, looking up at the poster we printed with the new logo for Mr. Feldman's company. It's gone through many iterations since our first meeting, but they still chose to keep the 80s magenta I'd pitched on day one. My heart swells at the sight of it.

"You did that," says a warm, husky voice behind me. Without looking away from the poster, I reach out my hand and a beer is placed in it, foaming at the top with a dark, rich color to it.

"I did that," I say, eliciting a chuckle.

I look to my left and see Cameron shaking his head as he raises the glass to his mouth. "You were supposed to be more modest and say 'we' did this."

"No," I muse, narrowing my eyes. "Because I did this." I look behind me and then back to Cameron. "Where's Ian?"

"Talking to Nia," he laughs. "What's new?"

I shrug. "Good point."

"You know what is new, though," he says, looking at the ground to shuffle his feet and then large swig of beer. "We have another client asking for you to head the next project."

"What?" I ask. My heart thumps in my chest. "I mean—I *am* an obvious choice."

"Hey," Cameron warns, and I grin.

"But they don't even know me."

"Apparently Mr. Feldman's been spreading your name around town like wildfire," Cameron says.

I try to open my mouth, but it keeps closing before I can speak. I can't find the words to form what I'm thinking. Holy cow, this is amazing? When do I start? Can I pinch myself because this seems like I'm dreaming?

"Are you serious?" I whisper, leaning in. Cameron's dimples deepen on one side as he has a lopsided smile.

"Yeah, Holmes." He looks left and right, seeing that most people have moved away from the back wall and have started playing beer pong. He steps up next to me, his arm hanging flush with my side, letting the outside of his pinky discreetly brush along mine. "You did that."

I'm taking deep, staggered breaths. I feel the electric sensation of his skin on my mine, traveling through me, lighting up every vein and setting my nerves aflame. My head feels like it's floating above my body, light and airy and disconnected from what may be right. But it's so beautiful in the clouds—who cares?

And then I look at our team's design—a design I had heavy influence in creating—and I'm proud of myself. I'm so proud that the sensation is less like floating, but maybe like an ocean with the waves rising and falling over my chest, the tide pulled me deeper into my passion.

But I also know that at any minute the tide could take me, and then where would I be?

"What's got Little Red Riding Hood in a daze?" asks Ian, making me jump.

Cameron's hand jerks from mine as we both turn from the

wall to face Ian, but it's too late. His gaze travels to our hands, his eyebrow lifting. One small exhale from Ian tells me everything I need to know.

"We should talk," he says, scanning between the two of us, but gesturing at Cameron, "Now. Right, Big Bad Wolf?"

40

CAMERON

I FEEL like I'm being reprimanded by my parents. They always said very general statements, emphasized as to why my mistake was an important lesson, but then never really went on to take any disciplinary actions. They were all bark and no bite—like Ian is.

Grace stands next to me, her arms crossed and mouth pursed. "And why do you think that?" she snaps, narrowing her eyes.

I don't sense the same vote of confidence in Ian from her.

"Cameron suddenly can't go to bars as much because he's staying later at the office," Ian says. "Ramona tells me that you're too busy with work to hang out with her and Wes."

"That's true," Grace says.

"I saw your tits," Ian says, rubbing his fingernails on his shoulder and looking at them absentmindedly.

Grace's eyes widen, and I feel my heart beat in my chest. He fucking saw Grace naked? When the hell did this happen? Grace's glare feels hot enough to burn straight through Ian's head.

"Genius here showed me pictures of his hotel build," he continues.

My chest puffs out a bit. I've admittedly been trying to draw more. I was proud of a mock-up I made and showed it to Ian, but then it suddenly hits me, and I'm deflated once more.

"Oh shit."

"Next in line was you, Grace. Right on display." Ian shoves his hands in his pockets and raises his eyebrows. "If you weren't my sister's best friend, I'd say those were fucking wonderful tits." He whistles low and I inhale sharply as a warning to him. He holds up a hand. "Relax."

Grace narrows her eyes. "Maybe you shouldn't snoop on someone else's phone. I'm sure whoever that was would be very upset."

I commend her for trying.

"Maybe don't send naked pictures to each other." Ian shrugs.

He's not the one on trial here so what does he care?

"How do you know that was me?" Grace asks, crossing her arms. She's not letting this die, but I know exactly what picture he's referring to, and there is no denying it is her. She sent it to me from her bathtub. The suds were strategically placed around her except where her chest stays afloat of the water. Apart from her ocean blue eyes staring directly in the camera with a "please come over and spank me" look (which I think was the exact text she sent with the picture), her bright red hair would give her away easily.

"Maybe he just has a thing for redheads." She shrugs. "In which case, thank you for the warning, Ian. Now I know to avoid him."

"Hey!" I say, pointing my finger at her.

"I refuse to be fetishized by my hair!" she says back, sticking out her tongue.

She can be fetishized for *much more* than the color of her hair.

"This is fun and all," says Ian, "but I know you guys are doing the dirty, so just stop it."

I run my hands through my hair, flopping it to the side. The humidity, combined with my own rising anxiety in being in this whole situation is doing me zero favors. "It's nothing," I lie. "We'll stop, Ian."

"No, hang on," Grace protests, shooting one arm out. "Don't I have an argument here? We"—she moves her index finger back and forth between herself and me—"are not doing anything."

"You also sext during work," Ian says with a sigh, as if he's done with these games, but Grace relents.

"Incorrect—I text my mom during work."

"In between sexting me," I toss in and she gasps, her hand slapping to her heart.

"Betrayal," she breathes out.

I hold back a smile.

"It means nothing," I repeat to Ian. "We did it once, we've been thinking about it since, but it's strictly been about the project."

The lies spill out of my mouth with difficulty. I've been seeing Grace's bare ass regularly for a little over a month now, and it's like I've been granted a gift every time she exposes herself. She has this habit of walking around the apartment nude, wide, freckled hips swinging side to side, and sending little insults my way every chance she can get. Nothing has changed since the day we met, and yet I get the added bonus of seeing her naked.

Fuck me for feeling like this is going well, right?

I look over at Grace and her eyebrows are stitched in toward the middle. I throw a grin at her, hoping to ease her concerns, and she gives me a slow smile. I know she has her worries. I know her career means the world to her. But Ian is not going to be the person who pulls this cancel card on us.

"I don't believe you," he says, staring at the both of us. "But that's because I'm a lawyer and you two are horrible liars. Just... be more careful."

There's a moment of silence and then Grace half-heartedly laughs. "My tits are pretty hot, right?"

41

CAMERON

WE SHOWER that night after sex and take a quick round two in the process, but the entire time my stomach is growling, Grace's as well, and we can't stop laughing long enough to finish up. I've never met a girl like Grace. Abby and I, whenever we did have sex, would do the deed and continue on with our lives. She would head to a different room and browse her phone, and I'd be left with a feeling of something missing. I'm now wondering if maybe that something had been Grace the whole time and I just didn't know it yet.

Grace runs to her apartment to bring over Hank, and then we're both moving through the kitchen, trying to scrounge up anything I may have for food that isn't for the dogs. Unfortunately, I've reverted to a bachelor lifestyle since getting my own place, and Grace is not much of a cook. All we're left with is sugary cocoa cereal. I expect her to be a bit put-off, but she brings out the bowls and spoons as if this were a gourmet meal ready for the taking. A girl after my own heart.

Buddy bounces between the two of us, rising on his hind legs, begging for food from anyone one who will bestow pity upon him, while Hank is in the corner of the living room trying his best to set a good example. Or maybe that's his clever way of playing the "good dog" card and conning us into food as well.

I go to the living room and plop into my bean bag chair, patting the brand new one next to me.

"You bought another chair?" Grace laughs, situating herself in it, adjusting my big t-shirt before it swallows her in the process.

"I bought it during lunch today." The new bean bag chair is bright red and not exactly the same shade of Grace's hair, as she's a bit more orange-y, but seeing her in it is exactly what I imagined when I picked it up. I knew that eventually I would need to provide some sort of accommodations apart from my bed. Plus, the end of a project seemed the right time to splurge on some new furniture.

I may not have enough design sense to buy a couch, but I can at least treat my lady to a bean bag chair.

"What a gentleman," she says, taking a spoonful of cereal and crunching it in her mouth, making her cheeks big.

"What are you, a squirrel?" I laugh.

"I was going for hamster," she mumbles through the bite before swallowing. "They're cuter."

"Nah, just be you. You're the cutest," I cheese, leaning forward to kiss her cheeks, but she recoils.

"Ew! Gross, you can't be mushy."

To be honest, I've never really thought of myself as a mushy type, but she brings it out in me. I want to adore her every second I get. And part of me wants to treasure every moment I can because eight hours of every day I have to pretend I don't even see her beyond being my employee, aside from the occasional sexy text she sends me, and I need to make up for that lost time.

"Speaking of mushy, you promised you wouldn't play favorites!" she says, pushing me.

My eyes widen and my smile falters. "What?"

"Telling me new clients want me," she scoffs. "Come on, Cameron. That was sweet, but—"

"I wasn't joking."

I had a meeting with a new client the day before and he had said exactly what I'd told her before Ian's interruption: "Mr. Feldman says you have a girl here that we would be stupid not to use." I found it hard to disagree. All I did was follow the necessary steps to get everything approved through HR so the ball could get rolling faster and admire the look on her face when she received the news.

She squints at me and smiles. "You're a liar."

"Not at all." I raise my hand in a boy scout oath and grin. "Your work speaks for itself and everyone knows it."

Her small smile turns into a wide grin. "So, I'm going to be a team lead?"

"Unfortunately for me," I say.

She lets out a small squeal and leans back into her beanbag chair, beaming up at the ceiling. I let her take in the feeling.

"Okay, so, now what do we do with you?" she asks.

My dick gets hard at the possibilities and I crouch out of my beanbag chair, resting my weight on my hand to get closer.

"What do you *want* to do with me?"

"No, Cameron!" she laughs, pushing my chest away to sit me back in my chair. I don't understand what she means by this now, but I'm still intrigued.

"What do we do about your architecture?" she asks.

Intrigue gone. I groan—and it isn't the type of groan I wish she'd elicited out of me.

Ian's pushed me about pursuing my architecture dream before, and he learned a long time ago that it was a lost cause. But Grace has been relentless. By the way her eyes dart between mine and the sketches hanging over every inch of my wall near the corner desk, I know we're diving into yet another one of those conversations.

"Let's not talk about it." I shovel more cereal into my mouth. "Let's talk about you some more."

She gets stern, arching an eyebrow. "No. I think you're so talented. Why do you go for it? What are you scared of?"

"It's too much risk."

"Ugh, you and your risk."

"I've built this career," I continue. "I've invested time. I'm a fucking director, for God's sake." She doesn't seem convinced.

"It was a lot of risk for me to quit my old job," she says. "I didn't even have a job lined up."

"Well now, that is just irresponsible," I tease, but she doesn't smile back. "Grace. It's complicated."

"It's really not."

"Hey, I just don't take chances," I say, huffing. "I don't like long-term, life-changing commitments. You know I've never gotten a tattoo?" I say.

"Well, of course," she says, her grin apprehensive. "I think I've seen most of you. I would have found one hiding somewhere by now."

"Exactly," I wink. "Why do you think I never married or had kids?"

She shrugs and I see her smile falter a bit. *No, no, don't make that go away.*

"You're the biggest chance I've taken in years," I say, setting my bowl down and taking her hand. It's soft, just like the rest of her. She may put on this act of a hardened soul, but if you get past her fire, she's just a golden retriever puppy waiting to come out. "And I'm not even sure if that was the smartest thing."

The words were meant to be a joke, but the moment I see her face, I know I've made a mistake. My stomach drops as she rips her hand from mine and gets up.

"No, Grace, wait." It's all happening so fast: She places her bowl in the sink and rushes to the bedroom. "You know what I mean."

"No, I don't." She pats her leg, harder than she probably should have in her fiery anger. "Come on, Hank."

Did I say she was soft? I definitely underestimated her. As usual. Hank looks at me as if apologizing and then follows his master. *Traitor.*

"Hey, let's get a time machine and restart," I plead.

"You can shove your time machine up your ass, Cameron Kaufman," she says, whipping around to me. "This was a shit decision. I know that. I've risked a lot sleeping with you. I love my career and I don't want to trade it for the world."

"Listen, I know," I say, lifting myself from the chair as if trying to tame the beast in front of me. "I get it. We both have—"

"No, you don't get it," she snaps. "I chose you. I had a choice and I chose you."

The apartment is silent. I can hear a car honking outside that breaks some of the tension, but the rising and falling of her chest and the heavy breaths that accompany them is a symphony of regret.

It dawns on me that she's right. I'd never considered it was choice, but now it's perfectly clear: It was a choice between our careers and each other. And we chose each other. The difference is that I don't care about my job. I wanted her and everything else was just noise.

"I need to choose myself for once," she says. "Joe made me think I was only good enough for dumb ass call centers, and now that I'm doing what I love—what I'm actually good at—I'm risking everything by sleeping with my boss. And for what? You don't even want anything more." Each word hits me harder and harder. Tears gather in her eyes but don't fall. "No kids? No marriage? Nothing?" She sounds so defeated it breaks my heart.

We hadn't discussed marriage or kids between us. After Abby, I've been left with this idea that bringing it up would only cause issues. But with Grace, it wasn't that I just didn't want to bring it up. It's that I hadn't even considered it. We've been so caught up in each other—in the pure happiness of being around each other—that kids or marriage hadn't even been on my radar. I've been too distracted by her. But now I'm considering these things and, as the words fall out of her mouth with pure disdain and disappointment, I can't help but feel slightly empowered by them.

"Have you even asked?" I say, and she exhales, closing her eyes and bringing one hand to her temple.

"What a dumb question to ask my boss," she breathes. "Want marriage to accompany this ass, Mr. Kaufman? Want to throw in kids, too?" Her voice is mocking. "Or how about you have some stupid two-month fling with your most junior designer and get all of it for free? Then, how about everyone finds out and your junior designer loses the one thing she's worked hard for and you're good to continue working your lost dream?"

I sit there for a few moments, taking in the headache of it all. I've been living in some make-believe fairytale for weeks. I've been soaking in this idea of a happily ever after, but what in the world am I thinking? That we run away and never go back to work? It's unfair to her and her dreams. And my selfish ass hadn't even considered that.

But I can't answer; the words just aren't there.

"Exactly," she whispers. And with that, she and Hank are out of my apartment.

I place my head in my hands and turn to pace the apartment.

Who even is Cameron Kaufman? I'm in a career I've grown to hate, doing less work and more management than I ever wanted, and I'm so unhappy that I almost threw it away for some fling? But is this even a *fling*?

No, it's not. Grace is the first woman to get me—really get

me. This is beyond some fun-fest between co-workers. It's something big and I know it. But she's right. She's getting her life in check, and maybe I need to rethink mine as well.

What have I always wanted? What would make me happy?

I take my hands from my face and look up to see all the blueprints hanging on my wall. The papers represent hours and hours of extracurricular work from the past couple years that have given me nothing. There's been no payout and no pats on the back. So why have I continued to do these?

I've put in so much effort. And for what? For them to just hang there?

I reach over to my phone and dial, putting it on speaker phone as I pace between the drawings, tracing a finger of their lines, analyzing their strokes. The phone continues to ring.

Shit, what am I doing?

I run back to my phone and my finger twitches over the red disconnect button, but I'm too late.

"Hello?"

I let out a small, desperate, laugh.

"Hey, Abby."

42

GRACE

"Scoundrel," Ramona hisses when I meet her for coffee during lunch the following week. "The damn scoundrel."

I caved and told her everything. If it truly was over, I figure if my best friend knew, then it wouldn't matter. Plus, her brother knows, so it would make it back to her eventually and she'd be less than happy that he had a leg up on her.

"He's not a scoundrel," I say. "And where are you from? The 1950s?"

"Was killing a man legal at that time?" Ramona asks.

"No, just easier to get away with." I shake my head and tip the decaf coffee toward my mouth. I've been trying not to overdo the amount of caffeine going into my body in the afternoons. I've been staying up later and I prefer to have only one mug in the morning and my trusty one at eight o'clock for good measure so I can make it through the night. Because that's totally healthy.

"Anyway," I say, "we're doing what we said we would do, I guess."

"Pretending like nothing happened?"

"Yep."

"How is he in meetings?" she asks. "Is it weird?"

I pause and rock my head side to side. "How do I word this... No, not really because we keep it professional, but also yes because we totally roleplayed screwing on the conference room table and now that's all I think about?"

I should have learned my lesson from the first time Cameron and I kissed: You cannot avoid the man you are in love with if you work for him.

We've been having daily morning meetings with only myself, Cameron, and our new client, Mr. Watts. As Cameron said, this new guy requested me as a design lead, and I could not have been more thrilled. But the moment was soured when I had to shake Cameron's hand in good faith to keep things on the down-low. It hit a bit too close to home.

We're biding time before we announce my promotion and new creative lead title. He's hoping that the team will be more enthused and less betrayed at how the new girl got a promotion so quickly. They're nice people, but I haven't proven myself nearly as much as maybe someone like Gary, whose been there for who knows how long. I once found a gummy worm under his chair that looked like it still had the smile design from the early '00s. Although, Gary already wished me a quiet congratulations with a small bag of gummies and a smiley post-it note, so I'm hoping this won't be too bad a transition. He's much too attentive for his own good.

During our morning meetings, Cameron stays behind his desk, scribbling notes on the white board, and I'm on the couch brainstorming with the client. We're both peering over each other's shoulders to hash out new ideas. Between Mr. Watts and I, the meetings aren't half bad. He's a goofy guy in charge of a skateboarding company and much less formal than Mr. Feldman was. But the second Cameron and I have to exchange words, it's like all the air in the room is sucked up and bottled tight.

Every word is carefully crafted, my movement is tense and jilted, and expressions are neutral with no room for misinterpretation. Whether Mr. Watts has noticed or not is beyond me, but he hasn't shown any signs of discomfort.

I feel like I wonder that a lot nowadays. Whether people notice us or not, I mean.

We had a rocky relationship and, from the outside, I'm sure it's jarring. First, we hate each other, then we're sort of friends, then we get lunches, then we stay late together, and now? Nothing. Not a single thing. It makes my own head spin just thinking about it.

"It's like I got a taste of something... real." I glance to Ramona.

Her eyebrows are furrowed inward and it's a look of borderline pity. She reaches out for my hand and I let her take it. I refuse to cry. I've spent a lot of time doing that lately. I watched all the best romcoms: *When Harry Met Sally, The Notebook, You've Got Mail...* I even watched *Love, Actually* and it's not the holidays, which is pure blasphemy. "Sounds stupid, I know."

Ramona shakes her head. "No, it doesn't." I laugh but her expression doesn't change. "There's a lot of relationships that felt, and still feel, real. To me, anyway. But then I go home, and I see Wes smiling back at me with his goofy grin and his dumb one-liners and I know that he's *the* guy. Not just *a* guy."

I smile and she winks.

"Maybe Cameron is the guy," she says. "But maybe he's not. And that's okay. But that doesn't mean what you guys had wasn't real."

I want to smile at Ramona and say, "Thanks, that made me feel better," but in reality, my chest feels heavier and the coffee I'm sipping feels like a time bomb. I'm going to be sick.

"He's *that* guy, Ray."

I GRAB my coffee for Wednesday's regularly scheduled meeting and make my way to Cameron's office with my tablet under my arm and my pen behind my ear.

I'm moving a bit slower than usual as I chose today to put on a long maxi dress with next to zero room for leg movement. Even though the weather is getting cooler as the end of summer closes, the office temperatures are somehow still on full blast. I'll need to talk to Nia about the possibility of turning that down. I've learned it's doubtful anything will come from complaints, as I'm sure she gets thousands as day, but at least she'll smile and make a good faith effort. She's reliable that way.

The door is cracked when I arrive, so I shove it open with my shoulder to find nobody sitting in Mr. Watt's usual spot on the touch. There's only Cameron, hunched over his desk with his head in his hands, running them through his hair. It's like they're on mess-up double duty today.

"Cameron?" I ask.

He looks up, his hair wild. He runs it through one more time to give it the usual purposefully-styled look.

It's not often that Cameron wears a suit, but when he does, it fits him better than any suit could on another man—I'm convinced of it. It's tailored so the shoulder stitching lands right where it should. The shirt beneath his jacket is crisp and the tie is completed in a perfect double Windsor. It's unlike him, while also accentuating everything that makes him wonderful.

"Grace," he says as if he's been expecting me—and not in a "we have a regularly scheduled meeting" kind of way. He seems exasperated and nervous. "Please shut the door."

"Why?" I ask, unmoving.

"Grace," he says with an edge to his voice, almost like a warning. I cross my arms.

"Where's Watts?" I ask.

"Will you shut the door?"

"And why are you wearing a suit?"

Cameron huffs out air and grips the edge of his desk, knuckles whitening.

"Will you please close the door?" he asks again. He's trying to be polite, but I can tell his patience is wearing thin.

"If you're trying for this whole 'I'm a brooding, hot boss in a suit' vibe, then you're failing," I say.

He laughs and I turn around to do as I'm told, but only because I refuse to give him the satisfaction of having us joke around again. And I don't need him seeing just how much I'm drooling at the sight of him.

I shut the door behind me and then we're alone. I used to have fantasies about being alone with Cameron in his office. He'd push me against the door; my hands would find their way under his shirt to run along his abs; I would hop on his desk just because he said so. It's a dream that can never be, yet here we are, alone with the blinds closed and just the distance from the door to the desk between us.

"We need to talk," he says.

"Where's Watts?" I ask again, ignoring his request.

"I told him we had to cancel."

"And why would you say that?"

"Because I need to talk to you," he says, standing and making his way around the desk. At the arch of one of my eyebrows, he raises his hands in innocence and leans back against the front to keep the unspoken requested space between us.

"Then talk to me and stop talking *about* talking to me."

He laughs at this, looking down at the floor and messing up his hair again. *Goddamn it, stop being so sexy.*

"All right then," He inhales and exhales like he's trying to find the words but there's something stopping him. "I... want you." He slaps his hands on his knees. "Yep. That's... all I got. I want you. I need you. I miss you. God, I miss you so much, Grace."

My knees buckle, and I'm trying to keep on my feet. This is everything I want to hear and yet everything I can't.

"What do you want from me?" I ask, sighing and tossing my tablet onto the couch. I walk closer to him. "Do you want me to lose my job? Is that what you want?"

"No," he exhales. "No, just let me finish."

"I don't know what else you can say."

"Holmes," He reaches out and grabs my arm, and I jerk it away.

"Don't call me that."

On his desk, I see his phone start to buzz. I don't mean to look but when I do, it's the last thing I would want to see: The incoming call is from Abby.

I look at him and he glances from the phone, back to me, then double taking once more. His expression drops. I can't process anything happening right now. Why is he getting a call from his ex? Why is he bearing his heart to me when we agreed —we fucking agreed—that this was not plausible? Careers first, we said. Careers fucking first.

I don't realize I'm quickly mumbling this out until he's reaching for my arm again. I'm too tired to fight it.

"I know we said that," he says. "But things have changed."

"What game are you playing at, Cameron?" I demand, probably a bit louder than I should, but the heat is rising in my face and to my temples, giving me a shooting pain through my head. It's too early for this. "You say you want me, but you're talking to your ex?"

"Damn it, sit on the couch and listen." His voice is demanding and though I'm increasingly getting turned-on the more serious this conversation gets, my temper is also rising.

"I don't want to listen," I spit out, sounding like some petulant child but feeling none-the-worse about it.

"It's not what it looks like."

"I've heard that before."

We both pause, staring at each other, our chests heaving. He walks closer to me, as slow as he can as if scared that any sudden movement will set me off. The tears threatening to fall from my eyes are pushed back with the bite of my lip as I let him approach. I should push him away. I pushed Joe when I saw the dating app on his phone. But when Cameron touches my shoulders and pulls me in for a hug, I close my eyes and let his warmth wash over me. My hands stay by my side, limp and unable to reciprocate. But his embrace is enough.

Then there's a *blam!* And a tall, muscular man busts through the door full-on sitcom style. From the corner of my eye I see it's Ian, which wouldn't normally be an issue, but my heart sinks when I notice a much shorter woman behind him with her mouth gaping open, her eyes darting between the two of us. We're stunned into holding the hug. I think neither of us are able to process just how much shit we're in.

"Nia," Ian is saying, still focused on the small, blonde HR woman next to him. "It's too damn cold in this building and Cameron says so too. He—"

I want to repeat the same sentiment Cameron just gave me. "It's not what it looks like" would seem to do the trick. But that would be a lie and we all know it.

Ian, still holding the door handle with his own expression of disbelief, shuts his eyes. "Fuck."

I can't tell if Nia is livid or disappointed. Her expression is a horrible mix of pursed lips, wide eyes, and eyebrows pulled so tightly in the middle of her forehead that they may as well be touching. I think the last time I saw a look like this was when my mom found me making out with my first boyfriend in ninth grade to the sounds of Boyz 2 Men's *I'll Make Love to You*. He was going through a weird phase and the album just so happened to land on the worst track it could in that moment.

Weirdly enough, this moment instills more terror in me than that memory does.

Nia nods as if she's finished assessing this HR nightmare. Once it appears like her brain has processed the appropriate course of action, she speaks.

"Would you like to discuss this in here or in my office?"

43

GRACE

I'VE ONLY BEEN in the principal's office two times in my life.

The first time was when I was seven and I fell during field day, hurting my knee. My mother took it all the way to the top and I sat there as she grew red in the face explaining that kneepads should be required. I tried inserting that it was my own negligence that caused the fall, but she wasn't having it.

For the record, my old elementary school now requires kneepads for all gym-related activities.

The second time was ten years later when I was seventeen. My friends and I cut class to work on our art projects during our allotted time for math class. Both our art teacher and math teacher couldn't care less what we did—we were seniors and we were going to leave in two months anyway. But the school's on-campus security guard caught us roaming the halls having a good old time and that just didn't seem to sit well with him. That ended with us being sent home with a note to our parents. Cue red-faced mother all over again. Once again, my fault.

It only makes sense that my next experience in an office with serious consequences would be yet another ten years down the line. I'm twenty-seven and I was fighting with my boss who also happens to be my lover. Is that the phrase? "Lover?" God, I'm too distressed to think straight.

Just like those other times, I'm practically shaking in my chair, gripping the sides so hard I could bust the stuffing right out, hoping to God I don't get expelled (well, fired, I guess), and knowing that this situation is entirely my fault.

Nia started by explaining the policy to us. It's all kind of a blur because I kept trying to discreetly glance over at Cameron, who has not moved an inch during this entire process. I'm sure my looks keep giving me away, but he's just as poised as ever. The power of the suit.

"Now, if you feel more comfortable speaking to me individually about what happened, then the topics we speak on will be kept between us," Nia assures the both of us. "Confidential."

I nod in response, but Cameron clears his throat.

"There's no need."

Nia's eyes whip to him and I hope to God he's not throwing in the towel.

He knows this job means the world to me. Us in a relationship? It would bring the entire team down. It would ruin both of us. "Of course that's why Grace got the promotion," they'll say, "She's sleeping with the boss."

"This is a very serious matter. Please tell me you understand this." She's almost pleading with him.

I've never seen Nia act beyond her HR façade—her forced smiles, generally good-natured conversations in the breakroom, and no-nonsense rapport with Ian. But this seems different. She doesn't want to be doing this. And I don't either.

"I understand," Cameron says. "And I'm quitting."

"What?" I spit out.

"I'm quitting," he repeats, pulling out his cellphone. "I don't care for this position, Nia. You know it. I know it. Promoting me was a mistake. But Grace is absolutely brilliant.

She deserves the promotion we've already discussed. So, I'm quitting."

What the ever-loving shit is he doing? I look from Nia to Cameron and back again. It doesn't look like she's buying his bullshit or appreciating the lack of respect he's showing her by pulling out a phone during such a serious meeting. He quickly types out a text before pocketing it again. I wonder if it's to Abby.

Nia snorts her frustration, trying to reconcile the next logical thing to come out of her mouth. "Cameron, we will need an investigation into what happened."

"Nothing happened," I blurt out, and then she's giving me the same incredulous look.

"It's okay if you're uncomfortable—"

"I'm not uncomfortable," I say, more defiantly than I have any right to. I straighten my posture and release my grip on the armchair. No more fear. Just confidence.

"I can leave right now," Cameron says rising up, but Nia snaps her fingers at him and points to the seat.

"Sit down, Kaufman."

He sits and crosses his legs. From the corner of my eye, I see the giraffe socks staring up at me. My stomach plunges and I'm filled with every emotion I've tried to suppress. I want to hug him and beg him not to do this.

"Now, I don't know what's going on and I don't know what I just saw," Nia says. "But what I *do* know is whatever you're comfortable speaking about needs to be out in the open right now."

Cameron has a plan. I don't know what it is, but with the way he keeps pulling his phone out, texting, and then locking it back, I can tell he's got something up his sleeve.

"I changed my mind. I'm uncomfortable speaking about this," I say.

Cameron's head turns to me and I see a faint smile tugging

at the corner of his lips. It melts me; I know I just read his mind.

On the flip side, Nia narrows her eyes and I'm reliving the same violent anxiety I got from the principal's office ten years ago.

"You just said you *weren't* uncomfortable," she says, a hint of accusation in her voice. She's polite enough to mask it well. It's that HR training at work.

"Well, now she is," Cameron says in my defense.

In that instant, as if by fate, Ian busts in the door, just as reliable as ever.

"Everybody doing okay in here?" he asks. "I thought I smelled HR frustration."

"Ian, are you *freaking* kidding me?"

If Nia had the capability to curse at work, I think she would have let one large profanity slip in that moment. But before Ian can answer, Cameron gets up, brushes off his pants and nods.

"Well, I'm glad we had this talk, Nia. Ian, walk me out?"

"Sure thing, man."

Cameron stops for a beat and looks at me. What words can be said now?

"I'm sorry, Holmes."

That wasn't exactly what I had in mind. I'm sorry for what? Our breakup? Leading you on? I bite my lip and he leaves just as quick as Ian came bounding in. His pull makes me want to leave with him. But the farther away he gets, the more my soul is left cold.

"No, I need you to—Cameron!"

Nia gets up from her chair and stumbles to get around her desk. The heel of her shoe catches on a stack of binders in the corner and she trips. I'm just close enough to stand up and catch her by the waist. She feverishly stands back up, huffs, straightens her pencil skirt, and looks at me.

"They're gone, aren't they?"

I lean back to peer out of the cracked door where I faintly see Cameron swaggering through the glass front doors. Ian salutes Saria and waltzes out behind him. Even though I'm so confused by the whole event, I have never been more attracted to a certain ex-boss, Cameron Kaufman.

"Yes, I think so," I say. "Gone as can be."

She buries her head in her hands. "Grace, is there anything you would like to discuss?"

"Nope," I say. Taking a cue from Cameron, I get up, nod my head, and exit the office.

44

GRACE

THE EVENTS of my day feel like a dream and I'm still trying to piece them together into something more palatable.

Cameron saying exactly what I wanted to hear, his borderline desperation to accept termination, and his sexy exit through the front doors... None of it makes sense. Well, him being sexy does, but that's beside the point.

I don't regret my decision to end things with him. At least, not entirely. I know I want to be a designer. And I've learned before that giving up your dreams for someone else is a slippery slope into self-loathing. I'm here to further myself. Cameron isn't going to be around forever. I know that now. But my passion for art will always burn like a fire in my soul. And that's a trade-off I'll have to learn to deal with.

I can't take back the words I said to him. I can't do anything to give him back his job.

I know that he quit because of our fight. He couldn't stand to spend one more day in the same office as me and his eagerness to leave only buried the stake deeper in my cold, dead heart.

I'm sorry, Holmes.

Fuck, that still hurts.

I should probably be working, but instead it's six o'clock and I'm sitting on the stool in my mom's kitchen just like I used to do after school, shoving down her new discovery of avocado fries and coming to terms with the fact that I will never see Cameron Kaufman ever again.

"These aren't half bad," I say, dipping one in a yogurt sauce she also whipped together. "I think you've really got a thing going on here." My tone is as light as I can make it. I don't need her pity. I just want to distract myself.

My mom, still donning her apron, beams at me as she removes more treats from the oven. "These are avocado brownies. I figure they're just as good as the real stuff, right? I know you normally like cake for celebrations, but..."

"It's perfect," I say.

The smell wafts through the kitchen. There were hints of cocoa when they were baking, but the second they're placed on the stovetop to cool, I know that those won't last long, and neither will my slim figure if I keep this up.

"Okay, next is..." Mom rushes from the fridge to the cabinets, wiping her hands over her apron and spinning through her new spice rack. "How about guacamole?"

I laugh. "I mean, I can never say no to guacamole, but did you somehow raid the store of all its avocados? What's with all the green?"

I dip another fry, locking my eyes at the brownies and wondering when they'll ever be cooled enough. As a kid, I always sat exactly where I am now, with my coloring book and crayons scattered in front of me, eyeing the exact same stovetop I'm looking at. Back then my mom didn't make fancy things like avocado brownies. We got the normal double chocolate mix right out of box and spent half the time licking the batter from the spoon than making the brownies themselves. Dad was the real chef.

"The farmer's market had a deal," she says, pacing to the fridge and pulling out cilantro and tomatoes. "It doesn't have anything to do with Nick."

My ears perk up. "Nick?" I ask. "Who is Nick?"

"Just a local seller." She is placing the ingredients on the island and notably not making eye contact with me.

"Is he a farmer?" A better question would be, is Mom dating? I suddenly feel like the parent in this situation. "Who is this Nick and what are his intentions?"

She laughs, smiling to herself. "Oh, hush, you."

"You wouldn't have mentioned that it didn't have anything to do with a man named Nick unless it had something to do with a man named Nick."

She cuts into the avocado and it's definitely a bit darker on the inside than it should be.

"How many weeks have you been going to see him?" I ask. "Because that looks old."

Her eyes meet mine and I can see her crow's feet crinkling as a smile spreads across her face. My mom is a hard woman. Even as her hair started to gray, she insisted on dying it back to a semi-natural looking red to maintain her feisty ginger. But a genuine smile? One that radiates from eyes to her ears? A small flush cover her freckles and it tells me all I need to know.

"A while," she admits. "I may have found an excuse to talk to him by buying from him."

"All of his avocados?"

"No," she protests. "But sure, a few. There's a lot of avocado recipes, you know."

"Uh-huh. And how many weeks have you been sleeping with him?"

"Oh, that is inappropriate, Grace!" She waves her hand at

me and goes back to slicing the avocado, but her face gets redder by the second. "I'm sorry."

"What do you have to be sorry about?"

"We had a pact and I broke it."

Oh, right. The pact. The pact that should have stopped me from sleeping with Cameron. The pact that did zero things to me. The pact that I'm sure has been worrying my mother sick for months. I had been so focused on my boss that I hadn't even considered my mom's love life. Not only am I cruddy employee, but I guess I'm not the best daughter right now, either.

"I should have asked more," I say. "If I would have stopped by more often, I would have known."

"No!" she says, dropping the knife and wiping her avocado-stained hands on her apron. She walks over and throws her arms around me in a giant bear hug. I settle into it. She may smell like a hint of coconut flour, but her natural mom-scent overpowers it—the one that smells like raspberries and lavender. I never know I need a mom hug until I get one, and the need for her comfort tightens my muscles as I hold back a sob.

The past few months come crashing down on me. Cameron. The job. All of my efforts and stress rebounding between my muscles and through my skin.

"You didn't do a thing wrong," she says. "You've got your own life to worry about—not mine, dear."

She pulls away with a smile and pats my hands. I feel tears well up behind my eyes for a moment, but then shake my head. "So, tell me about this man," I choke out. I place my chin in my hands as if ready to gossip.

My mom sighs, and it's the sigh of someone way too enamored to hide it. I wonder just how long she'd been dying to tell me, and I was too busy at work dreaming about my own forbidden romance. She needs my undivided attention far more than I need her as a distraction.

"He's a farmer," she says, walking back to her side of the island. "An avocado farmer."

"You've always liked the outdoorsy type."

Dad went hunting regularly, as well as fishing. Basically, all the hobbies where he could disappear and speak to nobody.

"Yes, and he's a good Christian man."

"Church, good, good. What else?"

"Red-headed."

"Well, haven't you just met your match." I laugh and she tosses part of an avocado peel at me.

"He takes my shit and sends it right on back," she says, throwing her hands to her mouth with a blush. "Oh, look at me. I'm just as bad as Ramona now. Bad, Lynette." She slaps her own wrist and places both hands on the counter to steady herself leaning forward. "He gives me this life that I can't really explain. It's been a while. And he's not your father, know that, but he's just the type of man I could see living the rest of my years with."

"Wow," I say. "How serious is this?"

She sighs. "More serious than I could have hoped for."

She turns on her heel and runs water over the cilantro, washing it probably too thoroughly. I can tell she's embarrassed, and it's sweet to see her like this. When Dad passed, she adopted this strong exterior—more so than she already had. It's nice that she's letting down the barriers she spent years building.

I think I may like this Nick guy.

"And what about you?" she calls over the sink. "I know by now you must have broken our pact."

I inhale, hoping the sound of the running water covers up the guilt that comes with it. If only she knew just how bad I broke our pact. I promised her no funny business with men, and then I made sure to double promise nothing with my boss. I guess I'm two for two on this one. Maybe I should have just gone to the farmer's market. Seems like there's some eligible bachelors there.

"No," I lie. My voice comes out a bit higher than usual. I sit up straight and swirl my finger into the yogurt dipping sauce, putting it my mouth. Damn it's good even without the fries.

"No?" she says, cutting off the water and circling back to the island to chop up the cilantro.

"I've just been focusing on work," I say. "You know me, staying late and all."

"Not staying late with your boss, are you?" Mom arches an eyebrow.

Got me there.

What do I even say to that? Yes, Mom, I got pounded by my ridiculously good-looking boss. Yes, I've never felt more pleasure in screaming a man's name before. Yes, I ended it all. And for what? For a promotion?

"Nope," I say.

She narrows her eyes at me as if trying to read my mind and then seems weirdly satisfied with my answer. Whether she actually believes me or if she's just giving me the benefit of the doubt, I'm not sure. Maybe she spoke to Ramona. Maybe she knows more than she's letting on. All I know is that dropping the subject is probably the best for both of us right now.

"Just checking," she says. "Is he still working there?"

"You're not as sneaky as you think you are. What did Ramona tell you?"

"Not Ramona, dear. Ian."

My heart stops. *What did Ian say?*

"You talk to Ian?"

"Darling, I talk to everyone." Shit, she totally does. "I know you've been focusing on your work, but I understand temptation. I was your age once."

"Kinda seems like you still understand it. How's Nick the farmer again?"

She raises the knife to me. "You're on thin ice, missy."

"It couldn't have worked out, anyway," I mumble.

She begins sliding in the cut cilantro and tomatoes from the cutting board to the bowl beside her. Next, she reaches for the cut browned avocado, but I reach my hand across the island to stop her.

"Seriously though, we cannot eat that avocado."

45

CAMERON

"I'm never going to hear the end of that."

Ian and I walked uphill on the sidewalk in the city's historical downtown area. The buildings we pass are quaint and home to small businesses that seem to only be found in these types of areas: Florists, antique shops, barber shops, local bakeries—the works.

I normally avoid coming downtown because parking is a bitch. To add insult to injury, this particular area is shaped like a bowl and the parking deck acts as the depressed center, making everything else one hundred percent an uphill walk.

Ian's forehead gathers sweat and his normally suave, curly hair melts into a damp mass. At least it's a breezy fall day?

"She'll get over it," I pant, ripping off my suit jacket and laying it over my forearm as we continue to climb this tiny Mount Everest. What is the point of running every day if I break out in a sweat this easily?

"Well no, probably not," he says. "Nia is a beautiful dragon from the hell fires of corporate America come to rain her fury onto me. But that's an issue for Future Ian. Why are we going to see Abby, again?"

"Because apparently, I love shoving my head into a wall"—I tilt my head from side to side considering—"which would honestly be preferable to this."

"Okay... so why take me, too?"

"I need a lawyer present."

"Ah."

Even though my decisions have been set in stone, I figure it would be best to have Ian close. If anything, he can be a buffer between the two of us. It'll stop her from making too many snide comments, and I may be smart enough to avoid losing this opportunity over a couple misconstrued words.

"Did you... mean to get caught?" Ian asks, flapping his suit jacket to let in cool air, but not succumbing to taking it off completely like I did.

"Why yes, I absolutely wanted HR to come in and accuse me, in so many words, of sexually harassing one of my direct reports." I roll my eyes. "All part of the plan."

That was definitely more hostile than Ian deserves at this point, given that he bailed me out of completing unnecessary harassment and termination paperwork. Plus, he's taking his lunch break to mediate between me and my cheating ex. I can tell he feels the same way about my snarky comment because he grabs my shoulder and forces me to turn and look at him.

Ian doesn't really get angry with me. He gets frustrated with people if they don't agree with him, but that's any lawyer for you. He wants to be right and will insist on it until he's convinced the other party according to his standards. But he's always been quite cordial with his close friends even if he is irritated. So even though I know Ian isn't about to lash out, it's clear he still isn't satisfied by my answers.

"You're gonna have to fill me in, man," he says, tightening his grip.

"Okay, I get it, you have questions," I say, moving my

shoulder away from his hold. I brush off my shirt and gesture with my chin back toward the hill. "Can we walk and talk?"

"Let's," he says.

So, I delve into everything I can fit during the next five minutes. I talk about how Grace and I were sort of dating, how there was no rhyme or reason to it, how suddenly it's like she became my best friend, and how I don't really believe in soulmates or anything but, "She's different."

"Never thought I'd hear *you* say that," Ian says with a smile.

We stop in front of a café. The storefront is all windows with a desaturated pink painted over the old-fashioned wood, adorned with white shutters that look so crisp it's as if they were painted just this morning. The company's logo is just above the window written in cursive with the end letter curling up into the shape of a heart. Looking inside, I spot Abby.

Even with her arms crossed and a look that could shrink your balls up to your scrotum, she's still as beautiful as always. Her long, curly black hair trails down her back, stopping just above her waist. She's dressed in a sharp suit, jacket and all. She's pure business with a look that tells me everything I need to know about how this will go down.

She is so similar and yet so drastically different from Grace.

"Je-sus," Ian says, shaking his arms in a mock shiver. "Never thought I could be so turned on and so terrified. Why are we here again?"

"Abby is helping me move on."

Ian guffaws behind me upon seeing her. "Yeah, sure she is."

I open the door and a tiny bell above it dings. The smell of bread and cheese wafts through the air with a hint of chocolate fudge that reminds me of those kitschy tourist traps that blindside you into buying a pound of fudge you only eat half of. The place could have been included in a Barbie funhouse with the amount of pink that's glaring at me from every wall, counter, and display case. Even the sandwiches inside have hints of pink to them. I read "*Daily Special: Pink Sugar Bread*" and I wonder how that could possibly be enticing to anyone.

At the sound of our arrival, Abby's already shaking her head, and I'm trying not to regret every life decision I've made up to this point. But then my thoughts drift to Grace, and I picture her smile, her tenacity, and the knowledge that she would be proud if she knew why I was here.

The restaurant is only big enough to hold three tea tables with two chairs at each so Ian pulls a chair to our side, swinging it around to sit in it with the back facing front and his arms hanging over.

"You brought Ian?" she snips. "I didn't know we were bringing a posse like opposite sides of war."

"Sweetheart, you *wish* you had a posse." Ian grins.

"This isn't about sides," I say.

Yikes, I hadn't anticipated them at odds. Although, Ian is right: He's nice to have in my corner. And I'd be lying if I said I didn't get slight satisfaction at seeing Abby roll her eyes in response.

"I brought Ian in case any contracts need to be written up."

She looks like she's staking out prey ready for the taking. On some women this could be hot, almost like a dare, but on Abby, I'm pretty sure she's like the cats that eat their owner's faces off seconds after they die. Except she probably wouldn't wait until they're dead.

How did I date her for five years again?

"Already done," she says, reaching into the black briefcase beside her. She pulls out a stack of papers about the size of a movie script.

I glance at Ian, who's already scooting the mountain of paperwork closer to him. He slides his glasses to the end of his nose and begins flipping through. "Hey, look at me, still being useful."

"It's pretty straightforward," Abby says through an exhale,

as if this meeting is already boring her. "Sign where the labels point, and you're locked in for a year. I'm not sure how much they offered you..."

"Two hundred thousand, it looks like," Ian clarifies, his finger scanning each line. I think I see hint of a smug smirk on his face.

"Right," she says through clenched teeth. "But unfortunately, no benefits with this being a contract position."

"With that much, who cares," I laugh.

I think a see a smile tug at the edge of her lips, too, but she just picks up her phone and begins sifting through anything she can use to distract herself while Ian reads the paperwork.

My lack of—no, my fear of—commitment has been stifling my happiness for too long. I'm happy that it didn't work out between Abby and me. Even without my aversion to commitment, I don't think we would have resolved our issues in the end. But it's high time I take control of my life—pursue what I want. Have the career I want. Have the woman I want.

Ian nods as he finishes flipping through the pages. He reaches into his chest pocket and clicks a pen, handing it to me. I take it and begin signing, turning pages every so often to double check I'm not missing anything. After a few minutes of silence, I scoot the papers back to Abby, giving another click of the pen to finalize the deal.

Ian claps his hands. "Well, as long as we're here, I'm getting some of that... what is that? Pink bread? Sure." He gets up to ding the bell on the counter, pointing to the pink sugar bread. He demands the entire loaf, and at first the employee laughs—at least until he throws his card down on the counter with a pointed "Do I look like I'm joking" face; she moves a little faster at that point.

I look over and Abby is already staring at me. I forgot how beautiful she was, hidden behind all my resentment for the last few months of our relationship: All the late nights arguing, the lack of physical intimacy, and, of course, my deep-rooted hate for how things ended. But it doesn't even matter now, and it's almost laughable how true that thought really is.

"Thanks, Abby," I say.

"Not a problem. Thank you for meeting me. They were going to kill me if I didn't get this signed today." She lets out a small laugh, and it's genuine. Now that it's just the two of us, she's let down her business façade.

I look around and sigh. "I actually thought they were going to come." It's more a question than a statement.

"You know how Mr. Feldman is. Busy man." He is, but Abby's recruiter skills made it easy to get a hold of him. "Sorry for the false alarm"—she looks me up and down—"nice suit, though."

"Lucky for him, I didn't intend on putting in a two weeks' notice."

"Run into a bit of trouble?"

"Something like that."

She tilts her head to the side. "Tell me something, Cam; I always asked you to pursue architecture. Why now?"

Because it's about time I grew up. Because I love it. Because I love Grace.

"I think I need to take a bit more chances," I say, shrugging and leaning back in my chair, both elbows propped on the back.

"I really do wish you the best," she says. "Even if you do still hang out with this guy."

We both look over to Ian and he's bagging up the giant loaf of bread and walking back over to us.

"I'm taking most of this back to Nia tomorrow. Think she'll notice?"

I laugh. "How could she not?"

46

GRACE

I'VE BEEN SITTING on my back porch for an hour, looking at the roads behind the apartments as cars fly by. I wonder where they're going. Are they headed home to meet their spouses? Maybe make dinner together, talk about their day? Or are they driving to a bar? Reliving the day? Praying tomorrow doesn't come?

Hank is lying on the ground under the porch table, letting out a huff of air. I lean down to pat his head. "Can't always get everything we want, huh?"

He tilts his head to the side and for a second, I wonder if he truly understood me, but I'm broken from my reverie with a knock at the door.

I exhale and drag my feet toward the front door. I'm sure it's Ramona and Wes, coming with some treats and a silly movie. Maybe that's what I need right now. Mom's avocado concoctions only did so much to my mood.

I pull open the door, but instead of my best friend, there he is: Cameron, clad in another stunning suit, looking sharper than ever, holding a stuffed giraffe in his hands.

"Hey, Holmes."

I shake my head in disbelief. "You're here."

"I'm here."

"And you brought me a giraffe."

"You bet your ass I did."

He hands it to me, and I notice the animal's arms are tied together with string and in the knot's middle is a small ring. The band is a bit dull and the gem is almost obnoxiously sparkly, as if it was painted over with gloss coating. But it's a ring.

"Oh my God," I somehow get out, looking from the giraffe to Cameron and back again.

Our relationship flashes before my eyes, and without a doubt, I can feel it in my heart. I love this man. I love him so much my heart bursts every time he's in front me. When he's gone, I need to be near him. When we hug, it's like even that is not good enough, and we need to be closer.

But I've only known him for three months. Could I *marry* him? My face feels hot, my hands are clammy as I hold the giraffe, and in a haze, the only thought running through my head is that I'm matting his makeshift fur with my sweat.

"Cameron... are you...?"

His eyes widen, realizing his unfortunate mistake. "No, oh, whoa, God no."

"Oh thank God," I exhale before I can stop myself. My body unclenches and I feel a relief wash over me. I let out a breath I didn't even realize I was holding. "Good lord." I shake my head side to side, still trying to take in the situation. "Wait—then why the heck is there a ring in this giraffe's hands?"

"I didn't really think about it." He shrugs and a grin bursts across his face, shining through the misunderstanding. Of course he didn't. Cameron's attention to detail is horrible. "I couldn't get the damn thing out of his hooves in time and it's the only giraffe toy the card store had."

I laugh, finally noticing the cheap plastic of the ring and

the shine of the fake diamond is indeed some type of polymer to give it the illusion of authenticity.

"Wow, you really thought I was proposing?" he grins. "You must feel so dumb."

"Excuse me for thinking that's what giving me a ring meant."

He chuckles and I can't help but laugh back. He's joking again.

Cameron takes a step forward, placing his hands on my hips and leaning his forehead against mine. I lean into him, taking in everything. His mesmerizing eyes, his cologne, and the soft touch of his beard against my lips as he leans forward to place a single kiss.

"I thought you were gone forever," I say. I feel his forehead move against mine in a shake of disagreement.

"Holmes, I hate commitment. I hate change. I hate pretty much anything that's going to turn my world upside down. But you wormed your way into me like some parasite before I could even notice my life was infected by you."

"Charming."

"Let me finish, damn it."

I smile and nod. "Go on, then."

"I'm not asking you to marry me," he says. "But I want you to know that I'm willing to do that for you"—he holds up his index finger in correction—"in the future, anyway."

I choke out a laugh. "Right. You know, I guess I could do a future with you, too."

He moves his forehead from mine and I want it back already. I want him to be close to him and never leave. I never want to stop my heart from beating to the sound of "I love you, Cameron Kaufman," over and over again.

He stretches out his hand to me, pinky sticking up, ready for the taking.

"Promise?" he whispers.

EPILOGUE
CAMERON

Most people call me Cam, but my fiancée calls me Cameron. If you needed to use it in a sentence, it could be said as: "Cameron, I love you," "Cameron, unload the damn dishwasher," and "Cameron, I need to have sex with you immediately." She loves that one. *I* love that one.

She's sitting on our couch, feet folded underneath her, tablet resting on her lap, red hair pulled into a loose bun on the top of her head. Our beanbag chairs are haphazardly resting on the floor in front of her with Hank's head lying on one and Buddy's tail whacking the other in anticipation to play.

I'm at my desk, sketching out a new floor plan for the warehouse at Treasuries Inc. They decided they needed an overhaul of the Beer Friday chapel, and I was happy to oblige. The work is pro bono, but it's the least I could do for the years of loyalty that company gave to me. Plus, I needed some way to pay my guilty debt to Nia for putting her through a recruiting nightmare after my sudden departure. Not sure she's fully forgiven me, but Grace stepped up immediately and, from what I hear, the department has been running smoothly since then. It doesn't hurt that Grace and Nia formed some special work bond after my departure.

Apparently, the HR Manager isn't as prickly as she seems. "At least not all the time," as Grace puts it.

I normally don't do a lot of freelance work, as I'm still full-time at Mr. Feldman's architecture firm. My contract was renewed after two years, and though I haven't quite gotten that promotion yet, I figure I'll just let things happen when they happen this time around.

Grace and I decided to move in together one month after I quit my job at Treasuries, Inc. I found a barren lot that Mr. Feldman's company wanted to break ground on, and I guaranteed my girlfriend and I could build a structure more worthy to stand there than just another set of cookie cutter apartments. For some reason, he believed me. I'm still unsure why he puts so much faith in Grace and me, but we made good on our word and built our unnecessarily extravagant house. I may have designed the layout, but Grace's unique décor ultimately makes this place feel like home.

Hank is still kicking, looking more white than golden at this point, but happy all the same. The two dogs have been decent roommates to each other, only with the occasional fight on which area at the foot of the bed to sleep on. While Buddy hasn't settled down in the slightest, we've given Hank an appropriate accommodation for escaping when he needs to. The first thing we added to our house was an under-the-stairs cave for him, just as he had before.

We separate our time nowadays by always finding something to renovate in the house, bouncing to and from dog parks, and prepping for our wedding. Eventually I bought a real ring. Weirdly enough, I still think she prefers the plastic one with the stuffed giraffe.

Do I regret sleeping with my employee? Fuck no. I'd do it again in a heartbeat. Hell, I'd do it many times over on every desk in that office if I could. But I'll just have to settle with the here and now with the beanbag chair that has been used again and again, proudly bearing an indentation of Grace's ass.

She lifts her head from her tablet and smiles to me—a glow exuding from every part of her. Her eyes crinkle and her freckles hide behind the flush spreading across her face.

"What?" she asks.

"Nothing," I shrug.

She starts to laugh. "No, what?"

"Just happy I took a chance."

"Me too, Cameron," she smiles. "Me, too."

THE END

NICE TO SEE YOU!

Hi there! Thanks for reading! I hope you enjoyed your time with Cameron and Grace. I'm sure they enjoyed spending time with you as well!

Sign-up for the Julie Olivia email newsletter to receive updates on upcoming releases!

www.julieoliviaauthor.com/newsletter

ACKNOWLEDGMENTS

Holy macaroni. I finished my first book.

If you just finished and you need to go to bed or go back to work from your lunch break or just go live your life somewhere else, please stay for one more second to accept my ABSOLUTE BIGGEST THANK YOU for taking a risk on a first time indie author. I hope it wasn't too much of a struggle. I can't wait to show you more!

Thank you to my editor and pal, Merethe Walther. This would be one mess of a book without you. You're not editing this acknowledgements page, and I'm willing to bet it is riddled with errors.

To my entire family who listened to me talk about this book for months on end. Not one single conversation went by without me saying, "SO ANYWAY, MY BOOK IS STILL TRUCKING ALONG…"

I am so grateful for my dad who raised me with the mindset that if you work hard enough you can do anything you want. And thank you for still sending weekly texts with this advice. You've never stopped parenting.

Thanks to both my mom and "evil stepmother." You two are

supportive, weird, and absolutely wonderful. I wouldn't have it any other way.

To my brother and his wife who started suggesting every weird kink under the sun after I said I wanted to write romance novels. For the record, no, I will not write about furries.

To Dr. Shira Chess who encouraged my creative writing throughout the end of my college years. You probably didn't imagine me writing romance when you told me to pursue this more, but that's okay.

And my English 1001 college TA who probably doesn't remember my name and whose name I don't remember either. Almost ten years ago, you told me to keep writing because you said I had a penchant for self-deprecating humor. Well, jokes on you; I did it and now I bet this book will flop.

A massive thank you to the Atlanta Writes Meetup group: Curt, Aaron, Mary, Bruce, and our haunted AirBnb. I had planned to visit other Meetup groups, but you guys were so darn cool that I didn't even bother with the rest. Plus, you have never failed to ask me, "So, have you been writing?" Thanks for keeping me in check.

And finally, the cherry on top of every day pie—every dot to my I, and cross to my T—is my biggest cheerleader and creative consultant. I've tried writing this paragraph for you almost fifty different times, but I can't do you justice, my dear. You were the last person I wanted to love, but isn't that how the most fantastic, life-altering love stories always begin? Thank you for being my number one supporter. Thank you for putting up with me. And thank you for asking me if you could do that for the rest of our lives.

ABOUT THE AUTHOR

Julie Olivia loves spicy stories with even spicier banter, so she decided to write them. Julie lives in Atlanta with her fiancé and their very vocal cat. She appreciates a good pair of boots and fresh lemon-filled donuts. She is easily bribed with either.

Sign up for release updates: julieoliviaauthor.com/newsletter

- facebook.com/julieoliviaauthor
- instagram.com/julieoliviaauthor
- amazon.com/author/julieoliviaauthor
- bookbub.com/authors/julie-olivia